THE 4TH REICH

- Book 5 -

Patrick Laughy

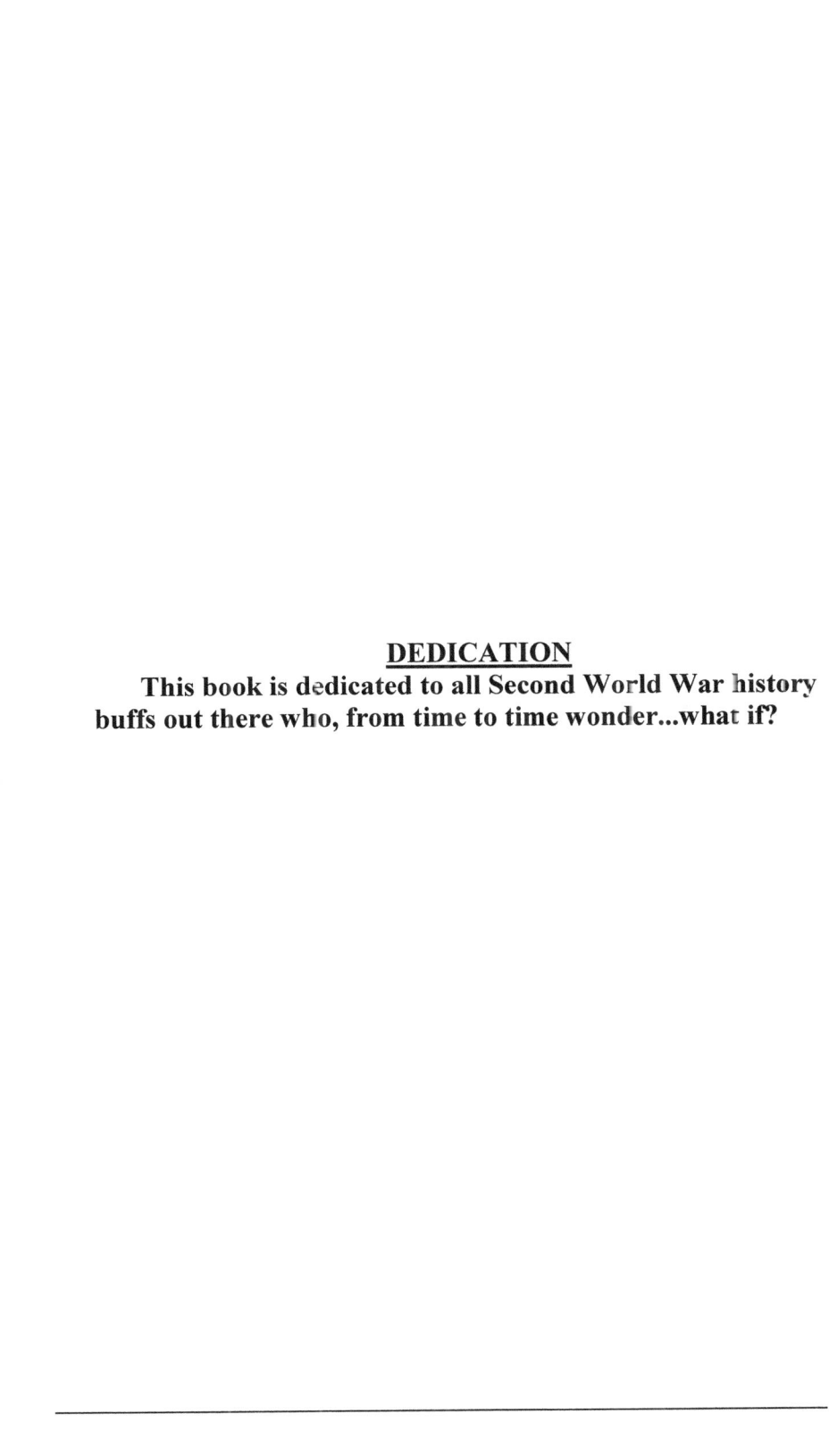

<u>DEDICATION</u>
This book is dedicated to all Second World War history buffs out there who, from time to time wonder...what if?

ACKNOWLEDGEMENT
Thanks to Suzy for her long hours of research and editing, David for another great cover and Linette for her continued support.

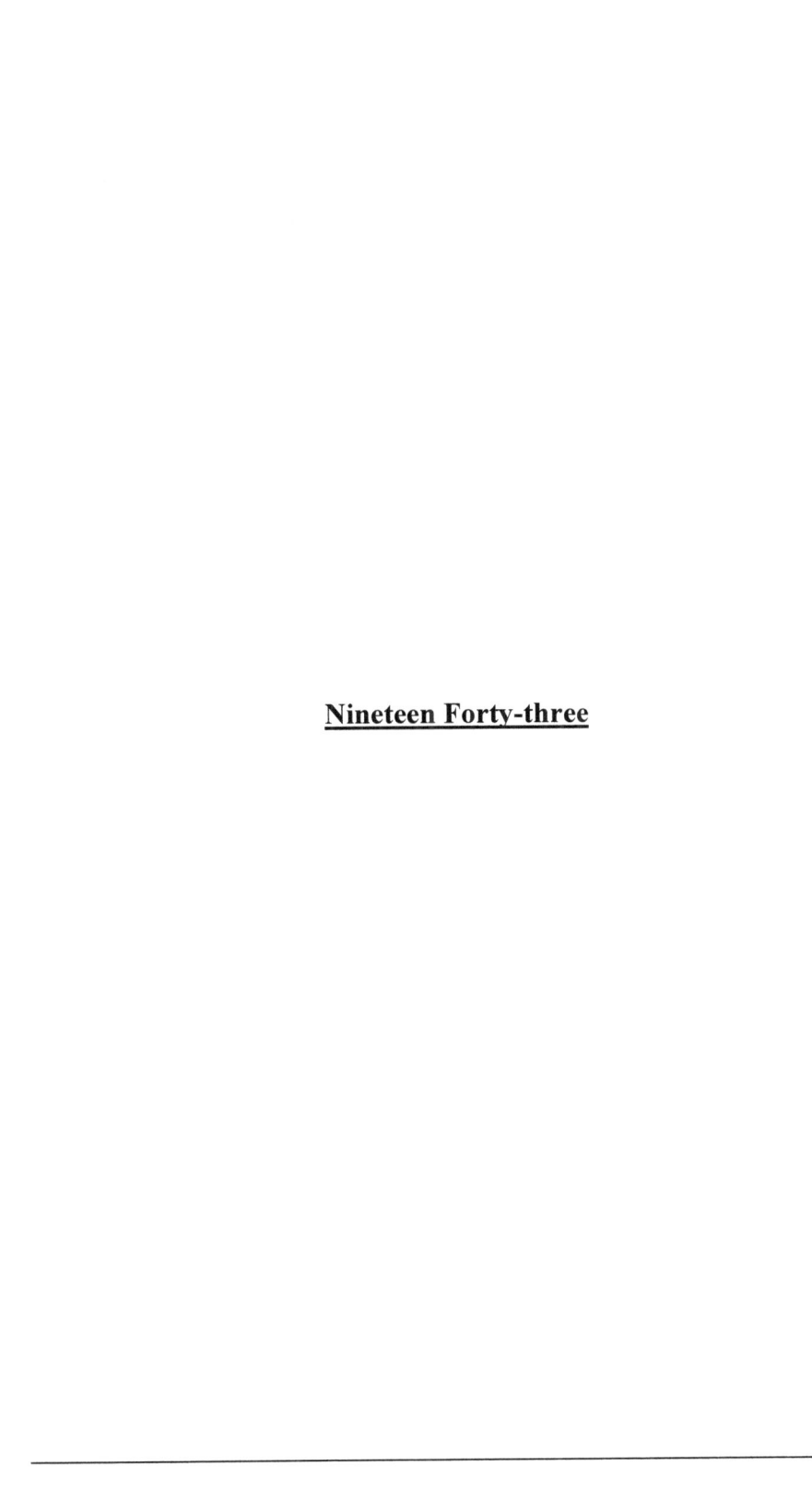

<u>Nineteen Forty-three</u>

CHAPTER ONE-

- January -

- Hitler -

In late December of nineteen forty-two Hitler sent his personal pilot, Hans Baur, into the Stalingrad pocket with orders to pick up the commander of the 14th Panzer Group, General Hans Hube.

When Hube arrived at the Fuhrer's command compound, Hitler asked him for a frank and unbiased report on the situation at Stalingrad. He expected and got exactly that, and listened quietly as it was delivered. He then said.

"Much of this is new to me."

For the next hour, the solemn Fuhrer outlined his plans to deal with the situation. He advised Hube that he would send the SS Panzer Group that was currently in France to relieve the forces in Stalingrad and promised to increase the airlift at all costs in the meantime. He left no doubt in Hube's mind that he was determined to move from defeat to victory at Stalingrad just as he had done after the previous winter's crisis.

He sent Hube back with instructions to instill renewed fortitude in his comrades. Convinced of the Fuhrer's determination to take the city, Hube arrived back in Stalingrad on January eighth of forty-three to deliver his message from Hitler, which was readily received by a desperate Paulus, who advised his commanders that help was on the way and no thought could be given to surrender.

The promise of increased airlift, based on Goering's optimistic promises to Hitler, soon resonated with a hollow ring as the amount of supplies making it into the pocket proved to be far less than had been promised by the Reichsmarschall. Subsequently Hitler's faith in Goering had hit rock bottom and the Fuhrer was now publicly heard to refer to him as *'This fellow Goering, this fat, well-fed pig!'* Hitler promptly made his feelings apparent to Goering by appointing a subordinate to reorganize the airlift.

For this task he selected Field Marshal Milch, in whom he had a great deal of faith.

In the middle of the month he summoned Milch to *'Wolfsschanze'* and ordered him to get three hundred tons of supplies per day into the troops at Stalingrad. He gave Milch special powers which included the authority to issue orders to any military command.

Within a short period of time, Milch was able to raise the daily drop from sixty to eighty tons but was unable to increase the amount of the airlift past that juncture. It was far from enough to maintain, let alone increase the fighting chances for the encircled German troops.

On the twentieth of the month, Paulus sent identical messages to both *'Wolfsschanze'* and Manstein, requesting the authority *'to avoid complete annihilation'* if the situation became untenable. Both Zeitzler and Manstein urged Hitler to grant this obvious plea for surrender if the conditions worsened even further. The Fuhrer's response was that the Sixth Army was *'to fight to the last man'*.

Manstein, in a last ditch attempt to sway Hitler from this death sentence for the pocket, arranged for a major by the name of Zitzewitz, to be flown out of Stalingrad and brought to *'Wolfsschanze'*. Hitler met with the man and after being given a horror story of starvation and frostbite, advised him of yet a new plan to break through, this one involving the use of a battalion of new Panther tanks.

Zitzewitz was dumbfounded by such a suggestion. His response was:

'My Fuhrer, permit me to state that the troops at Stalingrad can no longer be ordered to fight to their last round because they are no longer physically capable of fighting and because they no longer have a last round.'

Hitler appeared surprised by the statement and replied:

'Man recovers very quickly'.

He then dismissed the major and sent Paulus another message, which read:

'Surrender out of the question. Troops will resist to the end.'

On January thirtieth, Paulus informed Hitler that his men were hours from collapse. Hitler responded by delivering by radio a raft of field promotions to those officers encircled. Among those promoted was Paulus himself, who was elevated to the rank of field marshal. He went on to say that, historically, no Prussians of the rank of German field marshal had ever surrendered. He clearly implied the Paulus should commit suicide rather than surrender.

Paulus was a staunch Roman Catholic and had no intention of committing suicide.

The next day Paulus and his staff surrendered.

* * * * *

- Inner Circle -

- Joseph Goebbels -

Goebbels was still in Hitler's good books at this point in the war but the Propaganda Minister found himself out of the loop, now that the Fuhrer was so deeply embroiled in the actual day to day fighting. All the information about the progress of the war was actually coming to Goebbels second hand by those who participated in the military conferences Hitler held daily.

In the early stages of the war, Goebbels had aligned himself with Himmler in an attempt to thwart Goering's rising star with Hitler, and the Reichsmarschall's iron grip on Germany's economic development through his position of head of the Four Year Plan Ministry. This had been a beneficial if shaky alliance for both men in that Goebbels was wary of Himmler and the SS chief looked down upon Goebbels' position as Propaganda Minister.

Over time Himmler had begun to distance himself from Goebbels.

It therefore now behooved Joseph to align himself with others who found themselves in the same situation of being out of the loop and in December of forty-two, as the situation in Stalingrad became bleak, he began to invite three of his colleagues to call on him from time to time.

Being an academic, he chose from those who were not involved militarily and had similar educational backgrounds. He had already befriended Speer, who had been working together with him behind the scenes to undermine Goering's control of the economy during nineteen forty-two; the two men were doing their best to convince Hitler to remove the lethargic Goering from the control of the Four Year Plan, and he now added Walther Funk, the Minister of Economics and Robert Ley, head of the German Labour Front, to his friendly guest list.

At a meeting of the four men, held in early nineteen forty-three, Goebbels suggested that in a military sense, Germany had faced little failure at the beginning of the war, taking territory relatively easily and without seriously restricting the day to day lives of the every-day German citizen. He went on to point out that the British had taken a different tack in that, when they had suffered defeat at Dunkirk, they had immediately begun to tighten up on the civilian economy in order to support the war effort. The result of this difference meant that the British had tightened rationing and were now fighting an all-out war, while the Germans were still attempting to fight the war using only professional military forces while maintaining the civilian population on a peacetime footing.

He fortified this determination by pointing out to his guests that he knew for a fact that the German general public was asking for a ban on all luxuries and products which did not help directly with the fighting of the war. The people, he said, where displeased that they were not being asked to tighten their belts for the war effort; they wanted to do their part.

Speer advised that Hitler had ordered him to increase armament production, which was something he would find difficult to do unless the German economy was put on a full war-time footing.

Robert Ley piped in with the fact that eight hundred thousand men, many of them young skilled workers, were about to be drafted to replace the horrendous casualties and he would need to replace these workers. Where he was expected to get them from, he didn't know.

Speer countered with the fact that he had asked Hitler to allow German women to work in the armaments industry to free up men and allow for increased production but Hitler had refused such a suggestion outright.

* * * * *

- Ernst Kaltenbrunner -

On January thirtieth, nineteen forty-three, it was announced that SS-Obergruppenfuhrer, Dr. Ernst Kaltenbrunner, would replace Heydrich as *'und General der Polizei und Waffen-SS'*, Chief of the RSHA and President of Interpol.

* * * * *

- Resettlement -

By forty-three, six hundred and twenty-nine thousand repatriated *'Volksdeutsche'*, had been resettled, as Poles and French who had been living in the desired areas of occupied territory were transferred across borders. Work on bringing in a further three hundred and ninety-three thousand others was underway, with a long-term goal of five point four million to be resettled.

These would come mainly from Transylvania, Banat, France, Hungary and Romania. Candidates went through a selection process and each individual was classified as either racially or politically unreliable, (settled in *'Altreich'*), or of high quality, who would be settled in the annexed eastern territories or suitable for transit camps.

* * * * *

- Deportations -

On January twenty-ninth Himmler ordered that all gypsies be arrested and sent to extermination camps.

On January thirtieth, Ernst Kaltenbrunner succeeded Heydrich as head of the RSHA.

* * * * *

- Ghettos -

- Warsaw -

In January of forty-three, the Germans decided to resume mass deportations of the Jews interned at the Warsaw ghetto. A group of Jewish fighters infiltrated the initial column of Jews on its way to the *'Umschlagplatz'* and at a signal, broke ranks and fought their German escorts.

Their resistance was quickly put down and eventually in excess of five thousand internees were successfully deported, but the Germans had been shaken by the open revolt and temporarily suspended plans for further deportations.

* * * * *

- Bialystok -

In early forty-three, thousand of the Jews from this ghetto were deported to Treblinka. As these groups were being prepared for the trip, many who were deemed too weak or sick to travel, were summarily executed.

* * * * *

- Concentration Camps -

By the end of nineteen forty-two, many small sub-camps had been set up near factories in order to supply forced labour. IG Farben established a synthetic rubber plant at Monowitz (Auschwitz III) and other camps were set up next to airplane factories, coal mines and rocket propellant plants. Conditions were horrendous in these camps and prisoners either worked steadily and productively or found themselves on a one-way trip to the gas chambers.

In early forty-three Himmler ordered the end of Aktion 14f13, the T-45 Euthanasia Program that had been initiated to exterminate selected non-productive camp prisoners within the concentration camp system which had then transported them to facilities for *'special handling'* in order to reduce overcrowding. Gas chambers and crematoria had now been set up within the confines of the camps and it was no longer necessary to transport these undesirables outside the fences to dispose of them.

Although the furnaces used for cremation after *'special handling'* were referred to as crematoriums by those involved in designing and producing them, in reality they were not that, but were in fact incinerators. In a cremation oven, there is a heating cycle, an incineration cycle and a cooling cycle, after which the ashes are recovered.

What the Nazis ordered and received were incinerators. These furnaces offered no cooling periods to enable the recovery of ashes between cremations. New corpses were simply fed into the ovens as the old ones were consumed.

The cost of operating an incinerator was considerably lower than that of a crematoria and the volume that could be handled was also considerably higher. Coal and other fuels were in short supply in the Reich and with the substantial increase in the number of cadavers to be incinerated, these incinerators could run continuously and each oven could be designed to handle several bodies at one time. After all, at this point in the war, no one was going to receive the ashes that were left after the burning of these cadavers.

* * * * *

- Medical Experiments -

- Josef Mengele -

Mengele was born on March sixteenth, nineteen-eleven, in Gunzburg, Bavaria, Germany. His father was the founder of the Karl Mengele & Sons company which was a manufacturer of farm machinery.

7

Josef was a good student with an interest in music, art and skiing. He finished high school in April of nineteen-thirty and went on to study medicine and philosophy at the University of Munich.

In nineteen thirty-one, Mengele joined the *'Stahlhelm, Bund der Frontsoldaten'*, which was a paramilitary organization that was absorbed into the SA in thirty-four. In thirty-five he earned a PhD in Anthropology from the University of Munich and in thirty-seven, became the assistant to Dr. Otmar Freiherr von Verschuer, a scientist conducting genetics research, with a particular interest in twins. Here Mengele concentrated his research on the genetic factors resulting in a cleft lip and palate. His thesis on the subject earned him a *'cum laude'* doctorate in medicine in thirty-eight. It is likely that this bright young man would have become a professor if he had continued on in his chosen field.

Instead Josef joined the SS in thirty-eight and was called up for military service in the Wehrmacht in June of nineteen-forty. He then volunteered for medical service in the Waffen-SS where he served with the rank of *'SS-Untersturmfuhrer'* in a medical reserve battalion until November of that year. He was then assigned to the *'SS-Rasse- und Siedlungshauptamt'* (SS Race and Resettlement Main Office) in Posen, where it was his job to evaluate candidates for future *'Germanization'*.

In January of nineteen forty-two Mengele joined the *'5th SS Panzer Division Wiking'*, fighting in the Ukraine as a battalion medical officer. While in this posting he was awarded the Iron Cross First Class as well as the Wound Badge in Black and the Medal for the care of the German People when he rescued two soldiers from a burning tank. In the summer of that year he was seriously wounded in action near Rostov-on-Don, declared unfit for further active serve and after his recovery, he was transferred to the Race and Resettlement Office in Berlin.

In Berlin he resumed his research association with von Verschuer, who was then working at the Kaiser Wilhelm Institute for Anthropology, Human Genetics and Eugenics. Mengele was promoted to *'SS-Hauptsturmfuhrer'* in April of forty-three.

In early forty-three, encouraged by von Verschuer, Josef, who foresaw an opportunity to undertake genetic research on human subjects, applied for transfer to the concentration camp service. His application was accepted and he was posted to Auschwitz. Upon his arrival, 'SS-Standortarzt', Eduard Wirths, who was the chief medical officer at Auschwitz, designated him as chief physician of the 'Zigeunerfamilienlager' (Gypsy family camp), which was located in the sub-camp of Birkenau.

* * * * *

- Tiger 1 -

In direct response to what the Germans ran up against during the initial invasion of Russia, specifically the Russian T-34 and KV-1 tanks, which tended to outgun the current German Panzers; Germany immediately began to design a new tank which would be more heavily armoured and pack a bigger punch.

Production of this new 'heavy' tank, designated as the Tiger 1, began in August of nineteen forty-two and would go through several modifications over the next year. The initial production run was twenty-five per month. The Tiger I carried much heavier armour and a far larger gun than its predecessors. The gun that was fitted to the new tank was the 88 mm model originally manufactured for anti-aircraft use. And it was capable of piercing the armour on the current Russian tanks. When the Tiger went operational it quickly built a reputation as the best in the field.

* * * * *

- The Family -

- Eric -

Eric had returned to Bordeaux and his U-boat in mid-December.
There was now a shift in cargo for his boat and the other two large U-boats under his command as they were now to primarily carry

specialized supplies and machined parts for both the Brazilian mining operation and the *'Operation Fatherland'* complex beneath, as well as an array of looted treasure taken from the massive hoard that was being drawn from the European occupied territories.

As a result of the increase in Germany's domestic armament production which had been brought about by Speer's influence, and the resulting high demand for and control of raw materials, the Count had cancelled the building of the fourth super U-boat. He did this in a move to stem rising pressure, if tentative, from the Kriegsmarine, and Donetz in particular, with regard to the specifics of U-boat production needs.

Not surprisingly, the admiral was beginning to take exception to additional materials being syphoned off for the building of the massive U-boats, none of which had, as of yet, been judged operational and turned over to him. Karl thought it wise to offer this carrot in hopes of keeping well under the admiral's radar. *'Operation Fatherland'* would simply have to make do with three of the massive craft.

The weather had worsened with the season and Eric was more than a little relieved that he had no civilian passengers on this trip and could therefore afford to spend the majority of the trip travelling below the surface.

* * * * *

- Friedrichshafen -

Karl and Wilhelm were of necessity splitting their time between Berlin, visiting Hitler with updates on super weapons, and visiting Friedrichshafen where the remainder of the family had settled into day to day life at the castle.

Ursula had noticed some spotting of blood shortly after the family's celebration of the war-shortened Christmas holidays and after a few days had felt compelled to tell both her mother and Friedrich of the condition.

Konrad and Baron Heinrich von Kliest, the family doctor, had each examined her and suggested several days of bed rest and the

Countess Erika had quite determinedly taken that a step further. It was mutually agreed, despite Ursula's protests that she was to turn over her art responsibilities to her husband and spend all of her remaining time properly caring for herself in preparation for her delivery.

CHAPTER TWO

- January -

- Allied Air Operations -

The main thrusts of the Allied bombing runs for this month are the U-boat bases and their production centers. Additionally, the manufacturing towns of Dusseldorf, Cologne and Essen are raided.

The fledgling USAAF now had eighty bombers and for the first time ventures into Germany to strike against Wilhelmshaven late in the month as they continue to hit targets in France, including Brest and St. Nazaire.

RAF Bomber Command makes its first daytime raid on Berlin, sending in a force of Mosquitoes on the thirtieth.

The quality and effectiveness of Bomber Command has improved with the addition of new Lancaster and 104 Halifax's into the heavy category and seventeen of the new Mosquitoes, which have replaced the ageing Wellingtons. Only one hundred and seventy-eight of the old bombers remain operational.

Improvements in navigational aids add to the success rate of the RAF effort. Gee, Oboe and H2S are much improved systems and are now becoming widely available.

* * * * *

- Battle of the Atlantic -

The Germans have two hundred and twelve operational U-boats in the theatre and one hundred and eighty-one, either training or on sea trials. The Allies lose fifty ships for a total tonnage of two hundred and sixty-one thousand, four hundred tons. The U-boats sink thirty-seven of these for two hundred and three thousand, one hundred tons.

* * * * *

- January First -

- Eastern Front -

The Russians take Velikeye Luki, Elista and Chikola from the Germans. The German 1st Panzer Division pulls back from the Terek River in order to thwart encirclement by the Russians.

* * * * *

- January Second -

- New Guinea -

Joint Aussie and American forces take Buna from the Japanese.

* * * * *

- January Third -

- Eastern Front -

Russian troops take back Mozdok and Malgobek and in the north, Manstein is fighting fiercely to prevent the Russians from cutting Kleist's forces off in the Caucasus. The Stalingrad siege continues as the sixth army continues to starve and freeze to death.

* * * * *

- January Fourth -

- Eastern Front -

The Russians take Nalchik in the Caucasus and Chernyshkovskiy on the River Chir.

* * * * *

- January Fifth -

- Eastern Front -

Russian troops take Prokhladny in the Caucasus and Morozovsk and Tsimlyansk in the north.

* * * * *

- Tunisia -

Commanded by General Clark, the US Fifth Army goes operational.

* * * * *

- January Sixth -

- Berlin -

Under a cloud of suspicion, Admiral Raeder resigns his post as Commander in Chief of the German Navy.

* * * * *

- January Seventh -
- New Guinea -

The Japanese successfully land reinforcements at Lae.

* * * * *

- January Eighth -

- Eastern Front -

In the south, Zimovniki falls to the Russians.

* * * * *

- Madagascar -

The administration of the Island is taken over by Free French forces.

* * * * *

- January Eleventh -

- Eastern Front -

The Russians take Georgivesk, Pyatigorsk and Mineralnye Vody in the Caucuses and to the north Kuberle, which is situated on the Zimovniki to Proletarskaya railway line.

* * * * *

- January Fourteenth -

- Morocco -

The Casablanca Conference of Allied leaders begins. Churchill and Roosevelt open discussions on the eventual invasion of mainland Europe and the impending invasions of Sicily and Italy. The principle for the demand for *'unconditional surrender'* from the Axis forces is raised and deliberated.

* * * * *

- Eastern Front -

The Russians take Pitomnik airfield, the larger of the two airfields which had been held by the Germans at Stalingrad, and their forces move across the Chervlennaya and Rossoshka Rivers.

* * * * *

- Morocco -

Talks between Churchill and Roosevelt and their military planners continue. There is a certain amount of animosity on both sides.

Each is accusing the other of failing to support their specific concerns. The British want a stronger commitment from the Americans for a `Germany First` effort, while the Americans feel that the British are not throwing enough resources into the war being waged in the Pacific against the Japanese.

Each side has good reason to complain. However, the individual leaders know full well that they must settle their differences and come out of the conference with a determined public appearance of speaking with one voice and sharing a solidified position on the future course of the war.

* * * * *

- January Fifteenth -

- Libya -

Montgomery is ready to move the Eighth Army. He starts his offensive with the long term aim of taking far-off Tripoli. As he begins the advance the Germans retreat from their positions at Buerat.

* * * * *

- January Sixteenth -

- Declaration of War -

Iraq declares war against the Axis powers.

* * * * *

- January Seventeenth -

- Eastern Front -

The Russians capture Millerovo and Zimovniki.

* * * * *

- January Eighteenth -

- Eastern Front -

Russian forces have managed to clear a six mile wide supply corridor into Leningrad but it is tenuous and under continuous German fire. They fight fiercely to keep it open but are unable to push the Germans back in order to widen it.

In the Caucuses they take Cherkessk and Divnoe.

* * * * *

- Tunisia -

German forces use their new *'Tiger'* tanks for the first time. Neither the Americans nor the British have anything comparable that is capable of taking the on the Tigers on equal terms.

* * * * *

- January Nineteenth -

- Eastern Front -

The Russians take Voronezh and Urazavo and a pocket of Hungarian troops are driven from Ostrogozhsk. They have now taken a total of fifty thousand prisoners, of which only approximately twenty-five hundred are ethnic Germans.

* * * * *

- Libya -

Tarhuna is taken as the British Eighth Army continues its offensive.

* * * * *

- January Twentieth -

- Eastern Front -

In its offensive against Army Group 'A', the Russians push the German forces back as they take Nevinnomyssk and Proletarskaya.

* * * * *

- Libya -

The British take Homs, forcing the German occupiers to retreat.

* * * * *

- January Twenty-First -

- Eastern Front -

The last remaining German-held airfield in Stalingrad is taken by Russian troops. Any remaining hope that the Luftwaffe might be able to supply the trapped Sixth Army is dashed.

Voroshilovsk, which is located between Stavropol and Armavir in the Caucasus, is captured by the Russians.

* * * * *

- January Twenty-Second -

- Eastern Front -

In the caucus, the Russians take Salsk.

* * * * *

- Libya -

The Germans pull out of Tripoli. Before leaving they do extensive damage to the port facilities and manage to transport out the majority of their stores.

The Eighth Army moves in the next day and immediately goes to work on the repair of the port installations.

* * * * *

- New Guinea -

Allied forces take Sanananda and clear the Japanese out of Papua.

* * * * *

- January Twenty-Third -

- Easter Front -

The Russians take Armavir in the Caucasus.

* * * * *

- January Twenty-fourth -

- Morocco -

The Casablanca Conference wraps up. The participants put up a public show of a united front and it has been agreed that the allies will settle for nothing less than *'unconditional surrender'* from the Axis forces.

* * * * *

- Eastern Front -

Manstein makes a final request for authorization from the Fuhrer to order Paulus to attempt a breakout from the Stalingrad pocket but once again Hitler refuses. In the west, Starobelsk is captured by the Russians.

* * * * *

- January Twenty-Fifth -

- Tunisia -

US forces have advanced to Maknassy. They now threaten the Japanese positions at Sfax and Gabes.

* * * * *

- January Twenty-Sixth -

The Russians take Voronezh.

* * * * *

- January Twenty-Seventh -

- Wilhelmshaven -

The US makes its first air raid into Germany. They launch fifty bombers against the big naval base.

* * * * *

- January Twenty-Eighth -

- Eastern Front -

The Russians manage to cut off a segment of the German Second Army as they take Kastornoye east of Voronezh.

* * * * *

- Berlin -

Sauckel, the Director General of Labour, issues a decree for further mobilization. Conscription will now include all males between sixteen and sixty-five and females between seventeen and fifty.

* * * * *

- January Twenty-Ninth -

- Eastern Front -

Russian forces take Kropotkin in the Caucuses and Novy Oskol which lies just north of Valuyki.

* * * * *

- Berlin -

Ernst Kaltenbrunner is appointed to replace the assassinated Heydrich as the head of the SD.

* * * * *

- Guadalcanal -

In the battle of Rennell Island, the Japanese take the day and the heavy cruiser, USS *'Chicago'* is sunk by Japanese aircraft.

* * * * *

- January Thirtieth -

- Eastern Front -

Russian forces take Tikhoretsk in the Caucuses and overrun the Maykop oilfields.

Hitler promotes Paulus to the rank of *'Generalfeldmarschall'*, as the Russians locate his headquarters in Stalingrad and surround it.

* * * * *

- Berlin -

Celebrations of the Nazi party's tenth anniversary are held. Goebbels and Goering make speeches. Using their new Mosquito bombers, the British mark the occasion by sending in their first daylight raid over the city. It is timed to coincide with the speeches.

Donitz is appointed to the position of Commander in Chief of the

German Navy, replacing Admiral Raeder.

* * * * *

- Tunisia -

The newly reequipped 21st Panzer Division goes on the offensive near Faid, easily forcing the retreat of the inexperienced defending French and American forces.

* * * * *

- January Thirty-First -

- Stalingrad -

Paulus surrenders his part of the divided German Sixth Army forces trapped in the city. The German forces under General Strecker are still holding out.

CHAPTER THREE

- February -

- Hitler -

- Wolfsschanze -

On February first Moscow announces the surrender of Paulus and Schmidt.

At Hitler's midday military conference Zeitzler expresses his doubts that the broadcast is anything more than a propaganda tactic but Hitler dismisses such a thought, replying:

'They have surrendered there formally and absolutely. Otherwise they would have closed ranks, formed a hedgehog, and shot themselves with their last bullets.'

Complaining bitterly, the Fuhrer goes on to berate Paulus.

'What hurts me the most personally is that I promoted him to Feldmarschall! I wanted to give him this final satisfaction. That's the last field marshal I shall appoint in this war. You mustn't count your chickens before they're hatched. I don't understand it at all.'

On the second of February the remaining Stalingrad pocket to the north also surrendered. The Russians announced that they had captured ninety-one thousand prisoners which included twenty-four Generals and twenty-five hundred officers.

Few of these prisoners would ever see Germany again, and one of the main causes for this treatment could be laid at Hitler's door. His earlier treatment of Russian prisoners of war had appalled the Russians and they were in no mood to treat the captured German, Italian and Romanian prisoners they were now beginning to take on the Eastern Front, with any sense of sincere empathy.

Hitler's depression deepened.

At his military conferences he held himself aloof, raged often and attendance was kept to a minimum. His pronouncements were often lacking in reality and predictability. At mealtimes he isolated himself from his military advisors and invitations were primarily limited to those of his junior adjutants and his secretaries. He now refused to listen to music and instead ran to long monologues. These consisted of a reliving of his past, his early days in Vienna, the early days of the party and conversations about the war or world affairs were 'verboten'. Those in attendance got to the point where they had heard it all before, over and over again, ad nauseam.

Due to the deteriorating military situation, a depressed Hitler refused to speak publically at the upcoming Sportpalast meeting. He left the matter in Goebel's hands.

* * * * *

- Inner Circle -

- Speer -

Speer and Goebbels were convinced that certain austerities placed upon the German citizenry were essential and that the Nazi bureaucratic administrative apparatus had to be simplified, consumption brought under control and cultural activities restricted. Both men still had relatively free access to Hitler at this point but they were finding it difficult to convince the Fuhrer that these steps were necessary if Germany was going to have any hope of weathering an extended war.

Speer suggested to Hitler that Goebbels had a good grasp on the situation and should be placed in a position of authority over these matters. He and Goebbels were making some real headway in reaching that end when the ever present Bormann got wind of the idea and. sensing a challenge in the balance of power, immediately took steps to prevent what he saw as a power grab by his rivals.

Bormann convinced Hitler to instead appoint Dr. Hans Lammers, who was head of the Reich Chancellery and Bormann's strong ally, to look after solving the problems. Lammers was a man without imagination or initiative and one who Bormann knew would have no truck with any thought of interference with his sacred bureaucratic procedures.

A man Bormann could control with ease.

Since January, Lammers had served as President of the cabinet when Hitler was absent from their meetings. Now he, along with Bormann, moved to create a three man junta which would henceforth represent the Nazi Party (Bormann), the state (Lammers) and the army which would by represented by Field Marshal Wilhelm Keitel (Chief of the OKW).

They envisioned that this new *'Committee of Three'* would then be given exercised dictatorial powers over the home front.

Goebbels, Speer, Goering and Himmler, an unlikely alliance to be sure, all of whom had their own spies with ears attuned to what happened in Hitler's office, jointly saw this concept as a power grab by Bormann and a direct threat to their individual personal empires. They immediately joined forces and moved to block the formation of such a body.

Internal wrangling began in a battle that neither side could realistically hope to win. Lammers got the job and the *'Committee of Three'* was created. Speer, with Goebel's support, pushed them for these radical changes. Frick, the Minister of the Interior, supported by Lammers and Bormann expressed strong doubts as to the necessity of change and Sauckel boasted that he could supply all the workers needed from the conquered territories without such action, including those skilled workers required. Goebbels demand that the leading party members forgo their previous, limitless luxuries was met with silence and no action.

Hitler responded in his normal fashion. He listened to all and made no decisive decision. In the end little changed. The committee stayed. It had no additional powers. Yet another bureaucratic nightmare had been created and the power status quo was maintained.

* * * * *

- Goebbels -

Speer and Goebbels went at the problem from a different angle. Goebbels carried the ball. On the eighteenth of February Goebbels delivered a speech to the carefully chosen audience at the Sportpalast. Its theme was *'Total War'* and it was not only aimed at the leadership, which had bucked any changes but was also directed toward the world population in hope that it might motivate the democratic members of the Allies to turn against Russia and consider joining Germany in defeating the Bolsheviks .

Domestically, it was primarily a move to circumvent Bormann, Lammers and the others and gain acceptance for belt tightening from the people of Germany who would then hopefully pressure the naysayers into submission and force action on change.

There are many who consider Joseph Goebbels to be the greatest propagandist the world has ever seen and, of all his speeches, this particular event was his very best. The structuring and content of this particular oration can give one some insight into both the times and the man. An evaluation of this speech goes a long way toward understanding not only the ability of Joseph Goebbels to drive home a concept, but to help grasp his understanding of the mindset of the German citizenry of the day.

Goebbels had set the scene in the Sportpalast very carefully on the occasion of this speech, both from the point of presentation and that of audience. Those entering the Sportpalast on that day found themselves behind and under a massive banner bearing the all-capitals words in German *'TOTAL KRIEG - KURZESTER KRIEG'* (TOTAL WAR - BRIEFEST WAR) , and the massive enclosure was festooned with Nazi party banners set in a sea of Swastikas.

From start to finish, it was a carefully staged affair.

For several weeks beforehand, everywhere a German looked, he or she saw the slogan: *'The Wheels Must Turn Only for Victory'.* It was found on billboards, in shop windows, on walls and bannered on trains. The statement seemed to loom and take prominence everywhere the average Berliner travelled.

On the fifteenth of the month Goebbels issued a decree to Reichsleiters, Gauleiters and all army headquarters that demanded complete mobilization for victory. On the same day he gave a speech in Dusseldorf which was entitled: *'Do You Want Total War?'* In that speech he advised that: *'Two thousand years of Western civilization were in danger from a Russian victory, one forged by international Jewry.'* The crowd had responded with cries of *'Hang them!'* and Goebbels had gone on to promise that Germany would retaliate: *'with the total and radical extermination and elimination of Jewry.'* Those in the audience responded with wild shouts of agreement punctuated by waves of rolling laughter.

Goebbels alluded to the fact that the audience included people from *'all classes and occupations'*, while in fact the people invited were selected very carefully and were in fact far from representative of the German common man or woman of the time. The attending crowd was made up of trusted party members only and all wore civilian clothing rather than uniforms. The songs they broke into *'spontaneously'*, were orchestrated, as were their exquisite and perfectly timed *'comments'* and *'shouts of approval'*.

As he spoke, Goebbels skillfully brought the house to a frenzied crescendo and when he was finished, he asked.

'Do you want total war? Do you want total war? Do you want it, if necessary, to be even more total and radical than can even be imagined today?'

The response was a thunderous chorus of *'Ja's'*.

The epic speech, which had been widely broadcast throughout Germany, had achieved one of its goals certainly - that of firing up the German public and getting their support for an all-out effort to turn the tide of war.

* * * * *

- Hitler's Leadership Questioned -

To say that nineteen forty-three had started inauspiciously for Germany is a very distinct understatement. The country was suffering major military problems on all fronts.

On February second the Battle of Stalingrad had ended with the surrender of the Sixth Army. Germany's unconditional surrender had been demanded by the Allies at the end of the Casablanca Conference. The Russians were beginning to retake territory on the Easter Front and Rommel's Africa Korps had been reduced to a mere shadow of an Axis fighting force in North Africa.

The Axis forces were pinned in Tunisia, between two strong Allied forces, one advancing from Algeria and the other from Libya. Italy's forces in Africa had all but collapsed, turning it realistically into a German fight and in the Pacific, the Americans had just completed the retaking of Guadalcanal.

Goebbels' speech in the Sportpalast had pulled few punches as to the seriousness of the situation facing the Germans on the Eastern Front. While the average German man in the street had probably accepted that the fight was not going to be an easy one, he still felt that Hitler was a man who could not lose and that Germany could win the war if everyone did their part.

Those in the hierarchy of the Nazi Party and that of the German military machine however, could smell defeat and were scrambling to find an honorable way out of a very bad situation. It was now that many of these, in various different ways, began to express their serious concerns as to the Fuhrer's recent leadership.

Under the circumstances this was not done publically of course, but only between peers who could be trusted.

An example of this loss of faith took place on the evening after the speech given at the Sportpalast, when several ranking individuals of the Reich assembled at the expansive residence that Goebbels had built near the Brandenburg Gate shortly before the beginning of the war.

Several of the attendees, including Field Marshal Milch, Minister of Justice Thierack, State Secretary Stuckart from the Interior Ministry, and Goering's right hand man, State Secretary Korner, Funk and Ley met privately with Speer and Goebbels.

Milch and Speer raised the suggestion that perhaps those present could ensure better control of the domestic situation if they were to find a way of using Goering's powers as *'Chairman of the Council of Ministers for the Defense of the Reich' to* circumvent Bormann's iron grip and questionable involvement in every decision made in that regard. A lively discussion of the possibilities ensued.

Just over a week later, Speer was invited back to the Goebbels' extravagant domicile for another meeting. Funk and Ley were also invited. While liveried servants served French cognac and tea the conversation was light but once the servants were dismissed, Goebbels opened the serious conversation.

'Things cannot go on this way. Here we are sitting in Berlin. Hitler does not hear what we have to say about the situation. I cannot influence him politically, cannot even report the most urgent measures in my area. Everything goes through Bormann. Hitler must be persuaded to come to Berlin more often.'

He paused to let his words sink in and then continued.

'Domestic policy has slipped entirely out of Hitler's hands. It is being controlled by Bormann, who manages to give Hitler the feeling that he is still directing things. Bormann is guided only by ambition with his rigidly doctrinaire approach. He presents a great danger to any sane evolution of policy. First and foremost his influence must be diminished'

Surprisingly, considering he was in still in awe of Hitler, Goebbels did not spare Hitler in his remarks, as he'd always previously done.

'We are not having a leadership crisis, but strictly speaking, a 'Leader' crisis.

He went on to express his disbelief and serious concerns over the fact that Hitler had seemingly removed himself from the important task of politics and turned instead to personally taking the role of Commander in Chief of the armed forces. The failure at Stalingrad had driven this point home for him. In his estimation, if Germany was going to win the conflict, it needed Hitler to turn his attention back to the domestic Political situation where his strengths lay and let the military leaders see to the fighting of the war.

The other men in the room knew from long experience that when it came to political savvy, Goebbels was an exemplary judge of the situation and they readily agreed with his assessment.

Speer revisited his and Milch's earlier proposal that they attempt to bring Goering in and through him, use the exceptional powers that he had been given by Hitler before the war, to deal with Bormann. The powers Hitler had decreed at that time had given Goering, who held the highest military rank in the Reich, the authority to issue decrees even without Hitler's knowledge or collaboration. Over time, the majority of this power had been usurped by Bormann and his henchman Lammers and the indolent Goering had foolishly ignored what was going on.

Goebbels was currently feuding with Goering over Propaganda Minister's decree ordering that one hundred thousand restaurants and clubs in Germany be closed in order to encourage the civilian population to contribute more to the war effort.

While Goering clearly had no concerns about the fate of the other restaurants, he had taken great exception to having his own favorite restaurant closed down. He had then promptly taken Goebbels to task for it. Goebbels had held his ground, insisting that the restaurant be closed despite Goings whining, but Goering, who had tremendous powers, simply had it reopened as a private club for the Luftwaffe and there wasn't a thing Goebbels could do about it.

Therefore Goebbels was currently not on speaking terms with Goering. After discussion and despite admitting to each other that it seemed like an idiotic thing to do, those in the room asked Speer to speak to Goering about their idea.

Idiotic, in view of the fact that Goering had been doing little more than living an aimless life of excessive luxury for the last few years and during which time he'd given little thought to what was going on around him, unless of course it was something, however minor, that was personally important to him, his position or standing in Germany.

They were desperate men and, idiotic approach or not, they could see no other option that could be reasonably expected to successfully curtail Bormann's tremendous control over Hitler.

* * * * *

- Speer/Reichsmarschall Goering -

Up to this point in the war Speer had purposefully done his level best to keep out of the politics of the Nazi regime, a decision that had served him well and kept him out of the often intense infighting. He was now stepping out of the shadows and aligning himself with a faction of others within the tense inner circle. For the first time he was openly taking sides in the ongoing power struggles that permeated the group and was about to accept all the personal risks that decision could entail.

As it happened, Goering was currently taking a very long vacation. He was staying at his summer house which was located within the compound at Obersalzberg. The reason for the vacation was explained to Speer by Milch. It seemed that the Reichsmarschall had been horribly offended by Hitler's recent public criticisms over his leadership of the Luftwaffe.

Goering readily received Speer who arrived on the twenty-eight of February, the day after the meeting at Goebbels' mansion. Although Speer was by this time used to finding Goering dressed in his green velvet dressing gown sporting a large ruby brooch, he was somewhat taken aback by the Reichsmarschall's lacquered nails and, what appeared to be, rouged face.

Speer, conscious of the importance of his visit, promptly moved past the initial surprise of these idiosyncrasies and the two men soon entered into an open and honest discussion which lasted for several hours. Goering paid careful attention to Speer's recap of the meeting of the night before, occasionally removing a handful of large uncut gemstones from his pocket and letting them trail through his fingertips as he listened.

Speer recognized almost immediately that Goering was very pleased to have been chosen by the others as the man capable of taking on Bormann, whom he readily agreed, was largely responsible for the disarray of the domestic situation. While in the end he was on board with the concept of what needed to be done, it became clear to Speer during the discussions, that Goering was self-centred and petty enough to still be smarting over Goebbels' determination to close Horcher, his favorite restaurant. Goering kept pushing aside the topic of the need to curtail Bormann and coming back to his unhappiness with Goebbels' stubborn inability to see that his wish for the restaurant to remain open should have been accepted without question and certainly not in any way challenged, as had in fact been the case.

Speer danced around the incident of the restaurant, trying to come at it from different angles and was finally able to convince Goering that it had more than likely just been a misunderstanding between two very busy men. He then suggested that Goering demonstrate his graciousness by personally inviting Goebbels to visit him so that they could put the matter of the restaurant behind them and properly discuss the anti-Bormann plan now being studied.

After leaving Goering, Speer immediately called Goebbels and apprised him of what had taken place. Goebbels arrived at Berchtesgaden the next day and he and Speer went directly to see Goering. Speer exchanged greetings and then, confident that the golden-tongued Goebbels could quickly smooth things over between the other two men, left Goering and Goebbels to talk it out. A short while later he was called back into the room and as he entered he turned his gaze immediately to Goering in an attempt to read the Reichsmarschall's mood.

Goering's frame of mind was readily apparent. His appetite had clearly been whetted for a battle that he was sure he could win.

As he spoke, Goering's eyes were sparkling, and he was rubbing his hands with glee at the prospect of the power struggle that was about to begin.

'First of all the personnel of the Council of Ministers for the Defense of the Reich must be broadened. Goebbels and I ought to become members; the fact that we were not, by the way, indicates that the council was of little importance.'

The discussions on remedial action to be taken began and it was agreed that von Ribbentrop needed replacing, what was needed was a Foreign Minister who was pushing for a rational policy, not someone who simply acted as Hitler's yes man and one who was forever mouthing excuses for the sorry military situation Germany now found themselves in.

Goebbels quietly guided the direction of the conversation.

'The Fuhrer has not seen through Lammers any more than he

has seen through Ribbentrop.'

Despite his bulk, Goering suddenly sprang from his chair.

'He's always putting in a word edgewise, torpedoing me below the water line. But that is ending right now! I'm going to see to it, gentlemen!'

Obviously enjoying Goering's rage, but every cognizant of Goering's social ineptitude, Goebbels continued to fan the flames but counselled a cautious approach to the situation.

'Depend upon it, Herr Goering; we are going to open the Fuhrer's eyes about Bormann and Lammers. Only we mustn't risk going too far. We'll have to proceed slowly. You know the Fuhrer. At any rate we had better not talk too openly with the other members of the Council of Ministers. There's no need for them to know that we intend to slowly spike the Committee of Three. We're only acting out of loyalty to the Fuhrer. We have no personal ambitions, but if each one of us supports the others to the Fuhrer, we'll soon be on top of the situation and can form a solid fence around the Fuhrer.'

As Speer saw Goebbels to the door after the wrap-up of the discussions, the Propaganda Minister commented.

'This is going to work. Goering has really come to life again, don't you think?'

Later, Goering joined Speer for a long walk in the peaceful surrounds of the Obersalzberg. They talked about Bormann as they strolled. Goering had warmed to the theme and told Speer that it was obvious that Bormann was determined to be the man to step into Hitler's shoes and that he would stop at nothing to outmaneuver him in this regard as well as to cast doubt with Hitler upon the abilities of the others in the inner circle.

Speer took advantage of this opening to explain at great length to the Reichsmarschall what he had personally observed of Bormann's regular undermining of Goering's authority and stature with the Fuhrer. He spoke of the shared tea-times at Berchtesgaden with the Fuhrer, occasions that were no longer offered to Goering, during which he had experienced Bormann's repeated badmouthing of the Reichsmarschall and his fusillade of snide remarks directed at Goering whenever an opportunity arose. He punctuated this observation with the explanation that Bormann never worked by direct attack on anyone, but instead managed to weave little negative incidents into his conversation that, in the end, left Hitler with a very bad impression of that individual. That accomplished, the Fuhrer would express some negative assessment of the man himself and Bormann would then make no comment other than to issue some minor positive characteristic about the target, always one that left a bad taste in Hitler's mouth. It was a system that over time, and Bormann spent more time with Hitler than anyone else, would cause the Fuhrer to strongly dislike the individual in question.

Speer assured Goering that this was what Bormann was doing to him personally and was also trying to do in relation to the Reichsmarschall himself. By the time Speer left the Obersalzberg, Goering was wound up as tight as a spring and Speer was confident that the conspiracy was going to go well.

He was not the first, nor would he be the last man to underestimate Bormann.

* * * * *

- SS Expansion-

The Waffen-SS expanded again in February, when the 9th SS Panzer Division *'Hohenstaufen'* and its sister division, the 10th SS Panzer Division *'Frundsberg'*, were formed in France.

* * * * *

- Deportations -

- Romania -

The Romanian government proposed to the Allies that seventy thousand Romanian Jews should be transferred to Palestine. They received no response from either the British or the Americans.

* * * * *

- Greece -

Jews are ordered to move into Ghettos.

* * * * *

- Berlin -

Jews who had been working in the armaments industry in Berlin are deported to Auschwitz.

* * * * *

- Extermination Camps -

- Majdanek -

Like Auschwitz, Majdanek began its life as a concentration and forced labour camp. Unlike those constructed for *'Operation Reinhard'*, it had been built in nineteen forty-one, adjacent to and within sight of a major city, that of Lublin.

Up until mid-February of forty-three, it had been officially operated as a prisoner of war camp run by the Waffen-SS. It was now reclassified as a concentration camp.

* * * * *

- The Family -

- Operation Fatherland -

On February twenty-second, no longer believing that he could safely hold back a Kriegsmarine demand that the massive U-boats be brought into service for the Reich, Count Karl von Stauffer ordered that the next phase of *'Operation Fatherland'* commence.

For Eric this meant that he was to take on a more major roll.

The other two U-boats would temporarily continue to shuttle specialized equipment, small numbers of human cargo, and looted treasure garnered in the occupied countries, from France to Brazil. Eric's U-boat would now take up the task of shifting personnel and treasure that was already in Brazil, to the coasts of North America in the next step in the plan to prepare for the end of the war.

The first measure in this new phase was to remove both Eric and his massive craft from the Nazi radar. This was accomplished by means of transmitting a fictional message to U-boat headquarters. The radio message was brief, advising that the big U-boat was under murderous attack from two allied anti-submarine aircraft.

Simply put; on February twenty-third, nineteen forty-three the first of the three massive submarines was considered lost at sea with all hands and ceased to exist as part of the German navy.

Only a few of the top members of *'Operation Fatherland'*, and the immediate family were aware of the ploy and they each had a part to play in the public mourning process that followed the official announcement of the U-boats' demise.

It was planned that the two remaining craft would suffer similar fictional fates over the next few weeks and would then take part in missions similar to those Eric was now initiating. From that point on, all three of the big U-boats would work out of the hidden U-boat pens in Brazil on purely *'Operation Fatherland'* activities.

Under the plan put into motion by the Count, Eric, when not at sea, was now to remain in Brazil until the end of hostilities. It meant that he would no longer have direct contact with his immediate family in Friedrichshafen, nor could he visit Germany; but it freed him up to continue working toward the future development of the *'Operation Fatherland'* scenario.

It also meant that he and Heidi could be married and they did so in a small private ceremony on the last day of the month.

* * * * *

- The Count -

Karl von Stauffer knew he would be on pins and needles until all three U-boats had been crossed off the Kriegsmarine clipboard. Donetz had moved up in the world and it was becoming more and more difficult to hold him off.

The Count was sitting in his office mulling the situation over in his mind when he received the call from SS-General Dieter Bichler, *'Operation Fatherland's'* security expert. The General asked if they could meet for lunch. Karl had no difficulty in reading into the brief request, despite the relaxed tone, that something important had come up and they needed to talk. He immediately agreed to meet.

Thirty minutes later the two men faced each other across a small but relatively isolated table in their preferred restaurant. They ordered and when the waitress left, the General went right to the heart of the matter.

"Himmler must have taken offence at something you've done recently. He has been on to Goering suggesting that your son-in-law Friedrich should be relieved of his position at Friedrichshafen, in view of the fact that there is a pilot shortage on the Eastern Front. As you are aware he is a devious bastard and I'm afraid he intends to get back at you for whatever affront it was by directly damaging your family."

Karl swore softly and fired up a cigarette.

"I'd hoped that I'd been able to smooth things over. It's due to Hitler removing both myself and Wilhelm from the SS."

Dieter nodded and let out a sigh.

"Yes, well with Himmler, you must always expect the worst. Anyway, I've managed to go through Milch and have him whisper into Goering's ear that Himmler is simply trying to get loot from the occupied territories for himself. The SS and is taking this step in order to move in on the valuables stored at Friedrichshafen and see to it that they slip out from under the protection of Friedrich and his Luftwaffe contingent."

The strain evident in Karl's face slipped away as he took this in and the General allowed himself a self-effacing smile before continuing.

"…Well you know Goering well enough to understand how that

would go down, so I feel confident that Friedrich is safe in his current placement.   I would, however, advise that you be cognisant of Himmler's displeasure and keep an eye out for whatever other moves he may have in mind."

Beer arrived and they silently lifted their steins until they were alone again. Karl let his eyes meet and hold the General's.

"Thank you Dieter and you may rest assured that I will take great care to do whatever I can to bring the SS-Reichsfuhrer back on side. He is not an enemy any sane man would seek.

* * * * *

- Friedrichshafen -

Under Erika's watchful eyes, Ursula was living a very quiet life. She was forbidden any outside activities and, although bored to death, she was no longer spotting

To everyone's delight Gabriella announced that she believed she was again with child.

CHAPTER FOUR

- February -

- Allied Air Operations -

As a continuation of the previous month's activities, the Allied bomber offensive is targeted toward the U-boat pens in both France and Germany. St. Nazaire and Lorient receive the heaviest attacks while Hamburg, Wilhelmshaven and Bremen are also struck.

In the Mediterranean theatre, air strikes are made against Naples, Turin, Palermo, Spezia and Milan.

* * * * *

- Battle of the Atlantic -

Donitz has approximately one hundred operational U-boats in the Atlantic during the month. The Germans lose nineteen U-boats. Newly improved Allied radar comes into play with one squadron of modified Liberator bombers being supplied with the new equipment. Though only these few units are being used operationally, they are accredited with one of the U-boat kills.

The heavy bombing of U-boat pens is not particularly effective due to the fact that the bombs currently available do not have the hitting power necessary to penetrate the thick covers of reinforced concrete capping the pens.

In all theatres of war the Allies lose seventy-three ships for a total of four hundred and three thousand, one hundred tons. Axis subs sink sixty-three of these ships for three hundred and fifty-nine thousand, three hundred tons.

* * * * *

- February First -

- Eastern Front -

Russian forces take Svatovo.

* * * * *

February Second -

- Mediterranean -

The British submarine *'Turbulent'* sinks an Italian tanker near Palermo, before it can deliver much needed fuel supplies to the Italian naval squadron based on Sicily.

* * * * *

- February Third -

- Eastern Front -

The Russians take Kuschevka, fifty miles south of Rostov on the Soskya River, while their forces driving toward Kharkov, take Kupyansk.

* * * * *

- February Fourth -

- Eastern Front -

The Russians continue to advance on all fronts. They take Shcigny east of Kursk and Kanevskaya which is situated only thirty miles from the Sea of Azov.

The German Seventeenth Army is effectively cut off in the Kuban with no option but to seek resupply by sea from the Crimea.

* * * * *

- Tunisia -

Advance units of the British Eighth Army cross the border from Libya into Tunisia. Libya is now firmly in the hands of the Allies.

* * * * *

- February Fifth -

- Rome -

Mussolini removes his son-in-law from the post of Foreign Minister and assumes the role personally.

* * * * *

- Eastern Front -

Russian Forces take Stary Oskol and Izyum.

* * * * *

- February Sixth -

- Washington -

The African and European theatres are separated within the US command structure. General Anders is appointed to head up the European effort while General Eisenhower is to remain in charge in North Africa.

* * * * *

- Eastern Front -

In the Caucasus the Russians take Yeysk on the Sea of Azov and Lisichansk on the Donets River also comes under Russian control as their forces cross the river at Izyum and reach Barvenkovo. Manstein flies to a meeting with Hitler and is supported in his view that the German forces must retreat to a line behind the River Mius.

* * * * *

- February Seventh -

- Eastern Front -

The Russians take Azov at the mouth of the Don. Their forces in the Ukraine capture Kramatorsk.

* * * * *

- February Eighth -

- Eastern Front -

The Russians take Kursk.

* * * * *

- February Ninth -

- Guadalcanal -

Over several days the Japanese have removed their troops from the island giving the offensive US forces their first strategic win. The island is now firmly in American hands.

* * * * *

- February Tenth -

- Eastern Front -

Russian forces take Volchnsk and Chuguyev and are now only twenty miles east of Kharkov.

* * * * *

- February Eleventh -

- Eastern Front -

The Russians take Lozvaya.

* * * * *

- February Twelfth -

- Eastern Front -

The Russian offensive continues to push the German forces back. In the Caucasus they take Krasnodar. Krasnoarmeskoye and Kommunarsk are also seized.

- February Thirteenth -

- Tunisia -

Rommel launches a counter attack against inexperienced US forces, taking Sidi Bouzid and Gafsa, as the battle of the Kasserine Pass begins.

* * * * *

- Easter Front -

The Russians force the Germans out of Novocherkassk.

* * * * *

- February Fourteenth -

- Eastern Front -

Rostov-on-Don, Voroshilovgrad and Drasny Sulin fall to the continuing Russian offensive.

* * * * *

- February Sixteenth -

- Tunisia -

Forward units of the British Eighth take Medenine as they approach Rommel's Mareth line. The German offensive against the green American troops is proving very effective, having virtually destroyed a good two-thirds of the US 1st Armoured Division, including two full tank battalions.

* * * * *

- Eastern Front -

Hitler flies into Manstein's Headquarters at Zaporozhye and stays for two days reviewing and agreeing to the plan for a major counterattack.

* * * * *

- February Eighteenth -

- Tunisia -

German forces enter the Allied-abandoned city of Sbetla and Rommel, who has satisfied himself that the American forces aligned against them are no threat, pushes for an immediate expanded operation against them. His divided German/Italian high command dithers over the suggestion of an increase in the goals of the current offensive and, deeply frustrated, Rommel bites his tongue and holds his position.

* * * * *

- February Nineteenth -

- Tunisia -

Rommel finally gets authorization to expand his push against the American troops, but the Italian High Command disagrees with the Desert Fox's plan to attack Tebessa and instead orders him to direct his forces toward Le Kef. Contrary to Rommel's plan, which would have taken the American by complete surprise, this is what the Allies expect him to do and they are well prepared to defend. Additionally, while Rommel has been granted his request to have the 10th Panzer placed under his command, the important Tiger battalion is held back from him.

Collectively these changes in both target and equipment will effectively nullify the Desert Foxe's original audacious plan.

* * * * *

- February Twentieth -

- Eastern Front -

Russian troops take Pavlograd, entering into a salient bracketed by strong German forces on each flank.

* * * * *

- February Twenty-first -

- Solomon Chain -

American forces take the Russell Islands.

* * * * *

- February Twenty-Second -

- White Rose Movement -

The *'die Weiss Rose'* movement is a non-violent, intellectual resistance group active in Nazi Germany. It is made up of a group of students and their philosophy professor from the University of Munich. The students have been handing out anonymous leaflets and carrying out a graffiti campaign aimed at the Nazi government since June of nineteen forty-two and on this date the six top leaders are arrested by the Gestapo, tried and beheaded.

* * * * *

- Eastern Front -

Manstein's counterattack begins as the Russian troops continue to advance into the salient quickly outdistancing their supply lines. They come within twelve miles of Manstein's headquarters and then run out of fuel. Although outnumbered seven-to-one, the Germans go on the offensive. The First and Fourth Panzer Armies move northward from a line to the west of Krasnoarmeskoye while the Group Kampf, made up of three full divisional-strength panzer groups, drive south from Krasnodar.

* * * * *

- February Twenty-Third -

- Eastern Front -

Northeast of Kharkov, Russian forces take Sumy and Lebedin. In the south, Manstein's counteroffensive is making solid progress.

* * * * *

- February Twenty-Fourth -

- Tunisia -

A week too late, Rommel is appointed to command Army Group Afrika which will now include von Arnim's Fifth Panzer Army and the First Italian Army which is under the command of General Messe. The desert fox now skillfully pulls his forces back to the Eastern Dorsal, leaving a raft of booby traps in his wake.

* * * * *

- February Twenty-Fifth -

- Eastern Front -

In the Caucasus the Russians take Mingrelsk.

* * * * *

- February Twenty-Eighth -

- Norway -

A commando raid against the Norsk Hydro power station near Ryukan, conducted by Norwegian soldiers parachuted in from Britain under the codename *'Operation Gunnerside'*, causes heavy damage. This plant is being used by the German occupiers to create the *'heavy water'* needed for their strategic atomic research program.

CHAPTER FIVE

- March -

- Hitler -

As mentioned earlier, the sparkle of Hitler's rising star had begun to seriously tarnish by this point in the war. It isn't surprising then that, despite the inherent danger for anyone taking part in such overt activity, there was a slowly building resistance to his leadership.

Ludwig Paul Lochner was an American political activist and journalist who served for many years as head of the Berlin bureau of the Associated Press. When Germany went to war, he chose to remain in the country and he was one of the first foreign correspondent to follow the German forces into battle and report on the war from a relatively unbiased perspective. He continued to do so and in nineteen thirty-nine, based on his reporting from Nazi Germany, was awarded the Pulitzer Prize for correspondence.

In December of forty-one, when Germany went to war with the United States, Lochner, as were all American citizens remaining within the Reich, was interned by the Nazi government. He spent nearly five months behind bars before being released in May of forty-two as part of a prisoner exchange for interred German diplomats and correspondents. From nineteen forty-two to forty-four Lochner, now back in the US, worked as a news analyst and radio commentator for the National Broadcasting Company.

Lochner had many historic contacts within Nazi Germany and, still a serious anti-war political activist, he used these contacts to work toward a swift end to the war. He actively solicited those within Germany who he knew to be anti-Nazi, with a view to bringing the war to an end. Acting as a conduit for these early groups resulted in him making several attempts to inform President Roosevelt of the growing resistance movement against Hitler within Germany. He was hoping to give Roosevelt the radio code of two separate groups opposed to Hitler so that he could then inform the groups of exactly what type of political administration they proposed for a new Germany, without Hitler, that would be acceptable to the Allied powers.

He expected to be welcomed with open arms.

In fact he was rebuffed by the President's appointments secretary and eventually wrote a personal note to Roosevelt in which he revealed the existence of the codes and his willingness to provide them to the President. He eagerly awaited a response but after several days with none forthcoming, he was informed that his suggestion was viewed by official sources as *most embarrassing'* and would he please desist.

The policy of the American government of the time was that of *unconditional surrender'*, and that meant that there was to be no negotiation with Germany, therefore no encouragement of German resisters and no official contact with anyone in the Reich who held high office, either political or military.

* * * * *

- Anti-Hitler Plot -

- Hans Oster -

'Generalmajor' Hans Oster, like many other German officers, initially welcomed the Nazi regime. He had served in the army during the Great War until nineteen sixteen, after which he was appointed as a captain in the German General Staff. He moved from there to working under Goering in the Prussian police and in October of nineteen thirty-three he transferred to the *'Abwehr'* or (*'Amt Ausland/Abwehr im Oberkommando der Wehrmacht'*) (German Military Intelligence).

After the Nazi Party had come into power, Oster became more and more disillusioned with the Nazi's policies and had played a central role in the first military conspiracy to overthrow Hitler, which was based on Hitler's determination to invade Czechoslovakia. In August of nineteen thirty-eight, Chief of the General Staff, Colonel

General Ludwig Beck spoke openly at a meeting of army generals in Berlin about his opposition on a war with the Western powers over Czechoslovakia. When Hitler got wind of this, he demanded and received Beck's resignation. At the time, Beck was highly respected in the army and his removal shocked the officer corps. His successor as Chief of Staff was Franz Halder.

Beck remained in touch with Halder and Oster and, privately, considered Hitler *'the incarnation of evil'*. The three men worked toward bringing Hitler down with a military coup and during September, plans for such a move were formulated. This conspiracy involved the Field Marshal who was the army commander for the Berlin Military Region, and thus had a very good chance of success.

Oster, and his immediate co-conspirators, Hans Bernd Gisevius, a German diplomat and intelligence officer and Hjalmar Schacht, President of the Reichsbank, urged Halder and Beck to stage an immediate coup against Hitler, but the army generals hesitated, arguing that they could only guarantee support from among the officer corps for such a step if Hitler made overt moves towards war.

Halder nevertheless asked Oster to draw up plans for a coup. It was eventually agreed that Halder would instigate the coup when Hitler committed an overt step towards war. Therefore, emissaries of the conspirators travelled to England, with the assistance of Oster's *'Abwehr'*, to urge them to stand firm against Hitler over the looming Sudetenland situation. By September the twenty-eighth, despite these moves, Chamberlain agreed to meet Hitler in Munich and subsequently accepted the dismemberment of Czechoslovakia.

This Nazi diplomatic triumph undermined and thoroughly demoralized the conspirators and under the circumstances Halder would no longer support a coup attempt.

As war again grew more likely in late spring of thirty-nine, the efforts for a pre-emptive coup were revived. Oster was still in contact with Halder and the Field Marshal, who was the army commander for the Berlin Military Region.

However, many officers, particularly those from aristocratic Prussian backgrounds, were strongly anti-Polish and saw the recovery of Danni as justifiable. That being the case, the move to intervene was again placed on the back burner.

Once war had broken out, the resistance to a coup by military officers became more problematic since such a move could lead to the defeat of Germany. However, when Hitler decided to attack France soon after the Polish campaign had been won Halder, along with other ranking generals who were convinced they were not ready for such a campaign, were shaken to the core and yet again entertained the idea of a coup, which was now being strongly pushed by Oster and Canaris.

However, when Hitler vowed to destroy what he referred to as the *'spirit of Zossen'* (Zossen being where the headquarters of the Army High Command was located), by which he meant the nest of defeatism, Halder became convinced that their conspiracy was about to be discovered and immediately shut things down and destroyed all incriminating documents.

The period between nineteen forty and forty-two was the lowest point of German resistance. Germany under Hitler was doing just fine, thank you. Others who steadfastly opposed Hitler and the Nazi regime were of the opinion that the Fuhrer's enormous popularity with the people made taking any overt any action against him impossible.

Despite these setbacks, Oster nevertheless succeeded in rebuilding an effective resistance network. In nineteen forty-one, when the systematic extermination of the Jews began after the invasion of Russia, his *'Abwehr'* group opened communications with *'Generalmajor'* Henning von Tresckow's resistance cell, which was located within Army Group Center, and in forty-two he recruited General Friedrich Olbricht, head of the General Army Office headquartered at the Bendlerblock in central Berlin. This General commanded the control of an independent system of communications controlling reserve units all over Germany.

By forty-three Oster's apathy had jelled into intense dislike for both Hitler and the Nazi Party. He now headed one of the major military groups who had recognized that Germany, under the Nazi's, was not only on the path to destruction, but would remain so until Hitler had been permanently removed from the helm of leadership and a new political reality, acceptable to the Allied forces;, was firmly in place and prepared to lead the country along a different path.

At this point in the war Oster was a close confident of Admiral Wilhelm Canairs, the head of the *'Abwehr'*.

In March of nineteen forty-three, Oster's *'Abwehr'* group supplied British-made bombs to Tresckow's anti-Nazi group for the planned assassination attempt on Hitler, codenamed *'Operation Flash'*.

On a return flight from the Ukraine to Berlin, Hitler was scheduled to make a visit to the troops on the Eastern Front at Smolensk during a short stopover and luncheon. During the lunch, Tresckow asked Lieutenant Colonel Heinz Brandt, who was traveling with Hitler, whether he would be good enough to deliver a bottle of Cointreau to Colonel Helmuth Stieff at Hitler's headquarters in East Prussia. He explained that the bottle was payment for a lost bet. Brandt readily agreed.

The carefully wrapped *'bottle'* was in reality a bomb constructed of a British *'Plastic C'* explosive placed into the casing of a magnetic mine, with a timer consisting of a spring which would be gradually dissolved by acid. Before Hitler's Condor was to take off, Tresckow's adjutant, Fabian von Schlabrendorff, activated the thirty-minute fuse and handed the package to Brandt, who boarded Hitler's plane.

After the plane took off, a message was sent to the other Berlin conspirators by code that *'Operation Flash'* was under way. It was expected that the aircraft would explode in the area of Minsk. Probably due to the extremely low temperatures in the unheated luggage compartment, the fuse failed to detonate and Hitler's plane landed safely at his East Prussian headquarters.

The message of failure was quickly sent out and Schlabrendorff took immediate steps to have the package recovered. Thus the plot, which failed, was in any event, never discovered.

A second attempt was made on March twentieth. This was to be a suicide bombing mission undertaken by Kluge's Chief of Intelligence, Colonel Rudolf von Gersdorff. The Colonel was to sidle up to Hitler a week later, while the Fuhrer attended an exhibition of captured Soviet weaponry in Berlin, but due to a last minute change in Hitler's itinerary, this attempt had to be aborted.

These failures served to temporarily demoralize the conspirators. The Gestapo were unaware of these two attempts, but had come to strongly suspect that the *'Abwehr'*, was infested with traitors.

* * * * *

- Inner Circle -

- Speer -

On the fifth of March Speer flew to *'Fuhrerhauptquartier Werwolf'* in the Ukraine to meet with Hitler, ostensibly for the purpose of receiving several decisions on armaments questions.   His real reason, however, was to hopefully make some gains in the ongoing plan to take steps to curtail Bormann's influence over the Fuhrer.

As a first step, Albert suggested that Hitler invite Goebbels to join them for a visit. As expected Hitler, who was in the doldrums, welcomed the suggestion of a stopover by his intelligent and gregarious Propaganda Minister.

Three days later Goebbels arrived and quickly took Speer aside. *'What is the Fuhrer's mood, Herr Speer?'*

Speer told him that currently Hitler was not particularly enamored with Goering and had made several comments over the day about Goering's omissions and mistakes in the planning for air warfare, complaining that if the Allied bombing went on, not only would the cities be destroyed but the morale of the people would crack irreparably. He suggested to Goebbels that they tread very carefully in bringing up their plans for using Goering and the *'Council of Ministers for the Defense of the Reich'*.

While they shared qualms at bringing up the subject directly, the two men agreed that at some point they would have to at least introduce some mention of the concept into the conversation. They determined to wait for an opportune moment before doing so.

Hitler invited Speer and Goebbels to lunch. Strangely, the omnipresent Bormann was not invited to join them. Once the three of them were seated Hitler's oppressive mood appeared to fade and he became quite genial and talkative. He began to speak freely about his heavy burdens and, excluding present company, freely remarked on his dissatisfaction with all those others who surrounded and advised him.

Goebbels had a way with Hitler and after the meal Hitler courteously walked Speer to the door and then returned to spend some one-on-one time with Goebbels. The two men spent several hours in private conversation, which was not unexpected by Speer, in that Hitler regularly separated individuals and their areas of responsibility, when in a relaxed atmosphere.

At supper the three men met again. Hitler ordered a fire to be lit and offered wine to the others, while he took mineral water. In this warm atmosphere they spent several hours during which Speer took a back seat to Goebbels, who knew only too well how to entertain the Fuhrer.

The Propaganda Minister spoke at length on varying topics that had nothing to do with the war and Hitler's day to day concerns. Theaters, movies, old times, his family, casually dismissing the current problems Germany was facing, drawing on past periods of challenge that the Fuhrer had, in the end, easily overcome. Slowly at first and then firmly, Goebbels positive attitude and idolization of Hitler's leadership qualities hit their mark and soon Hitler was cheerfully responding in kind, lavishly praising his Propaganda Minister's achievements.

Things had mellowed out considerably. Exchanging glances, Speer and Goebbels silently agreed the time was opportune to raise the issue of the *'Council of Ministers for the Defense of the Reich'*.

Unfortunately, at that very moment an aid entered to advise the Fuhrer that Nuremburg was under heavy bomb attack, and in response Hitler's mood turned from relaxed and mellow to absolutely infuriated.

He ordered the aid to summon Goering's chief adjutant, Brigadier General Bodenschatz, immediately and had the man hauled out of bed to attend him. When Bodenschatz reached the room Hitler informed him of the attack on Nuremburg and immediately began to berate him and his master, who he referred to as the *'Incompetent Reichsmarschall'*.

Under the circumstances, any thought of raising Goering's name in relation to their plans for an expanded *'Council of Ministers for the*

Defense of the Reich' was suddenly out of the question.

Instead Speer and Goebbels threw their joint efforts into calming Hitler down and getting Bodenschatz dismissed from the room, something which took some time to accomplish.

With Goering under a cloud, the two men did not bring up the matter of an expanded council with the Fuhrer during the remainder of their visit.

* * * * *

On March seventeenth, Goebbels, Speer, Ley and Funk met with Goering at his palace on *'Leipziger Platz'* in Berlin. They were ushered into Goering's office and found him ensconced behind his massive desk. His earlier fervor over the plans to reign-in Bormann's power over Hitler, which had been expressed at their last meeting, seemed to have chilled somewhat since that time and with it, his cordiality.

Seemingly having forgotten how angry the Fuhrer had been at Goering only a few days previously, Goebbels, who did the talking for the others, soon had Goering aroused once again. In short order he and the corpulent Reichsmarschall were actively trading barbs aimed at Bormann and his two cohorts, actively devising plans for dealing with the problem and bringing Hitler out from under the man's ironfisted control.

The vacillating Goering, who was proficient at shifting back and forth between lethargy and exhilaration, suddenly saw no reason why, working together, they could not solve the problem of the control being exercised by the headquarters team, headed by Bormann.

'We mustn't overestimate it either, Herr Goebbels! Bormann and Keitel are nothing but the Fuhrer's secretaries, after all. Who do they think they are! As far as their own powers are concerned, they're nobodies.'

Goebbels ventured the opinion that control of the Gauleiters was the first step that must be taken once they had joined the *'Council of Ministers for the Defense of the Reich'*. These men currently functioned under Bormann's lash and requiring them to be responsible to the *'Council'* would immediately strip Bormann of his greatest hold on power. It was agreed that Goering would preside over the newly expanded organization and that Goebbels would be the vice chair, stepping in for Goering if he was unable to make a meeting.

Goering arranged to have Lammers, who was the host for the next meeting which was to take place on April twelfth, invite him and his new group of conspirators, as well as Sauckel and Milch, to the next meeting. Speer had carefully briefed the *'Reichsmarschall'* again on what needed to happen at the meeting and Goering had responded.

'That will soon be taken care of!'

* * * * *

- Deportations -

In March the Germans start the deportations of forty-nine thousand Jews from Greece to Auschwitz.

On March fourteenth the Krakow Ghetto is liquidated.

On March seventeenth, the Bulgarian government tells the Germans that they opposed the deportation of their Jews.

On the twenty-second the newly constructed gas chamber/crematorium, IV opens at Auschwitz.

On March thirty-first the next combination gas chamber/crematorium, number II, comes on stream at Auschwitz.

* * * * *

- Concentration Camps -

Transports to Chelmno cease in March as most of the Jews in the Warthegau, other than those in the Lodz ghetto, have been dealt with. The camp is dismantled.

Four new crematoria buildings, two of which begin their work this month, and the other two still under construction at Auschwitz are arranged, as the facilities previously in place are deemed insufficient for the scale of gassing anticipated. Each is to consist of three components, a disrobing area, a large gas chamber and crematorium ovens.

* * * * *

- The Roman Catholic Church -

The role played by the Catholic Church and their support for the Axis powers has been touched on earlier, but some insight into what transpired in that regard helps to understand what motivated this stance.

The vast majority of Italians were Roman Catholic when Mussolini came to power in Italy and to hold power he needed the support of the Pope and his church. As a Fascist dictator, Mussolini governed the political side of Italy, but the Roman Catholic Church governed the spiritual side.

Personally, Il Duce had little use for the Church, referring to priests as *'black germs'*. However, once in power in nineteen twenty-two, he could not ignore the fact that the Pope represented four hundred million individuals worldwide. He saw only two choices: he could take on the power of the Church and risk his fledgling government or he could work with it.

He needed the Pope's support for a Fascist state and, knowing what the Church wanted, he came up with a long-term plan to get it. He began to curry favor with the Church. In nineteen twenty-three he had his children baptized. Previously married to his wife Rachele in a civil ceremony in twenty-six, he now went through a religious marriage ceremony. The Church preached for women to stay at home and look after the family while men worked, so Mussolini pushed for the same end and he supported the Church's disapproval of the use of contraception, and suggested that divorce be outlawed in Italy.

Before long, the earlier jaundiced eye of the Pope for fascism began to wane somewhat and it was then in twenty-six when Mussolini made his move to settle the ongoing dispute between state and Church over the education of children. Mussolini wanted the State to control education so that all Italians could grow up to be good

Fascists. The Church wanted to control the education system so that all Italians could grow up as good Roman Catholics.

The two sides began to negotiate and by nineteen twenty-nine they reached a compromise with the Lateran Treaty.

The pacts consisted of two documents, the first of which had four annexes:

1. A political treaty recognizing the full sovereignty of the Holy See in the State of Vatican City, which was thereby established, a document accompanied by the annexes:

... A plan of the territory of the Vatican City State

... A list and plans of the buildings with extraterritorial privilege and exemption from expropriation and taxes

...A list and plans of the buildings with exemption from expropriation and taxes

...A financial convention agreed on as a definitive settlement of the claims of the Holy See following the loss in eighteen-seventy of its territories and property. (The Italian state agreed to pay seven hundred and fifty million lire immediately plus consolidated bearer bonds with a coupon rate of five percent and a nominal value of one billion lire. It thus paid less than it would have paid under the eighteen seventy-one *Law of Guarantees'*, which the Holy See had not accepted.

2. A concordat regulating relations between the Catholic Church and the Italian state.

The Concordat made the Roman Catholic Church in Italy the state religion. The pope was to appoint bishops, albeit with the blessing of the government, and religion had to be taught in both primary and secondary schools. The Roman Church was given full control of marriage.

For the Church this agreement was the redemption for what had taken place historically. During the unification of Italy in the mid-nineteenth Century, the Papal States had resisted incorporation into the new nation, even as all the other Italian countries, except for San Marino, joined it.

Italy's first prime Minister, Camillo Cavour's dream of proclaiming the Kingdom of Italy from the steps of St Peter's Basilica did not come to pass. The nascent Kingdom of Italy invaded and occupied Romagna (the eastern portion of the Papal States) in eighteen sixty, leaving only Latium in the Pope's domains.

Latium, including Rome itself, had then been occupied and annexed in eighteen seventy. For the following sixty years, relations between the Papacy and the Italian government were hostile, and the status of the Pope became known as the *'Roman Question'*.

Yes, Mussolini knew what the Church wanted.

Negotiations for the settlement of the *'Roman Question'* began in twenty-six, between the government of Italy and the Holy See, and culminated at a meeting, which took place in the Lateran Palace. The agreements referred to as the *'Lateran Pacts'*, were signed on February the eleventh, nineteen twenty-nine.

They included a political treaty which created the state of the Vatican City and guaranteed full international relations and abstention from mediation in a controversy unless specifically requested by all parties. In the first article of the treaty, Italy reaffirmed the principle established in the March fourth eighteen forty-eight *'Statute of the Kingdom of Italy'*, that *'the Catholic, Apostolic and Roman Religion is the only religion of the State'*. The attached financial agreement was accepted as settlement of all the claims of the Holy See against Italy arising from the loss of temporal power in eighteen seventy.

The sum thereby given to the Holy See was actually less than Italy had declared it would pay under the terms of the *'Law of Guarantees of eighteen seventy-one'*, by which the Italian government guaranteed to Pope Pius and his successors the use of, but not sovereignty over, the Vatican and Lateran Palaces and a yearly income of three million, two hundred and fifty thousand lire as indemnity for the loss of sovereignty and territory. The Holy See, on the grounds of the need for clearly manifested independence from any political power in its exercise of spiritual jurisdiction, had refused to accept the settlement offered in eighteen seventy-one, and the Popes thereafter, until the signing of the Lateran Treaty, considered themselves prisoners in the Vatican, a small, limited area inside Rome.

To commemorate the successful conclusion of the negotiations in nineteen twenty-nine, Mussolini commissioned the *'Via della Conciliazione'* (Road of the Conciliation), which would symbolically link the Vatican City to the heart of Rome.

Mussolini had known exactly what the Church wanted in exchange for the public recognition of his Fascist regime - an ally against communism, two billion in cash and a sovereign territorial base. He gave it to them happily.

* * * * *

- Ratlines -

As discussed earlier, the origins of the first ratlines were connected to various developments in Vatican-Argentine relations before and during the Second World War. As early as nineteen forty-two, Monsignor Luigi Maglione had contacted Ambassador Llobet, inquiring as to the *'willingness of the government of the Argentine Republic to apply its immigration law generously, in order to encourage at the opportune moment European Catholic immigrants to seek the necessary land and capital in our country'*. In time, this concept was to turn into the escape routes which fascist exiles would exploit, both with and without the knowledge of the Catholic Church.

After those discussions, a German priest, Anton Weber, the head of the Rome-based Society of Saint Raphael, traveled first to Portugal and then continued on to Argentina, to lay the groundwork for future Catholic immigration.

Spain, not Rome, was to be the *'first center of ratline activity that facilitated the escape of Nazi fascists'* once the war was lost. The Rome ratline would be formed later.

The exodus itself was planned within the Vatican. Charles

Lescat, a French member of *'Action Francaise'* (an organization suppressed by Pope Pius XI and then rehabilitated by Pope Pius XII and Pierre Daye, (a Belgian with contacts in the Spanish government, were among the primary organizers). As fate would have it, Lescat and Daye were the first able to flee Europe, using the system, with the help of Argentine cardinal, Antonio Caggiano.

* * * * *

- The Family -

- Eric -

Eric and Heidi, immensely pleased with themselves and with eyes only for each other, had set up housekeeping in her Grandfather's mansion after their marriage.

Late in February, Eric was preparing to take his massive U-boat to the coast of Florida on its first trip to offload a human cargo of several specialist members of *'Operation Fatherland'*. These individuals, who had been furnished expertly forged papers, would now fan out over the United States to selected locations. Once there, operating independently, they were to assimilate into their various locales in preparation for taking up their duties at the end of the war.

Each of his passengers, some in *'married teams'*, and others acting individually, had been furnished with a fortune of uncut gemstones looted from the occupied territories. Once in place they would sell these over time, in order to set themselves up in preparation for receiving the ongoing transshipment from Brazil, of addition artwork and treasures. These would be forwarded to them by way of consigned shipments arriving in North America aboard neutrally flagged ships originating in South American ports.

The plan was for these individuals, once securely in place and accepted into their communities, to act as future intermediaries for the sale of the treasures and initially transfer the resulting cash initially back to Brazil, and after the war, to Germany. Here it would be used to finance the future operations of *'Operation Fatherland'*.

Eric's main job from this point on until the end of the war was to repeat this operation, travelling to the east coasts of both Canada and the US, unloading his human cargo until sufficient numbers had been safely and deeply entrenched into the two countries.

The night before he was scheduled to leave on the trip, Heidi took him aside after their evening meal and led him quickly out to the mansion's three car garage.

She was obviously excited and was acting mysteriously.

At first, newlyweds being what they are, Eric thought she might have some type of sexual adventure in mind, so he held his tongue until they had entered the garage. Once inside and out of sight of the mansion, he kicked the door closed, took her into his arms and pressed her firmly up against the wall.

His voice was husky and he gave her an exaggerated lubricious look as he spoke.

"And what exactly did you have in mind my love?"

Heidi flushed and then laughed coquettishly.

"Not what you seem to think I'm afraid. I just want to show you something before you leave in the morning and we will need one of the cars to get there."

A little disappointed but immediately curious he smiled, released her and stepped back.

"What is it?"

Heidi playfully shoved him in the direction of the four-wheel drive vehicle that they often used to travel over the area.

"It's a secret; you mustn't let the others know that I showed you. Come on, open the door, I'll drive."

He quizzed her periodically as they drove but she refused to give in to his questions and after about thirty minutes she turned off the main road leading to the mining complex and began to follow a secondary gravel road which climbed as it wound its way around the bottom of the mountain in the direction of the ocean. After another fifteen minutes they began a steadier climb up the lower ridges of the mountain itself. After they'd travelled along this narrower tract for a few minutes and with Eric's patience rapidly disappearing, Heidi brought the vehicle to a sudden stop.

"Now close your eyes and don't open them until I tell you."

Eric gave out a loud sigh for effect and then did as he was bid. He felt the vehicle being to move again. He sensed that they had come over the top of a rise and as they did she braked again.

"Alright - you can open them now."

As Eric opened his eyes and began to refocus, Heidi spoke.

"It's the house your father had us build for your family to use when they are here in Brazil. It's not quite finished, but I wanted you to see it before you sailed again. Isn't it fantastic? And just wait until you go inside and see the view - you can see the ocean from one side and the whole valley below from the other. On thirty acres!"

She put the four-wheeler in gear and quickly picked up speed as they shot down the hill and through an open gate situated in the imposing stone wall fronting the property and approximately one hundred yards away, the impressively large four story dwelling which nestled in the center of a wildflower-filled meadow, on what was otherwise a heavily forested plateau came into view.

* * * * *

- Berlin -

Karl and Wilhelm were spending a lot of time in trains and planes. They saw Hitler several times a month, keeping him abreast of new developments in weaponry and had added Himmler to the travel circuit whenever possible, in an attempt to assuage the SS-Reichsfuhrer's injured attitude toward them. This in an attempt at rebuilding the sense of partnership which had earlier been carefully fostered and had then crumbled when Hitler had granted their request to move out from under the control of the SS and re-uniform into the Wehrmacht rank structure.

When not keeping the two men apprised of advances, they often returned to castle von Stauffer and spent time with the rest of the family.

* * * * *

- Friedrichshafen -

Friedrich was still safely in place with his Luftwaffe team despite whatever Himmler had told the Reichsmarschall. Karl had worried about the situation for a good week but was now convinced that SS-General Dieter Bichler had been correct in his assumption that Goering would not allow the Luftwaffe to give up control of the treasures being stored at the von Stauffer castle.

Some astounding gains had been accomplished in the genetic research and Konrad was now deeply involved on his studies with the Baron at the new facility in the city of Friedrichshafen, and although often working late into the evening, still managed to make all the daily family dinners at the castle.

Ursula, who was bored stiff and now sporting a very large stomach and a sore back, had nonetheless graciously accepted her new sequestration from the work world and was now quite looking forward to the imminent arrival of her baby.

Somewhat to everyone's surprise, Gabriella was actively spending a great deal of time with her mother, something that had not occurred for a good decade. Erika found herself very much enjoying her matured youngest daughter's company and spoiling her grandson, with glee.

CHAPTER SIX

- March -

- Allied Air Operations -

British Bomber Command drops eight thousand tons of bombs in ten large raids over German territory. Essen and Berlin are hit hardest. The new navigational tool, codenamed *'Oboe'* is used early in the month for the first time in the attack on Essen. In addition the RAF bomb St. Nazaire in France, as attacks on the U-boat pens continue unabated.

The Americans strike at Vegesack and Wilhelmshaven.

* * * * *

- Battle of the Atlantic -

This month is likely the best month the German U-boats will have over the entire war. Six hundred and twenty seven thousand, four hundred tons of Allied shipping are taken by the U-boats. This is out of loss of one hundred and twenty ships for a total tonnage of six hundred and ninety-three thousand four hundred.

* * * * *

- March First -

- Eastern Front -

The Russians take Demyansk which is situated north of Moscow.

* * * * *

- New Guinea -

The battle of the Bismarck Sea begins and over the next three days, the combined Australian and US naval forces sink eight Japanese troop ships.

* * * * *

- Berlin -

General Heinz Guderian is appointed Inspector-General of the Armored Troops of the German Army.

* * * * *

- Burma -

Wingate's *'Chindits'* (British Airborne deep-penetration guerilla troops) continue localized strikes.

* * * * *

- March Third -

- Eastern Front -

After several days of hard fighting, the Germans pull out of Rzhev and the Russians move in. The Russians also take Lgov which is situated on the River Seim west of Kursk.

* * * * *

- Burma -

The Chindits cut the Mandalay-Myitkyina railroad line just north of Kyaikthin.

---

* * * * *

- March Fourth -

- Eastern Front -

Russian troops take Olenion and Chertolino to the west of Rzhev and in the area of Kursk, they take Sevsk and Sudzha.

* * * * *

- March Sixth -

- Eastern Front -

The Russians take Gzhatsk south of Rzhev.

* * * * *

- Tunisia -

Contrary to Rommel's wishes, and without his input, the *'Battle of Medenine'* begins. This ill-planned and executed major German attack fails hopelessly. The Germans lose fifty of their tanks for no gain.

* * * * *

- March Eighth -

- Eastern Front -

The Russians capture Sychevka in the central sector between Rzhev and Vyazma.

* * * * *

- March Ninth -

- Tunisia -

A disgruntled `Desert Fox'* leaves North Africa for good. On his trip back to Germany, Rommel meets Mussolini in Rome and Hitler in East Prussia. On both stops he tries to convince the fascist leaders to withdraw their forces from Africa. His pleas fall on deaf ears.

* * * * *

- March Eleventh -

- Eastern Front -

The newly formed SS Korps enters Kharkov amidst fierce fighting.

* * * * *

- March Twelfth -

- Eastern Front -

In the central sector the Germans are forced to retreat on a wide front. The Russians take Vyazma.

* * * * *

- March Fourteenth -

The German SS forces recapture Kharkov and in so doing reach a very favourable new position in Hitler's mind.

* * * * *

- March Fifteenth -

- Eastern Front -

In the central sector, the Russians take Kholm and Zharkovskiy.

* * * * *

- March Sixteenth -

- Poland -

The first reports of the Russian NKVD's (closely associated with the secret police), *'Katyn massacre',* where the Russians had executed approximately twenty-two thousand men, leaks out to the western powers.

With Stalin's consent, it had been decided that all members of the Polish Officer Corps should be executed in the area of Poland that the Russians had occupied in their joint venture with Hitler earlier in the war. In the end the Russians executed eight thousand captured officers, six thousand police officers and the majority of the Polish intelligentsia, which included lawyers and priests.

Stalin denies the executions when confronted by his new allies and responds with demands for a second front against the Germans.

* * * * *

- March Eighteenth -

- Tunisia -

US II Corps, under the command of General George S. Patton, takes Gafsa.

* * * * *

- March Twenty-Third -

- Tunisia -

US forces push the Germans out of El Guettar.

* * * * *

- March Twenty-Fourth -

- Germany -

On this date, seventy-six Allied prisoners of war escaped from *'Stalag Luft III'*, (Stammlager Luft or main camp for aircrew). We know of this escape today as the *'Great Escape'*. The camp was located near the town of Sagan in Lower Silesia.

As a result of the escape, an enraged Hitler ordered that fifty of the recaptured men be executed. Only twenty-three men were returned to prison. Three managed to make it successfully back to Allied territory.

* * * * *

- March Thirty-First -

- Eastern Front -

The Russians capture Anastasyevsk

CHAPTER SEVEN

- April -

- Hitler -

On a clear, mild evening early in the month, Hitler left *'Wolfsschanze'* for Berchtesgaden.

His personal train slipped out of the dismal snow-shrouded compound and through the Rastenburg forest transporting the Fuhrer and his entourage in relative luxury when compared to the facilities they had left behind. The train afforded every comfort, the seats converting to comfortable beds in its heated interior and the food served was excellent. It also boasted a car containing showers and bathtubs.

On the first leg of the trip, the main topic of conversation among the secretaries and servants was Eva Braun who was to board the train at Munich. Braun was referred to by these individuals as *'the lady at the Berghof'* in that, whenever Hitler took up residence in the alpine compound, Eva joined him.

* * * * *

- Berghof -

- Hitler's Personal Family Circle -

The Berghof in the Bavarian Alps was where Hitler went to unwind. Hitler's personal quarters were on the second floor of the large residence. Here, sharing a common bathroom which separated them, were Eva and the Fuhrer's bedrooms. Magnificent artwork from the old masters and beautiful sculptures adorned the halls and walls of the building and custom furniture filled its rooms. Those of the staff who were visiting at the time found the *'Berghof'* wonderful to view, if somewhat cold and impersonal.

The daily routine, while the Fuhrer was in residence, rarely varied. A typical day would run as follows.

At noon, Hitler got his military briefing which usually dragged on into late afternoon. When the last of the officers had left, the Fuhrer would enter the living room to join his current houseguests and secretaries, those he considered as his personal family circle, where he transformed himself from the heavily burdened leader he'd been just minutes ago into the good-humoured host.

As a practice Hitler compartmentalized his activities with regard to specific subjects in regard to allowing the sharing of knowledge, information and discussion on various topics. For example, when he was at the Berghof, he forbade that any military or government topics be raised while he was surrounded by his personal inner circle. Because of this, only banal pleasantries would be exchanged by all in attendance on these occasions.

Immediately after Hitler arrived in the room where the inner circle waited, Eva would join them in the company of her two black Scotch terriers who roamed freely. Hitler would welcome her to the mix, kissing her hand and then greet his other guests with an individual handshake.

After entertaining conversation, Hitler would eventually extend his arm to one of the women and offer her escort to the dining room table. Hitler and the chosen female would be immediately followed by the omnipresent and toad-like Bormann. Bormann would often choose to escort an unenthusiastic Eva, who was well aware of his reputation as a committed skirt chaser, although he never dared attempt any such move on her.

The meal would consist of a variety of meat dishes, side plates and wine for the others, while Hitler would consume a vegetarian meal with mineral water. Conversation around the table would normally begin with light and frivolous topics, but at some point, would almost inevitably shift to one of the Fuhrer's two pet peeves: those who ate meat or those who smoked. He would then begin a personal tirade against one of those topics.

Once lunch was out of the way Hitler, accompanied by chosen

guests, would go for his daily walk to his tea house. This took just under a half hour. The round stone building situated below the Berghof featured six large windows that presented beautifully unencumbered riparian and forested panoramas. Here tea was served.

After tea Hitler would lead the parade back up to the Berghof and everyone would go on their own way for a short time. Hitler would then receive various bureaucrats and non-military hierarchy to discuss the business of government.

At approximately nine o'clock Hitler would leave that conference and join his guests to lead the way into the dining room where he would eat mashed potatoes and a tomato salad while the other were provided a selection of cold meats. He would then dominate the conversation during the meal, which would centre on the days of his youth and early manhood.

After dinner, Hitler would be advised that the parade of vehicles had arrived at the manse, pulling up one at a time in a line at the bottom of the stairs and disgorging group after group of military officers who were destined to make an appearance at the evening military conference. The Fuhrer would excuse himself and his secretaries from the dining room, directing those remaining at the table to take in a movie in the basement while he attended the conference. He was always careful to keep the military separate from his house guests. An adjutant would call down to the theatre when Hitler was free and the guests would be directed to attend him in the main hall. Knowing they would have a few minutes before the Fuhrer reached the room, Eva would quickly return to her room to refresh her makeup while others would take the opportunity to grab a last cigarette. They would all be arranged around the fire in the great hall at around midnight when Hitler came down the stairs and seated himself next to Eva.

Alcoholic beverages were available but Hitler took only tea and apple cake while the group sat silently around the flickering blaze in the subtlety lit room. When he was ready Hitler would take the floor once again. Various non-military topics would be discussed with the Fuhrer having the last word.

At approximately four in the morning Hitler would ask to see the nightly air raid reports and after having read these he would retire and his guests, many of whom were exhausted, could finally go to their beds.

* * * * *

On the seventh of April Hitler left for a meeting with Mussolini at Salzburg. The Fuhrer's intention in calling the meeting was to raise Il Duce's flagging fighting spirit. Mussolini had come as bid, but dispirited by the way things were going; he arrived with every intention of urging Hitler to seek peace with the Russians and determined to demand the complete withdrawal of all Italian forces abroad.

The two men met privately over the next four days. Neither man seemed to accomplish his aims. Hitler did his best to animate and rouse the Italian but had little real success. On the other side of the coin, Mussolini didn't have the intestinal fortitude required to make requests or demands of the German leader.

As the two of them came down the stairs together at the end of conference several onlookers commented on how drawn and lethargic they looked, especially Mussolini who was now sixty and in poor health.

* * * * *

On the afternoon of the last day of the meeting, April tenth, a Hitler aid contacted the Berghof to announce that Hitler and his entourage were leaving Klessheim and advised that when the Fuhrer arrived it was his wish that all his guests meet him at the tea house so he could again take up his calming position as head of his personal family circle.

When the long procession of cars arrived, Hitler, happy to be home and again out of the limelight, led the others down to the tea house. He was immediately freed from the pressures of leadership and slipped quickly and gratefully into his regular routine of playing the role of benevolent father, to whom, to all intents and purposes, he now considered to be his extended family.

* * * * *

At this adjunct in the war, even when taking a break at the Berghof, Hitler was unable to completely cocoon himself and others around him from what was going on in the world around him. During this month, on two specific occasions, his self-induced protective screen was shattered, indicating expanding chinks in both his personal ability to control his anger and the ability of others to isolate themselves from what was happening in German controlled territories.

The first came when his youngest private secretary, Traudl, who had joined his staff in December of forty-two and was one of those sharing a meal with him, asked Hitler when the war would be over.

Hitler had just been affably apologising to everyone present for the fact that he had to wear a uniform at all times and explaining that this would no longer be necessary once the war had been won. Despite the fact that Traudl was a favorite of the Fuhrer's, the instant she asked the question the others in the room cringed and held their breath.

After a strained silence the Fuhrer turned on the young woman and snapped harshly.

'I don't know. But only after victory!'

The ambiance of the meal was instantly shattered and a chill settled over the room. Everyone ate quickly, eager to end the torture of enduring Hitler's sudden coldness.

The second occurred on Good Friday, when Henriette von Schirach, the daughter of Heinrich Hoffmann, Hitler's personal photographer, was visiting the Berghof.

'Henny' as Hitler called her, had spent her childhood in Schwabing. Her home had been an early National Socialist stronghold, and in nineteen twenty her father, a staunch nationalist and anti-Semitic DAP (German Worker's Party) member, joined the National Socialist Party.

'Henny' was nine years of age she first met Adolf Hitler, who frequently came to the Hoffmann house for dinner.

From nineteen twenty-three onwards, her father became the personal photographer of Hitler and held a lucrative business selling busts of Hitler. By nineteen thirty, while undertaking her studies at the University of Munich, Henriette worked as Hitler's secretary. For a short period Hitler dated Henriette.

In thirty-one she met Baldur von Schirach, the former leader of the Nazi Student League and the youngest of Hitler's entourage. The couple was married on March thirty-first of nineteen thirty-two in Munich. Both Adolf Hitler and Ernst Roehm acted as best men.

'Henny' had then taken up the goals of her husband, who held sole control over the educational system of the German Reich. Von Schirach was appointed by Hitler to the position of Gauleiter and Reich Governor in Vienna and the family had then moved to the prestigious Vienna Hofburg.

In nineteen forty-three *'Henny'* was invited to the Netherlands by friends in the German occupation forces. While there she bore witness to an occurrence.

'I heard screaming outside the hotel late at night so went out to investigate. I saw Jewish women and children being bundled into transportation to be deported. I then asked a German Officer what they were doing to which he replied, 'What Hitler is doing in Holland is wrong, we are making enemies of the Dutch which is a big mistake, make sure you tell him this the next time you visit the Berghof.'

What she had witnessed troubled her deeply. She broke off her visit and telephoned the Berghof to make an appointment to see Hitler.

She arrived at the Berghof for her visit, on which she described as:

'A splendid, somewhat sultry fall evening when we joined the regular company by the large open fire at the Berghof.'

'Henny' was upset and unsure of exactly how she would should approach Hitler with her concerns. She later described the incident in question, as follows.

'Long after midnight Hitler turned to me and asked in a friendly tone: You have just come back from Holland, have you not?'

She had taken a deep breath and answered:

'Yes, that is why I am here. I wanted to speak to you about some

terrible things I saw; I cannot believe that you know about them. Helpless women were being rounded up and driven together to be sent off to a concentration camp and I think that they will never return.'

A painful stillness fell; all color had left Hitler's face. His face looked like a death mask in the light of the flames. He looked at me aghast and at the same time surprised and said:

'We are at war'. He very cautiously stood up. At that moment he screamed at me: 'you are sentimental, Frau von Schirach! You have to learn to hate! What have Jewish women in Holland got to do with you?'

The rest of the company were quiet as mice. Nobody looked at me. I walked out of the room and once in the vestibule I began to run. One of Hitler's adjutants came running after me. The Führer was furious. I was asked to leave the Obersalzberg immediately.

Neither Henriette von Schirach nor her husband was ever invited to the Berghof again.

* * * * *

- Inner Circle -

- Speer -

When the Fuhrer was in extended residence at the Berghof, rather than being held in the Chancellery in Berlin, the meetings of the Berlin Chancellery secretariat were held in a large building that Hitler had ordered constructed near Berchtesgaden.

It was here that Speer, Goebbels and Goering had wangled an invitation to join the April twelfth meeting as guests and where they intended to curtail Bormann's powers in a bloodless expansion of the Chancellery secretariat, through Goering's use of the authority provided in his position as *'Chairman of the Council of Ministers for the Defense of the Reich'* .

Unfortunately, upon his arrival, Speer found that the deck had been carefully stacked against them. He and Goering and Goebbels were not the only guests who had been invited. Himmler, Bormann and Keitel were already in the conference room when Speer arrived and he was then advised that Goebbels had sent his apologies.

The Propaganda Minister had fallen ill it seemed. The entire plot fell apart in short order. When Speer made the planned pitch demanding that Sauckel provide an additional two million, one hundred thousand workers for the economy, Sauckel replied that he had already delivered the needed forces. Speer challenged him, suggesting that the man's figures simply could not be substantiated.

As part of the plan, Goering was then supposed to step in and force Sauckel to agree to changes in his labour-assignment policy.

And what did the corpulent *'Reichsmarschall'* do?

Instead of supporting Speer's position, he began to pugnaciously attack Milch who was Goering's direct subordinate and who was also aligned with Speer.

To Speer's horror, Goering said that it was outrageous that Milch was making so many difficulties.

'Our good party comrade Sauckel who is exerting himself to the utmost and has achieved such successes...'

He then addressed Milch directly and stated.

'I at any rate feel a great debt of gratitude toward him. You are simply blind to Sauckel's achievements.'

A lively discussion over the whereabouts of the missing workers ensued. Each of the ministers present offered up possible explanations for the differences between the official and actual number of workers available. Himmler, who for the most part calmly watched the proceedings with satisfaction, suggested that perhaps the missing hundreds of thousands had died.

From Speer's perspective, both Goering's performance and the meeting were a disaster. Not only did they fail in their attempt to curtail Bormann, but they hadn't even been able to successfully justify their first move against Sauckel before they were shut down.

After the meeting Goering took Speer aside.

'I know you like to work closely with my state secretary, Milch. In all friendship I'd like to warn you against him. He's unreliable; as soon as his own interests are in question, he'll trample over even his best friends.'

Speer later passed this information on to Milch, who laughed and responded.

'A few days ago Goering told me exactly the same thing about you.'

What had brought about Goering's overt act of sabotage at the meeting?

Over time, Speer was to learn that in addition to the standard posturing by those in the inner circle, which he had come to expect, and their learned tendency to hold few permanent alliances among each other, there were a couple of other explanations for Goering's failure to play the part he'd previously staunchly agreed to play.

Milch was later to advise him that the Gestapo had proof of Goering's drug addiction. Himmler had thereby been in a position to apply pressure to the *'Reichsmarschall'*. As well, Bormann had made Goering a present of six million marks, from the industrialist's *'Adolf Hitler Fund'*. A few months later Speer ran into Himmler at headquarters, the *'SS-Reichsfuhrer'* exchanged peasantries and then stated curtly.

'I think it would be very unwise of you to try to activate the 'Reichsmarschall' again.'

After leveling that clearly unveiled threat he turned on his heel and left Speer standing alone.

Speer's newfound alliance toward the curbing of Bormann's powers had been effectively blown out of the water shortly after it had been formed.

* * * * *

- ME 262 -

The Messerschmitt ME 262 Schwalbe (Swallow) was the world's first turbo-jet fighter aircraft. Design work on this craft had begun in Germany prior to the start of World War Two.

Although one of the most advanced aviation designs to be developed during the war, engine problems and top-level political and military interference in its creation were to keep the aircraft from reaching operational status until mid-nineteen forty-four.

Initial plans for the plane were drawn up in April of nineteen thirty-nine. Development of the original design had been stagnated repeatedly by technical issues arising with the new jet engine. In addition to this problem, military funding for research and development of the fledgling jet engine program was initially lacking, as many high-ranking German officials, both political and military, including the commander of the Luftwaffe, Hermann Goering, thought the war could easily be won with conventional aircraft.

Early in the development stages, Goering had cut the engine development program to just 35 engineers. In February of nineteen-forty, Willy Messerschmitt, who wanted to maintain the mass production of the piston-powered BF 109 and his projected ME 209 fighter aircraft, was not particularity interested in using resources in the direction of the new 262 development

Later, Messerschmitt's interest in this new design gathered speed and Major General Adolf Galland, a flying 'ace' and German hero, took a strong interest in the proposed 262. Galland flew a prototype ME 262 himself on April twenty-second of nineteen forty-three, by which time, the problems with engine advancement had slowed development of the aircraft considerably.

One particularly acute problem by that stage was the lack of an alloy with a melting point high enough to endure the high temperatures created by the engine itself, a problem that 262 manufacturers would never completely overcome.

By mid forty-three Hitler had worked his way into the development of the craft. Hitler was not particularly stimulated by weapons that were designed for defensive warfare. He much preferred offensive weapons. It was not surprising then that the Fuhrer envisaged the ME 262 as an offensive ground/attack bomber rather than a defensive interceptor.

At this point in the war Hitler was looking for a high-speed, light-payload 'Schnelbomber' (fast bomber) which could be used to penetrate enemy airspace during the anticipated Allied invasion of France.

He ordered that the 262 should be developed toward that end and production and development for such a variant, the Hitler *'Sturmvogel'* (ground support) version, immediately took precedence over that of the fighter. Development of both versions went ahead.

Test flights continued over the next year, but engine problems continued to plague the project, the Jumo 004 being only marginally more reliable than the BMW 003. Airframe modifications were complete by nineteen forty-two but, hampered by the lack of engines, serial production of this innovative and outstanding fighter would not begin until nineteen forty-four.

* * * * *

- Horten Ho 229 -

The 229 wars a German prototype fighter-bomber designed by brothers Reimar and Walter Horten and which some experts have called the world's first stealth bomber.

The initial designs for this aircraft came about as a direct response to Reichsmarschall Herman Goering's nineteen forty-three proclamation that the Luftwaffe needed a plane that could meet his *'three times one thousand'* performance requirements.

Goering specified that the plane must be capable of carrying a one thousand Kilogram bomb load, a distance of one thousand kilometers and do so at a speed of one thousand kilometers per hour. It was also to have a ceiling of fifteen thousand meters.

Walter and Reimar Horten were German aircraft enthusiasts and pilots. They had little, if any, formal training in aeronautics or related fields, but that did not stop them from designing some of the most advanced aircraft of the nineteen forties, including the world's first jet-powered flying wing, the Horten Ho 229.

Between the First and Second world wars the Treaty of Versailles severely limited the construction of German military aircraft. Those Germans interested in circumventing the restrictions and who wished to take up military style flying, had of necessity to become clandestine. Civil aviation *'clubs'* where students could train on gliders under the supervision of decommissioned Great War veterans popped up around the country and as teenagers, the Horten brothers became deeply involved in such flying clubs.

This, *'start-from-scratch'* type of instructing the education of pilots, coupled with the boys' strong admiration of German aircraft designer Alexander Lippisch quickly led the Hortens away from the dominant design trends apparent in the twenties and thirties. They were much enamored with the idea of experimenting with alternative airframes. They subsequently built many models and over time began to fill their parents' house with full-sized wooden airplanes.

Their first Horten glider flew in in nineteen thirty-three. When this event took place, both boys were members of the Hitler Youth.

The Hortens' glider designs were extremely simple and aerodynamic and for the most part consisted of a huge, tailless albatross-wing, fixed with a cramped fuselage, in which the pilot was required to lay prone. These machines proved to create little drag and were well ahead of the times. In thirty-seven, the Hortens began flying motorized airplanes.

Hitler rejected the restrictions of the Treaty of Versailles in nineteen thirty-nine and Walter and Reimar had immediately entered the Luftwaffe as pilots. Despite the fact that the Hortens were looked upon by the members of Germany's aeronautical community as rash outsiders, the young men were both were committed members of the Nazi parties and as such they soon found themselves being called upon as aircraft design consultants.

The Luftwaffe did not actually use many of the Hortens' designs until forty-two. However, when the two men came up with the proposed design for their Ho 229, the Luftwaffe gave enthusiastic support to the proposed twin-turbojet powered fighter/ bomber design, which was then designated under wartime protocols, as the Horton H.IX.

* * * * *

- Special Handling -

On April fourth gas chamber V came into operation at

Auschwitz.

On April ninth, the exterminations at Chelmno temporarily ceased.

On April nineteenth, the SS began an all-out attack against Jewish resistance in the Warsaw ghetto.

* * * * *

- The Family -

- Karl and Wilhelm -

SS -General, Dieter Bichler, arrived at Friedrichshafen toward the end of the month for a two day visit at the castle. Officially the General was on a brief holiday and simply a guest of the von Stauffer family.

In reality the Count had asked him down in order for them to have the time, in the relatively safe confines of the castle, to discuss the best way *for 'Operation Fatherland'* to take the next step, which was to begin spiriting selected individuals out of Germany and into the compound in Brazil.

He and Wilhelm spend the best of two days discussing the matter with Bichler.

In opening the considerations, Karl had explained to the General that it was now necessary for them to begin recruiting additional experts from within Germany for future use in *'Operation Fatherland'* activities. Specialists with expertise in the fields of art, gems and precious metals, needed to travel to Brazil for onward relocation to North America in order that they could be deeply imbedded in both the US and Canada before the end of the war.

After the war these men were to become active and begin the task of selling the accumulating treasures, some of which were already at *'Fatherland'* headquarters in Brazil and much that was still being regularly shipped there from Friedrichshafen across Lake Konstanz and into a family owned warehouse in Neutral Switzerland, for onward shipment by way of Neutral-flagged shipping.

The sales proceeds of these valuables and treasures were then to be used to finance the furtherance of future *'Operation Fatherland'* activities.

The Count had the wherewithal to look after the continuing shipment of these treasures from Friedrichshafen to Brazil, but his ability to ship human cargo out of Germany was no longer possible. Did the General have any ideas as to how this could now be accomplished?

Bichler, who had anticipated this problem, smiled as he replied.

"Yes Karl, as a matter of fact I do."

He'd then gone on to explain the two recently created ratlines to them.

"By taking advantage of the Church's decision to assist good Catholics to migrate, to the extent that they are prepared to go as far as to provide false identity papers for those concerned, coupled with the willingness of certain South American Governments to welcome these new immigrants with open arms, it is expected that we will now be able to arrange for the escape from Germany to South America of pretty much anyone.

The system is currently in its infancy, but it goes without saying that, due to the current war situation, certain members of the SS have shown interest in the possibility of resettlement if the war is lost. If I were to suggest that I implement an experiment to test the waters of these escape routes, so to speak, I am sure that such a suggestion would not fall on deaf ears. In fact, I would venture to guess that I would find a great deal of assistance, should I require it, in bringing about such an experiment. If you would be kind enough to provide me with a list of people you are interested in having migrate to South America, I will carefully see to their vetting and then put these ratlines to the test."

* * * * *

- Eric -

Eric had waited for the sea to calm somewhat before surfacing off the coast of Florida.

Lookouts around him used binoculars to scan the horizon and skies as he stood in the conning tower observing several members of his crew carry out the much-trained-for exercise which was taking place below him on the deck.

The black rubber boat was already in the water and the selected individuals, who were about to begin their new lives as Americans, were being assisted into the bobbing craft by the shore party.

* * * * *

- Friedrichshafen -

On April eighteenth, amidst much celebration, Ursula delivered her first child, an overdue but healthy and robust eight pound girl.

CHAPTER EIGHT

- April -

- Allied Air Operations -

A better organized and growing bomber offensive continues to increase in intensity. RAF Bomber Command drops just under ten thousand tons on Germany and the US Eighth Army Air Force, one thousand. Primary German targets are Duisburg and Essen. The bombing runs against the U-boat bases at Brest, St. Nazaire and Lorient continue.

In the Mediterranean, La Spezia is heavily attacked as part of the all-out war on the U-boats and in Italy and Sicily bombers and fighters target communication links and air transports carrying Axis supplies to North Africa.

* * * * *

- Battle of the Atlantic -

German operational U-boat strength has reached four hundred and twenty-five vessels. Fifteen U-boats are lost this month. Allied losses are sixty-four ships for a total tonnage of three hundred and thirty-four thousand, seven hundred tons. U-boats account for fifty-six ships, totalling three hundred and twenty-seven thousand, nine hundred tons.

* * * * *

- April Ninth-

- Tunisia -

Advancing British Eighth Army forces have the Axis forces on the run and take Mahares which lies fifty miles north of Gabes.

* * * * *

- April Tenth -

- Tunisia -

Advance units of the Eighth Army enter Sfax as the Axis retreat continues. The British IX Corps manages to break out of Fondouk Pass, but are too late to complete the encirclement of the retreating Axis forces.

* * * * *

- Sardinia -

Eighty-four Liberators attack La Maddalena. They sink the Italian heavy cruiser *'Trieste'* and damage the heavy cruiser *'Gorizia'*.

* * * * *

- April Twelfth -

- Berlin -

The German government announces to the world that they have discovered a series of mass graves in the Katyn Forest and accuse the Russians of committing war crimes by way of executing forty-one hundred Polish officers.

* * * * *

- April Fifteenth -

- Finland -

The Finnish government officially rejects the Russian terms for peace.

* * * * *

- April Eighteenth -

- Moscow -

The Russians respond to German claims of war crimes, claiming that the whole thing is simply German propaganda.

* * * * *

- Tunisia -

An armada of one hundred German transport planes leaves Sicily with much needed supplies for the harassed Axis forces. A full half of these aeroplanes are shot down by Allied fighters.

* * * * *

- Bougainville -

The plane carrying Admiral Isoroku Yamamoto, the chief architect of Japanese naval strategy, is shot down by the Americas. The intelligence allowing them to pull this off is provided by information from broken Japanese codes and great care is taken to hide this fact from the Japanese, who believe their codes are safe. After the fact, the Americans make no public announcement of their success in order to pretend complete ignorance of the incident.

* * * * *

- April Nineteenth -

- Bermuda -

The Bermuda conference is held in Hamilton, Bermuda. American and British leaders discuss the plight of the European Jews over the next several days. Nothing positive comes out of these talks as there is general agreement that little can be done until the war is won.

* * * * *

- Warsaw Ghetto -

On the eve of Passover, German forces initiate the final phase of the transport of Jews from the ghetto to Treblinka.

By this point it had become common knowledge within the ghetto that, contrary to the earlier belief that previous transports from the ghetto where destined to end in resettlement in the east, the transports had in reality been to death camps. As a result, the remaining internees, approximately seventy thousand in number, decided to revolt against the new transport orders and fight to the last man.

In the end the revolt failed to prevent the transports from being carried out but turned out to be the longest and strongest rebellious effort made by ghettoized Jews during the war.

* * * * *

- Belgium -

In occupied Belgium, partisans attacked a railway transport containing Belgian Jews which was en route to Auschwitz. This was to be the largest and most successful attack against a German Jew Transport during the war and a total of two hundred and thirty-six Jews escaped as a result.

* * * * *

- April Twenty-Third -

- New Guinea -

Unopposed Australian troops take up position around Mubo.

* * * * *

- April Twenty-Sixth -

- Tunisia -

The British take Longstop Hill, a key position on the breakout road to Tunis.

* * * * *

- April Twenty-Seventh -

- Tunisia -

British forces take Djebel Bou Aoukaz.

* * * * *

- April Twenty-Eighth -

- Atlantic -

Allied long range bombers begin to remove the previous mid-Atlantic gap in aircraft convoy protection.

* * * * *

- April Thirtieth -

- *'Operation Mincemeat'* -

'Operation Mincemeat' was a successful British disinformation plan executed on this date as part of *'Operation Barclay'* which was the Allied plan to spread a cloud of deception intended to cover the planned future invasion of Italy from North Africa. *'Mincemeat'* was intended to help to convince the Germans that the Allies planned to invade Greece and Sardinia in forty-three instead of Sicily, the actual objective. This was to be accomplished by persuading the Germans that they had, by accident, intercepted *'top secret'* documents giving details of future Allied war strategies.

The documents were attached to a corpse deliberately left to wash up on a beach in Punta Umbria in Spain.

Of necessity, the planning for *'Mincemeat'* was intricate and involved. It included securing the body of a man who appeared to have died at sea by hypothermia and drowning, creating a believable military history for the man, cuffing a briefcase holding the false documents to his arm and fitting him with a life jacket, transporting him by submarine to the coast of Spain and launching him.

A Spanish fisherman found the corpse a short while later and informed the authorities.

As anticipated, the Germans, who were tight with the Spanish intelligence agencies, were soon given an opportunity to examine the corpse and the briefcase. The Germans bought the idea that the Major had been the victim of an airplane crash at sea and believed the false information in the briefcase.

The British operation was deemed a great success.

CHAPTER NINE

- May -

- Hitler -

On May seventh, after traveling to Berlin for the funeral of Viktor Lutze who had succeeded Rohm, Hitler hosted the Reichsleiters and Gauleiters at a luncheon held at the chancellery. After the meal Hitler gave a speech.

In the speech, he reviewed the military situation since nineteen thirty-nine. He told his audience that at the beginning of the war Germany, as a revolutionary state, had faced only bourgeois states. These, he intoned, had been easy to occupy, in that they were inferior to the new Germany in both upbringing and attitude and a country with an ideology would always have the edge over a bourgeois state, since it was founded upon a firm spiritual base.

This advantage had ended with Barbarossa, where the German forces found themselves up against a state which also sponsored an ideology, albeit one that was wrong. He went on to praise Stalin for his purges of defeatists in the military and imbedding political commissars within his troop formations. Added to this was fact that Stalin had expunged the *'High Society'* of Russia by way of liquidation to ensure that Bolshevism could devote all its energies into fighting the invading Germans.

He went on to explain that another reason for difficulties in the East was that Germany's allies, particularly the Hungarians, had proven to be poor fighters and that Germany was the only power in Europe who could defeat the Russians because victory in battle was linked with ideology.

He told his captive audience that the anti-Semitism, which had formerly invigorated party members, must once again become the focal point in the spiritual struggle. That it must be the rallying cry for

German troops and that if Germany did not stand as firm as a wall, the hordes of the East would sweep into Europe. A constant, invincible effort must therefore be concentrated on taking the necessary measures needed to ensure the security of European culture.

'If it be true today that the Bolshevism of the East is mainly under Jewish leadership and that the Jews are also the dominant influence in the Western plutocracies, then our anti-Semite propaganda must begin at this point.'

That is why there could be no possibility of any compromise with the Russians.

'They must be knocked out, exactly as we formerly had to knock out our own Communists to attain power. At that time we never thought of a compromise either.'

Although this speech was delivered with fervor, it was apparent to those in the audience that Hitler's physical health was failing and that he was a pale shadow of his former self - that despite the fact that Hitler's personal doctor, Morell, had recently doubled his hormone injections as well as adding another drug, Prostakrin, to the Fuhrer's daily intake. He had also convinced Hitler to take another electrocardiogram, which indicated a worsening of his heart condition, something that the doctor, once again, withheld from the Fuhrer.

Morell attempted to deflect Hitler's worsening condition away from himself by suggesting that the diet regime for the Fuhrer, which was overseen by Dr. Zabel, was aggravating matters and recommended that Hitler hire a special cook. This was done and a woman from Vienna, Frau von Exner, took up the position.

On May twelfth Hitler, satisfied that his leadership had staunched the military withdrawals after Stalingrad, returned to *'Wolfsschanze'*. The next day he was informed that two German/Italian armies in Tunisia, consisting of three hundred thousand men, had been taken prisoner by the Allies. Seven days later came the news that Mussolini's regime was close to collapse and that on the streets of Rome German soldiers were being openly cursed.

During this month Hitler received no positive reports of any significance and his mood darkened considerably.

* * * * *

- Inner Circle -

- Goebbels -

Goebbels, who had been too ill to attend the conference in support of Speer and Goering, had by the beginning of May, written Goering off and managed to ingratiate himself with Bormann, in whom he suddenly claimed to find the merits he had attributed to the *'Reichsmarschall'* only weeks before. The two men had come to an agreement whereby Goebbels would pass all his reports to Hitler that required a determination from the Fuhrer, first through Bormann, in return for Bormann's pledge to see to it that the *'right decision'* (from Goebbels point of view) would be made by the Fuhrer on each occasion.

* * * * *

- Speer -

Speer, who had had his faith in Goebbels as a co-conspirator in the battle against Bormann completely dashed by this turn of events, was still unable to convince himself that Goebbels had completely abandoned him. In addition he could not risk the loss of his only supposed friend from within the inner circle and it was difficult for him to break out of his fascination with the Propaganda Minister's impressive comradeship, perfect comportment and levelheaded reasoning.

As a result he and Goebbels continued to meet regularly and assist each other in achieving their attempts to make the utmost use of Germany's domestic reserves.

* * * * *

- Bormann -

There was no doubt that Bormann had been alerted to the plans hatched by Goebbels and Speer to reduce his influence with Hitler, or that Bormann had quickly acted to counteract them. Despite this fact, Bormann, having had little difficulty in counteracting the move and sensing that he might need Speer's support at some point down the road, graciously took the whole thing in stride and continued to behave amiably toward Speer while suggesting that he might find it advantageous to come over to his side, as Goebbels had done. While Speer had not immediately taken the bait, Bormann was a patient man who liked to leave his options open.

* * * * *

- Goering -

Shortly after mid-month, Goering, who was now doing his best to repair his sinking reputation with Hitler, approached Speer with a suggestion that they make a joint speech on armaments at the Sportpalast. Speer, who was eager for an opportunity to press for his vision of what needed to be done in that regard, readily agreed.

Goering then sent the suggestion for such a speech to Hitler by way of his new friend Bormann. Everyone in the inner circle, with the exception of Bormann, was somewhat surprised when Hitler agreed to the speech, but appointed Goebbels to replace Goering as one of the two speakers.

Goering was depressed beyond words but knew he had no recourse to the decision.

* * * * *

- The Sportpalast -

As a matter of principle, Hitler demanded that he pass judgment on all speeches before they were given.

When Speer and Goebbels sat down together to co-ordinate the speech texts, Goebbels told Speer that he would probably have to shorten his speech since the Propaganda Minster would be speaking for an hour and that *'If you don't stay considerably under half an hour, the audience will lose interest'.*

Speer, who was scheduled as the second speaker, was prepared to do this.

When the manuscripts of the two featured speeches, (Speer's containing a note that it would be cut by a third), were forwarded to Hitler they had to first pass through Bormann's hands.

Speer was immediately ordered to attend the Fuhrer who was in residence at the Berghof. When he arrived, he and Hitler sat down, with the omnipresent Bormann hovering about as usual. Hitler was handed the draft manuscripts for the speech and began to read them. In a matter of a few minutes the Fuhrer slashed Goebbels speech by half and handed the two documents back to Bormann with the comment.

'Here Bormann, inform the Doctor and tell him that I think Speer's speech excellent.'

In so doing, in Bormann's presence, Hitler had determined Speer's prestige as higher than that of the Propaganda Minister and had made it clear to both men that Speer could still command the Fuhrer's confidence and strong support in all things, even, if need be, against those holding the highest of offices.

While this buoyed Speer considerably, his speech at the Sportpalast did little to change the status quo. He was able to make known the sizable increases he had been able to bring about in the area of armaments production; however, this only brought about later comments from the hierarchy to the effect of; *'So it can be done without the big sacrifices you were asking for.'*

At the same time, the General Staff and the front line commanders largely dismissed Speer's figures, suggesting that; *'they had often suffered from supply difficulties with ammunition or ordinance.'*

* * * * *

- Special Handling -

In May, seven thousand Jews who were employees of the Jewish council in Amsterdam were ordered to assemble in an Amsterdam city square for the purpose of deportation. Only five hundred of these individuals complied with the order. The Germans responded by sealing the Jewish quarter and systematically rounding up the Jews.

For the next five months this process continued. The Germans efficiently confiscated all the property left behind by those forced to deport.

SS Dr. Joseph Mengele arrived at Auschwitz.

On May nineteenth the Nazi government declared Berlin to be Judenfrei (cleansed of Jews).

* * * * *

- Concentration Camps -

Deportations to Treblinka had continued until May, with a few isolated trains arriving after that date. The SS then moved to obliterate all traces of mass killing (Aktion 1005) from the site. The mass graves were opened and internees were forced to remove and burn the corpses on huge pyres. It was a massive undertaking and was not completed until the end of July.

* * * * *

- Ghettos -

On May sixteenth the SS complete the destruction of the Jewish resistance effort in the Warsaw ghetto which has been reduced to rubble. The SS commander, Stroop, orders the destruction of the Great Synagogue on Tlomackie Street to symbolize the German victory. Stroop reports to Berlin that he has captured fifty-six thousand Jews and destroyed six hundred and thirty-one bunkers. He estimates that between five and six thousand have been killed in the bombardment and resulting fires and that he has shot more than seven thousand and has sent the same number to Treblinka for special handling. The remaining Jews have been deported to Poniatowa and Trawniki forced-labour camps and to the Majdanek extermination camp.

* * * * *

- Medical Experiments -

- Josef Mengele -

SS Doctor Mengele, nicknamed *'The Angel of Death'* was perhaps the most infamous of the Nazi doctors. In May he arrived at Auschwitz to take up his duties as a replacement for another doctor who had fallen ill.

Here he became medical officer of the Auschwitz-Birkenau *'Zigeunerfamilienlager'* (Gypsy Family Camp). He filled this position until August of nineteen forty-four.

By July of nineteen forty-two, the SS had begun systematically conducting *'selections'* upon the arrival of each trainload of deportees which reached the camp.

Incoming Jews were segregated upon arrival. Those deemed able to work were admitted into the camp, and those deemed unfit for labour were immediately sent to the gas chambers. The group selected to die, normally about three-quarters of the total, included almost all children, women with small children, pregnant women, all the elderly, and any of those who appeared, during a brief and superficial inspection by an SS doctor, to be completely unfit for work.

Mengele was a member of the team of doctors assigned to do the selections. He often undertook this work even when he was not assigned to do so, in the hope of finding subjects for his medical experiments.

He was particularly interested in locating sets of twins. Unlike most of the doctors, who viewed the undertaking of selections as one of their most stressful and horrible duties, Mengele undertook the task with a flamboyant air, often smiling or whistling a tune while he made his judgments.

Mengele and other SS doctors did not actually treat inmates; however they did supervise the activities of inmate doctors who were forced to work in the camp medical service. Mengele made weekly visits to the hospital barracks and readily dispatched to the gas chambers any prisoners who had not recovered after spending an allotted two weeks in bed. He was also a member of the team of doctors responsible for supervising the administration of 'Zyklon B', the cyanide-based pesticide that was used to execute individuals sent to the gas chambers at Birkenau. He served in this capacity at the gas chambers located in crematoria IV and V.

When an outbreak of noma, (a gangrenous bacterial disease of the mouth and face) broke out in the Gypsy camp in forty-three, Mengele initiated a study to determine the cause of the disease and develop a treatment. He enlisted the aid of prisoner, Doctor Berthold Epstein, a Jewish pediatrician and professor from Prague University. Mengele ordered the patients isolated in a separate barrack and had several afflicted children euthanized so that their preserved heads and organs could be sent to the SS Medical Academy which was located in Graz, as well as other facilities for study.

In response to a typhus epidemic in the women's camp, Mengele cleared one block of six hundred Jewish women and sent them to the gas chamber. The building was then cleaned and disinfected, and the occupants of a neighboring block were bathed, de-loused, and given new clothing before being moved into the clean block. He repeated this process until all the barracks were disinfected.

Mengele oversaw a similar disinfection used for later epidemics of scarlet fever and other diseases, but on this occasion he ordered that all the sick prisoners be sent to the gas chambers.

Using inmates for human experimentation, Mengele looked at Auschwitz as an opportunity to continue his anthropological studies and research on heredity. The experiments he carried out were unscientific and had no regard for the health or safety of the victims.

Mengele saw to it that his research subjects were better fed and housed than other prisoners and held temporarily safe from the gas chambers. He established a kindergarten for the children that were the subjects of these experiments, along with all Gypsy children under the age of six. The facility provided better food and living conditions than other areas of the camp, and even included a playground. When visiting his child subjects, he would introduce himself as *'Uncle Mengele'* and often offered them candies.

Despite these niceties, he was committed, without empathy, to his need for human experiments and personally supervised or dispatched via lethal injection, shootings, beatings, and through selections and his deadly experiments, thousands of individuals.

He was sadistic and extremely anti-Semitic - an individual who staunchly believed that the Jews, as an inferior and dangerous race, should be entirely eliminated.

He was particularly interested in identical twins, people with heterochromia iridum (eyes of two different colors), dwarfs and people with physical abnormalities. Von Verschuer, who received regular reports and shipments of specimens from Mengele secured a grant from the *'Deutsche Forschungsgemeinschaft'* for his pet doctor. The grant was used to build a pathology laboratory attached to Crematorium II at Auschwitz II-Birkenau. Dr. Miklos Nyiszi, an inmate Hungarian Jewish pathologist who arrived later at Auschwitz, performed dissections and prepared specimens for shipment in this laboratory.

Mengele's twin research was in part intended to prove the supremacy of heredity over environment and thus bolster the Nazi premise of the superiority of the Aryan race and a desire to enhance the reproduction rate of the German race by improving the chances of racially desirable Aryan couples of producing twins.

Twins involved in Mengele's experiments were examined from head to toe. Measurements of the entire body were meticulously taken. Dr. Mengele demanded specific and careful exams. If any detail was missed, the staff, usually a prisoner doctor, would be punished severely.

Twins were allowed to keep their hair for the first several days of the examination. After all the living data was taken, the twins would be routinely euthanized by a single injection of chloroform in the heart. Care was taken to insure the twins died simultaneously. They were then dissected with the organs being sent to research centers.

Twins were subjected to weekly examinations and measurements of their physical attributes by Mengele or one of his assistants. The experiments performed by Mengele on twins included unnecessary amputation of limbs, intentionally infecting one twin with typhus or other diseases, and then transfusing the blood of one twin into the other. Many of the victims died while they underwent these procedures. Often, after an experiment was over, the twins were immediately euthanized and their bodies dissected.

On one occasion Mengele personally killed fourteen twins in one night by using chloroform injections into their hearts. When one twin would die of a disease, Mengele would routinely euthanize the other so that comparative post-mortem reports could be prepared.

Mengele's experiments with eyes included attempts to change eye color by injecting chemicals into the eyes of living subjects and euthanizing others who had heterochromatic eyes, so that their eyes could be removed and sent to Berlin for study.

His experiments on dwarfs and individuals with physical abnormalities included taking measurements, drawing blood, extracting healthy teeth, and treatment with unnecessary drugs and X-rays. A large number of these victims were sent to the gas chambers after about two weeks and then their skeletons were then sent onward to Berlin for further study. Mengele also selected pregnant women, on whom he would perform experiments before sending them to the gas chambers.

On one occasion, Mengele sewed two Gypsy twins together at their backs in an attempt to create a set of conjoined twins. After several days of suffering, this pair of unlucky children died of gangrene.

A specific example of one of Mengele's procedures with twins has been recorded by prisoner doctors.

'The train arrived at the camp in the very early morning. Three sets of twins were found aboard. They were taken to the experimental block. Dr. Mengele ordered that a set of Hungarian twins be placed in the examination room. The Hungarian twins, young men, eighteen

years of age, were described as 'extremely athletic and handsome.' They had much body hair and were allowed to keep it for the first few weeks.

After a quick initial examination, this set of twins was showered and returned nude to the examination room. There the examination began, starting with their heads. All parts of their heads were examined and the head examinations took days. The two subjects were then completely X-rayed.

The next stage of the examination consisted of tubes being forced through their noses and into their lungs. The men were then ventilated with a gas which caused them to cough so severely they had to be restrained and then their sputum was collected from their lungs for examination.

After this procedure, the twins were photographed for several days. The purpose of these photographs was to show hair patterns. The young men were each forced to stand, bend and kneel in many positions to accomplish the taking of the photographs. At one point they were required to stand with their arms lifted for several hours straight in order that the under arm hair could be photographed.

After the photographs had been completed the twins were allowed to rest and then awakened very early the next morning. They were taken directly into a room with tables and a large tub containing very hot water. They were made to sit in the water for a long period of time, until they were beginning to pass out from the heat. They were then each strapped to tables where their hair was plucked in an attempt to save the hair root. This procedure was repeated several times. After enough hair was collected, they were totally shaven of every hair on their body. The twins were then again extensively photographed without hair.

In the next phase of experiments the twins received several painful two liter enemas. They were then strapped over a bench table and their rectums were hyper distended after which they received an extensive lower gastric-intestinal examination. This procedure was performed without the use of any anesthesia. The young men were crying so loud that Doctor Mengele ordered they be gagged so he could continue his work in relative peace.

A day later they received urological examinations. During these examinations, tissue samples were taken from the kidneys, prostate, and testicles. Several semen samples were also forcefully taken over next two days.

After this three week period of medical examinations they were taken to the dissection laboratory. Using two doctors, each twin was simultaneously given a fatal injection in the heart. They were then dissected and their organs were sent on to the Institute of Biological Racial and Evolutionary Research in Berlin.'

* * * * *

- The Family -

- Karl and Wilhelm -

General Bichler, true to his word, found those of the SS junior leadership extremely interested in his suggestion that trial runs be quietly and secretly undertaken in relation to the potential safety of the newly created ratlines.

No official recognition of this undertaking was forthcoming from the elite members of the SS, of course. Any such idea would be considered defeatist. However, a short verbal report as to how the tests went was, as Bichler had predicted, eagerly anticipated at this level as well.

Two groups of six had been arranged from the list that Karl had earlier provided and although these men were still moving through the system, reports were that, so far, the forged documents provided and the line of safe houses along the way were well organized and proving effective.

All was going smoothly.

Karl instructed Bichler to report to him when the first group had safely reached Brazil and if and when that occurred, to begin sending similar sized groups of specialists to Brazil at regular intervals.

* * * * *

- Eric -

The big U-boat was making good time on its return trip to Brazil after dropping its human cargo on the Florida shoreline.

The trip had been uneventful and Eric decided to surface and allow the crew an hour or two in the open air when evening had set in.

As the U-boat breached the surface he followed the lookouts up into the conning tower and after checking to see what cloud cover was available to shield his craft from the brightness of the moon, he raised his head and turned slowly, using his binoculars to sweep the surface.

Almost immediately one of the lookouts shouted a sighting and bearing and Eric spun to have a look. He rapidly spotted the small shore-patrol craft and as he watched, it abruptly changed course and started towards them. The vessel was still some distance away.

While Eric was certain that the U-boat had been spotted by those aboard, he doubted that they could have easily gauged its size and uniqueness with any certainty. The situation was unfortunate but only a minor irritation.

Unlike other German U-boats, his advanced craft had a streamlined and hydro-dynamically clean hull design and was fitted with powerful twin diesel electric engines. It had the ability to outrun most surface ships even while submerged, and was capable of much improved dive times over its predecessors, due to the new hull form.

This combination also gave the boat a *'sprint ability'* when required and the new hull design not only significantly reduced visibility by marine or airborne radar when the U-boat was on the surface, but was far less noisy when operating underwater.

If push were to come to shove, the massive U-boat also featured a hydraulic torpedo-reloading system that allowed all six bow torpedo tubes to be reloaded faster than a Type VIIC U-boat could reload a single tube, making it capable of firing eighteen torpedoes in under twenty minutes. It also featured a very sensitive passive sonar-system, not seen on earlier U-boats.

Eric gave the order to crash dive and the massive craft began its rapid descent as he and the lookouts cleared the conning tower.

Running under full power below the surface, the U-boat could do close to thirty-two kilometers per hour.

Eric knew it would likely be unnecessary for the big submarine to have to fight and that it could quickly draw away for its pint-sized pursuer.

* * * * *

- Friedrichshafen -

Erika was in her element and very busy from morning to night as she bustled about, fulfilling her duties as matriarch and grandmother.

The large bright rooms resulting from the renovations that had been made to the old nursery were full of activity and she found herself happily spending as much if not more time there than did her daughters and the two newly hired nannies.

Friedrich was now deeply involved in his eugenic research with the Baron, which was from all reports, progressing astonishingly well. Subsequently he often spent his time at the new facility seven days per week. Surprising everyone, Gabriella was seamlessly usurping her mother's initial tightfisted control over the operation of the nursery and, with Ursula spending more and more time in the lower levels of the castle, the youngest von Stauffer daughter had begun efficiently organizing and taking charge of overseeing the day to day activities of the children and their nannies.

Ursula, after three weeks of recovery, was again involving herself more in the cataloguing, storage and forward shipment to Brazil of the treasures which were still making their way to the castle from the occupied territories.

CHAPTER TEN

- May -

- Allied Air Operations -

Bomber Command's attacks against the German industrial production of the Ruhr valley continue. In excess of two thousand tons of bombs are dropped in a single night on Dortmund and Essen. Wuppertal and Duisburg are also targeted.

The Americans concentrate their efforts on the continued destruction of the U-boat facilities, dropping two thousand, eight hundred tons on Kiel, Antwerp and St. Nazaire.

In the Mediterranean theatre, Allied aircraft fly over twenty five thousand missions against targets in Sicily, Sardinia and southern Italy and in support of the ground operations in Tunisia.

* * * * *

- Battle of the Atlantic -

Only forty-eight Allied ships are sunk for a total of two hundred and ninety-nine thousand, four hundred tons. Of that total, U-boats sink fifty ships for two hundred and sixty-four thousand, nine hundred tons.

Although the month begins very well for the Germans, due to increased British anti-submarine air operations, it ends with the loss of forty-one U-boats and Admiral Doenitz orders the withdrawal of his forces form the north Atlantic routes.

* * * * *

- Greek Resistance Forces -

The Allies encourage the Greek Resistance to step up their operations in an attempt to draw German attention away from the upcoming *'Operation Husky'*, their invasion of Sicily. The resulting increase in Greek activity is effective, with the Nazis sending two additional German armored divisions into Greece. Once these forces are in place, a strategic viaduct on the Athens/Thessaloniki railroad is destroyed, isolating the units and placing them in the position of having to travel under their own power rather than by rail if they choose to leave. A choice to move these isolated units now would result in a great deal of wear and tear on the amour and take a good deal of time to complete.

* * * * *

- May First -

- Tunisia -

American forces manage to take Hill 609 but are unable to continue their push against the Germans.

* * * * *

- May Second -

- Australia -

Japanese bombers hit Darwin.

* * * * *

- May Third -

- Tunisia -

The Americans force their way out of Mousetrap Valley and capture Mateur but are then again halted by the Germans.

* * * * *

- May Fifth -

- Eastern Front -

The Russians take Krymsk and Neberjaisk.

* * * * *

- Tunisia -

British forces retake Djebel Bou Aoukaz.

* * * * *

- May Seventh -

- Tunisia -

The British capture Tunis and the Americans take Bizerte.

* * * * *

- Burma -

The Japanese take Buthidaung, forcing the British forces to retreat.

* * * * *

- May Ninth -

- China -

The Japanese slaughter of thirty thousand civilians begins in Changjiao. Now referred to as the *'Changjiao Massacre'*, this operation also included the rape of thousands of Chinese women and girls.

* * * * *

- May Thirteenth -

- Tunisia -

The remaining German *'Africa Korps'* and Italian forces in North Africa surrender. Over two hundred and fifty thousand prisoners are taken by the Allies.

* * * * *

- May Sixteenth -

- Warsaw Ghetto -

The Jewish resistance is quelled by the SS. The Ghetto has been destroyed and fourteen thousand Jews killed outright with another forty thousand transported to Treblinka for *'Special Handling'*.

* * * * *

- Germany -

RAF special Squadron 617, later known as the *'Damn Busters'*, successfully bomb two German dams in the Ruhr Valley, the Mohne and Eder cutting off electricity to major war industries.

* * * * *

- May Seventeenth -

- Yugoslavia -

The Germans begin their fifth major offensive against Tito's partisans in Yugoslavia. Codenamed *'Operation Schwarz'*, this offensive will be provided by the SS Division Prinz Eugen, primarily supported by the 1st Mountain Division and 4th Brandenburg Regiment. In total, it pits one hundred and twenty thousand troops against Tito's force of approximately twenty thousand.

* * * * *

- May Twenty-Fourth -

- Auschwitz -

Josef Mengele becomes the Chief Medical Officer.

* * * * *

- May Twenty-Sixth -

- Canada -

Meat rationing is introduced countrywide.

* * * * *

- May Thirtieth -

- Aleutians -

American forces take the politically important, but strategically insignificant island of Attu. The Japanese invaders have lost two thousand three hundred and fifty troops and only twenty-eight Japanese prisoners are taken. The Americans have taken heavy losses to take back the island, with six hundred dead and twelve hundred wounded

CHAPTER ELEVEN

- June -

- Hitler -

- Wolfsschanze -

In spite of the destruction of the Axis fortunes in North Africa and Milch's strong opposition to the idea, Hitler is still considering a major offensive in the Eastern Front against Kursk.

Guderian, Germany's expert in armored warfare, arrives from Berlin and after studying the situation, sides with Milch. He points out that the new Panther tank has, as yet, only a limited supply of spare parts.

Hitler responds by stating that the attack is necessary now for political reasons. Guardian replies that it would do nothing for general morale in that few Germans even know where Kursk is.

Hitler admitted that he was unsure about this major move and said he would give it further thought.

After Guardian left, both Kluge and Zeitzler pushed strongly for the launch of the offensive move against Kursk, urging Hitler to put it into motion while there was still time.

Hitler spent the month waffling back and forth on the issue and became easily frustrated and angry during the military conferences held in June.

* * * * *

- Hitler's Personal Family Circle -

By this time in the war, the atmosphere within the *'Wolfsschanze'* compound had become dark and depressing.

Hitler' non-political and non-military, *'family inner circle',* those he surrounded himself with when having his meals and when not directly involved with military matters and who he sought out to remove himself from his worries, could no longer ignore the gloomy sense of impending doom that permeated the entire complex.

These feelings of universal dissatisfaction and the fear of an uncertain future created a sense of *'cabin fever'* on a scale that could no longer be dismissed. A general veil of despondency was rampant and even those among them who had always viewed the Fuhrer as infallible and Godlike, were having misgivings.

Hitler could not help but be aware of these changes and the current situation did nothing to help him maintain anything like a positive attitude. He needed the ongoing diversion that the *'family inner circle'* provided him in order to maintain his mental balance and lift him out of his growing depression over the progress of the war.

Central to, and the mainstay of that group, were his young private secretaries.

For the most part, these women had come into Hitler's life early in his political career. Initially Hitler had only two secretaries, Johanna Wolf and Christa Schroeder.

In nineteen thirty-seven, as Hitler's work load had increased, the two secretaries had complained about having too much work. They asked for assistance. At first Hitler resisted as he was a man who disliked change and did not wish to see a new face in his inner sanctum. Eventually however, he realized that the girls were simply unable to keep up with the increased workload and he agreed to take on a third secretary.

He chose Gerda Daranowski, nicknamed *'Dara',* who came to work for him in thirty-seven.

Gerda had worked for Elizabeth Arden before coming to work for the Fuhrer. After coming to Hitler's staff she became engaged to his driver, Erich Kempka for a short period of time and then on February second of nineteen forty-three she married a Luftwaffe officer named Eckhard Christian. None of Hitler's secretaries were married, and once 'Dara' had taken her vows, she left Hitler's *'family inner circle'* to take up her wifely duties.

Traudl had been promoted from the secretarial pool at that time to fill *'Dara's'* shoes.

When *'Dara'* left the *'family inner circle'*, so did the wonder of her outgoing spirit and the streams of positive energy and a real sense of fun that seemed to follow her wherever she went. Traudl had soon become a Hitler favorite. However her innocence, and awe, while beguiling for him, did not make up for the loss of *'Dara'*.

It was therefore suggested to Hitler that perhaps this would be a good time to convince her to return to his service and bring the total list of personal secretaries up to four in order to liven things up within the close-knit group.

The Fuhrer thought it might be just what was needed to improve the atmosphere at *'Wolfsschanze'* and in June of forty-three; *'Dara'* Christian arrived at the compound, accompanied by several traveling trunks and suitcases, to great fanfare.

* * * * *

- The Panther -

The German Panther tank was a direct response to the appearance of the Russian T-34 and Kv-1 tanks.

These were first encountered on June twenty-third of forty-one. At that time, the T-34 definitely outclassed the existing models of the German Panzer III and IV, so much so that at the time, General Heinz Guderian, had insisted that a special *'Panzerkommision'* be dispatched to the Eastern Front to assess the T-34.

Among the features of the Soviet tank considered to be most significant were the sloping armor, which gave much improved shot deflection and increased the effective armor thickness against penetration, the wide track, which improved mobility over soft ground, and the 76.2 mm gun, which had good armor penetration and fired an effective high explosive round.

As a result of the report generated by the *'Panzerkommision'*, Daimler-Benz (DB) and Maschinenfabrik-Nurnberg AG (MAG) were given the task of designing a new thirty to thirty-five ton tank (Designated VK30.02), by April of nineteen forty two.

The DB design resembled the T-34 in both hull and turret. It used a leaf-spring suspension, in lieu of the T-34s coil-spring-suspension. The main advantages of the leaf springs over a torsion bar suspension were lower hull silhouette and a simpler shock damping design. This leaf spring suspension lay outside of the hull. Subsequently, the hull was narrower and offered a smaller turret ring.

Like the T-34, this DB design had a rear drive sprocket and a forward situated turret, but unlike the T-34, the DB design had a three-man turret crew consisting of commander, gunner, and loader.

As the planned L/70 75 mm gun was much larger than the T-34's, mounting it in the Daimler-Benz turret proved difficult and in order to address the space limitations, DB considered reducing the turret crew to two men but this idea was eventually discarded as experience had shown it to be a less effective.

The MAN design represented more conventional German thinking. It placed the transmission and drive sprocket in the front and envisioned a centrally mounted turret. It had a gasoline engine and eight torsion-bar suspension axles per side. Because of the torsion bar suspension and the drive shaft running under the turret basket, the MAN Panther was higher and had a wider hull design than the DB.

In the MAN proposal, the Henschel firm's original design concepts for their earlier Tiger I tank's suspension/drive components was used. This concept used its characteristic *'Schachtellaufwerkformat'*; large, overlapping, interleaved road wheels with a *'slacktrack'* using no return rollers for the upper run of track and these were to be repeated with the MAN design. These large, rubber-rimmed steel wheels added to the protection of the hull from a lateral penetrating shot.

The two designs were reviewed from January through March of forty-two. *Reichminister* Todt and later, his replacement Speer, both recommended the DB design to Hitler because of its several advantages over the initial MAN design. However, having learned from the DB proposal, prior to the final submission, MAN had improved their design, and a review by a special commission appointed by Hitler in May of forty-two ended up selecting the MAN design.

Hitler approved this decision. One of the principal reasons he did this was because the MAN design made use of an existing turret, which had been designed by Rheinmetall-Borsig, while the DB design would have necessitated the design of a brand new turret and to do so would substantially delay the commencement and cost of production on the new tank.

Though light in weight, its motor was to be the same as the Tiger's, which meant it could develop superior speed.

Since the Tiger had gone from a fifty tone tank to a mammoth seventy five tons, it was decided to develop this new faster and more maneuverable thirty ton tank, which would be named, *'Panther'*, in order to signify its greater agility when compared to the *'Tiger'*.

Hitler was always very interested in new weapons and often dabbled in their design. Predictably, the Fuhrer did exactly that with the *'Panther'* and by the time it went into production, this new tank, at his order, had inherited heavier amour and larger guns. It now came out at forty-eight tons.

After testing a prototype, the MAN design was accepted for immediate production, but this was delayed due to the time required to produce the specialized machine tools needed for the machining of the hull. The demand for this tank was so high that the manufacturing had to be expanded beyond MAN to include Daimler-Benz, Maschinenfabrik Niedersachsen in Hanover (MNH), a (MNH) subsidiary, and Henschel & Sohn in Kassel.

The initial production target was for two hundred and fifty tanks per month at the MAN plant in Nuremberg, but his had been increased to six hundred per month in January of forty-three.

* * * * *

- Forced/Slave Labour -

Shortly after Hitler came to power, the party began a policy of garnering and maintaining a supply of forced or slave labourers.

This official party policy had begun with the formation of labour camps within the Reich, which were made up of what the new government considered to be German *'undesirables,'* individuals who needed to be rooted out from within the unproductive ranks of its own citizenry.

The new order introduced by the party initiated the forced euthanasia for all its own citizens who were considered unable to work productively for the state, due either to some form of mental or physical disability. Additionally they believed that all who could work must work to their full potential, for the good of all of Germany.

The Nazis considered that those Germans termed as *'undesirable',* should include all homeless, homosexuals, criminals, political decenters, communists, Jews and anyone that the regime saw as *'not pulling their weight for the state'*.

It really isn't surprising then, that after the war had started and as it continued, this policy of seeing to it that the state get the most out of those falling under the Nazi boot was, with certain tweaks, expanded into the occupied territories.

The whole purpose of Hitler's *'lebensraum'* policy of conquest of new lands in the East was to exploit those lands to provide cheap goods and labour for Germany. Of course, the idea that those who had now been conquered should enjoy any better treatment than their own citizens did not even occur to those in the Nazi hierarchy. Subsequently, over time, several categories of *'Arbeitslager'* (labour camps) were created for different categories of inmates drawn from the newly occupied territories.

As had been done in Germany, those *'undesirables'* discovered. in what was now German land, who were capable of work were placed into labour camps with the sole purpose of being worked by the state for the remainder of their lives and those who were unable to work, were promptly euthanized.

These new categories were based on a newly created class system, for all *'Fremdarbeiter'* (Foreign workers) transported to Germany to work for the Reich. The system was based on layers of increasingly less privileged workers, running the gamut from those of well paid workers from Germany's allies, those taken from neutral countries, to those who were to be considered as slave labourers and originated from conquered *'untermensch'* (subhuman) populations.

'Gastarbeitnehmer' (guest workers), were workers brought into Germany from Germanic and Scandinavian countries, Italy, other German allies (Romania, Bulgaria, Hungary), and friendly neutrals (e.g. Spain and Switzerland). This amounted to a very small group of workers, not even one percent of all the foreign workers in Germany.

'Zwangsarbeiter' (forced workers), were forced labourers who came from countries who were not allied with Germany. This class of workers was broken down into the following specific designations:

'Militarinterniete' (Military internees), in reality prisoners of war. The Geneva Conventions allowed captor nations to force non-officer prisoners of war to work within certain restrictions. For example, almost all Polish non-officer prisoners who had been taken by German invasion troops, amounting to approximately three hundred thousand men, were forced to work in Nazi Germany. By nineteen forty-three almost two million prisoners of war were employed as forced labourers in Germany.

Compared to other foreign workers, the prisoners of war were relatively well-off, especially if they came from western countries that were still at war, like United States or Britain, as the minimum standards of their treatment for these individuals were mandated by the Geneva Conventions. Russian prisoners of war, however, were treated with utter brutality, as the Nazis did not consider them subject to the protections guaranteed under the Conventions.

In the case of the Russians, their working conditions and well-being were subject to supervision by the International Red Cross. In cases of Russian POW mistreatment, retaliation against German prisoners held in US and Britain who were likewise performing forced labour, was almost certain.

In reality the treatment of these workers varied greatly depending on their country of origin, a given period in the war and their specific workplace.

'Zivilarbeiter' (civilian workers), who consisted primarily of Polish captives who had been transported into Germany by the occupying *'General Government'*. These workers were regulated by strict *'Polish Decrees'* and they received much lower wages and could not use public conveniences, such as public transport or visit many

public spaces and businesses , including German-church services, swimming pools, or restaurants. These workers were to work longer hours and were assigned smaller food rations as well as being subject to a definite curfew.

Poles were routinely denied holidays and had to work seven days a week. They could not marry without a permit, nor possess money or objects of value. Bicycles, cameras, even lighters were *'verboten'* to them. Additionally they were required to wear: the Polish *'P'*, on their clothing.

At the start of the war, the number of Polish workers in Germany numbered about three hundred thousand and by the end of forty-three there were nearly one and a half million.

'Ostarbeiter' (Eastern workers), consisted of those transported from Russia, primarily from the Ukraine. These workers were also required to display their ethnic identity on their clothing, in this case with *'OST'* (East) and were forced to live in camps that were fenced and under guard at all times. Under such conditions they were often exposed to the arbitrariness of the SS and the industrial plant guards used by German industry. By the end of forty-three there were well over four million of these workers in Germany.

Generally speaking foreign labourers who originated from Western Europe had similar gross earnings and were subject to similar taxation as German workers. The central and eastern European forced labourers received approximately one-half the gross earnings paid to German workers and far fewer social benefits. Forced labourers, who were prisoners of labour or concentration camps, received little if anything.

True to form, the Nazis issued a ban on sexual relations between German civilians, both men and women and foreign workers and worked diligently to propagandize a, *'Volkstum'*, racial consciousness, to prevent such relations from occurring.

German soldiers and SS officers however, were exempt from any such restrictions. The flip side was that approximately thirty-four thousand Eastern European women taken in *'Lapankas,'* (military kidnapping raids), were forced to serve as sex slaves in both German military brothels and similar camp establishments.

About twelve million forced labourers, most of whom were Eastern Europeans, were employed in the German war economy inside Nazi Germany throughout the war. Over time the German need for slave labour grew to the point that even children were transported in to work in Germany. Hundreds of German industries readily and routinely made use of Nazi government supplied forced/slave labourers during the war. Many of these companies are still successfully operating in Germany today.

* * * * *

- Special Handling -

On June the eleventh Himmler orders that all Jewish ghettos in occupied Poland are to be *'cleansed'* of all inmates.

On June twenty-fifth, the newly built gas chamber/crematorium III, goes into full operation at Auschwitz. The camp now has the capacity to process four thousand, seven hundred and fifty-six bodies each day.

* * * * *

- Concentration Camps -

In the summer, the Germans force prisoners to reopen mass graves in Rumbula and burn the bodies and deport the Riga ghetto inhabitants to the new camp that had been built at Kaiserwald in March.

* * * * *

Beginning in mid-forty-three, the Germans begin dealing with the sixty thousand Jews remaining in Paris. Deportations begin at Jewish children's homes, homes for the aged and from the Rothschild Hospital.

* * * * *

At the Natzweiler-Struthhof concentration camp located in France, approximately thirty-one miles southwest of Strasbourg, prisoners work in nearby granite quarries and on construction projects. At this point in the war, this relatively small camp begins to be used to house suspected European anti-German resistance members, many of whom are involved in the French resistance movement.

* * * * *

- Medical Experiments -

- Auschwitz -

Doctor Carl Clauberg, who had arrived at the camp to begin his horrific experiments on the sterilization of women with Himmler's blessing in Decembers of forty-two, wrote to the Reichsfuhrer.

'The non-surgical method of sterilizing women that I have invented is now almost perfected . . . As for the questions that you have directed to me, sir, I can today answer them in the way that I had anticipated: if the research that I am carrying out continues to yield the sort of results that it has produced so far (and there is no reason to suppose that this shall not be the case), then I shall be able to report in the foreseeable future that one experienced physician, with an appropriately equipped office and the aid of ten auxiliary personnel, will be able to carry out in the course of a single day the sterilization of hundreds, or even 1,000 women.'"

* * * * *

- The Family -

- Karl and Wilhelm -

Karl, Wilhelm and SS-General Bichler were enjoying a leisurely, after-lunch stroll on what was a balmy Berlin afternoon. The park they'd chosen was in an area that had so far escaped any heavy bombing, which made it, at this point in the war, not particularly representative of the general beating the German capital was taking.

En route to the park, however, the three men had been unable to miss the destruction resulting from the incessant RAF raids and as they quietly spoke to one another, their moods reflected the seriousness of the situation in which Germany now found itself.

Bichler had just begun his report on the results of his ratline tests.

"The first six have reached their destination without incident and as of today the second group is nearing the conclusion of their trip. It appears that what is in place is well thought out, and well supported with regard to the requisite forged documentation and the modes of travel being employed."

Karl nodded.

"Your news comes none too soon. There can no longer be any doubt that the turning point in the war has arrived. It will be all downhill from here. Our first priority must be the transport of a sufficient number of gem and art experts out of Germany and into Brazil, so that we can get them safely into place while we still have the capability to physically manage it." Having them prepared and ready to sell our material in the North American underground market for such material, at least a year or so before the war ends, is paramount. We have to expect that our current source of funds will dwindle quickly and be eventually completely cut off as the war comes to an end. Without the planned income from our overseas sales these experts will ensure, we would be unable to continue in our aims for *'Operation Fatherland.'*

Bichler hunched his shoulders as he responded.

"No doubt about that. Those in industry and business who currently financially support our goals will soon find little profit coming out of their repeatedly bombed factories."

Wilhelm picked up the topic.

"Yes, and we had better get our people through fast, because unless I miss my guess, demand for the use of these ratlines is going to expand exponentially as the war deteriorates and Germany becomes a poor choice for residency. Many will gather what they can and wisely head for greener pastures."

Bichler paused to light a cigarette and both Karl and Wilhelm responded by joining him.

It was the General who reopened the discussion.

"Wilhelm makes a good point. It goes without saying that many of those in the SS are already beginning to realize that if this war is lost, the activities in which they have been involved, when known, are not going to be well perceived by the victorious armies once they march into Germany. There may be only minor interest in these ratlines now from this group and the SS lower echelon, but as Germany's forces continue to lose their chosen battles and the expanded Reich subsequently begins to shrink, these men will flee in droves."

Karl exhaled a cloud of smoke as he raised and nodded his head in agreement.

"Yes, and while they will be the mainstream of those rushing to leave the sinking ship, there will be many others who have been instrumental in questionable activities under the Nazi government and who will also hasten to leave the Fatherland, where common sense tells me that once the war ends, they will have to atone for their misdeeds.

Not only will we have to use the ratlines quickly, but we will also have to speed up the shipment of treasure from the castle. The closer we get to the end of this damned war, the harder it is going to be to move any material, human or otherwise, out of Germany."

The ever cautious SS-General raised his head slightly before lowering it and then ground out his cigarette under his boot before responding.

"Yes foresight has given us an edge, but although I agree we need to get these things moving at top speed, I caution that we must also remain vigilant in our precautions as we do so.

Of late Himmler has been using the Fuhrer's paranoia and deteriorating confidence to further his own fortunes and that means that he is looking for any chance to expose those who are in any way acting in a defeatist manner. In short order, he will be looking for signs of anyone attempting to leave Germany and he will also be looking for anyone who is shipping valuables out of the country. Each time he pulls one of these prominent people down, he gains points with Hitler and a subsequent expansion of his own little empire; he is not a man one should underestimate."

* * * * *

- Eric -

On his arrival back in Brazil Eric found himself in the position of having to feign surprise when several senior members of his extended family greeted him with a motorcade and joined him and Heidi on a trip into the countryside to view a *'surprise'*.

As the trip got underway Eric leaned close to Heidi, who was seated behind him in the backseat of the lead car and whispered into her ear.

"I wonder what they would think if I told them that I'd already seen the house and that we'd already broken the place in?"

She paled visibly and shook her head in an adamant *'don't you dare'*

When he smiled broadly down at her, enjoying her reaction, Heidi frowned and promptly elbowed him.

Two of his ribs were still aching slightly when they reached their destination. Holding her secret, he forced his mind back to the first time he'd seen the massive property and managed to repeat his first impressions based on what had transpired on that occasion.

* * * * *

- Friedrichshafen -

Without the need of a formal agreement, the division of responsibilities at castle von Stauffer had settled into a routine.

Seemingly becoming her Mother's shadow, Gabriella had

stepped in to assist in the management and operation of the big household. She had also assumed the primary responsibility of supervision of the nannies and their charges.

Ursula now spent most of each day seeing to the accelerated need to store and forward shipments of the goods that arrived at the castle by train. The flow was slowing noticeably as the fortunes of the German military faltered in the east, but although diminished, it did continue.

Her father had confided the need to ship out as much as possible of the *'Operation Fatherland'* wealth to Brazil over the next few months and both she and her husband were fully occupied with attempting to accomplish this while taking great care to arouse no suspicion about what they were doing.

Friedrich managed to breakfast and sit down to dinner with the family on most days, but was otherwise consumed by his work.

On the night of June twentieth the RAF had instituted a new type of bomb run. This new bombing tactic was coined *'shuttle bombing'*. In this new style of targeting, the bombers flew from their home base to bomb a first target and then continued on to a different location where they were refueled and rearmed. The aircraft then bombed a second target on the return leg to their home base.

On this night, while participating in the first of these shuttle bombing missions of the war, which was codenamed 'Operation *Bellicose'*, the RAF bombers departed from their bases in the United Kingdom and bombed industrial targets in Friedrichshafen prior to landing in Algeria, where they refueled and rearmed. On the return leg they bombed the Italian naval base at La Spezia.

Needless to say, the citizens of Friedrichshafen, including those residing in the von Stauffer castle, where taken by complete surprise by this new endeavor. The bombers had been right on target and as a result, little damage to the civilian areas was sustained and those in castle von Stauffer, although awakened and presented with quite a light show, never considered themselves in serious danger.

CHAPTER TWELVE

- June -

- Allied Air Operations -

Bomber Command drops in excess of fifteen thousand tons, the majority on the Ruhr Valley targets. Cologne, Mulheim and Oberhausen receive major hits.

The US Eighth Air Force delivers a total of twenty-five hundred tons of bombs, concentrating on Cuxhaven, Wilhelmshaven, Kiel and Bremen in a continuation of the attack against the U-boat threat.

Allied air units target Pantelleria and Lampedusa early in the month and then shift to concentrate on Sardinian and Sicilian targets.

* * * * *

- Battle of the Atlantic -

Early in the month, U-boats try sailing in groups across the Bay of Biscay in order to improve their chances of beating off air attacks. However, this proves ineffective and they soon receive orders to travel the area submerged.

The Germans lose seventeen U-boats this month while total Allied shipping losses amount to only twenty ships out of a twenty-eight ship total overall.

* * * * *

- June Third -

- Free French -

Generals De Gaulle and Giraud bury the hatchet and agree on the structure of a Committee of National Liberation under their joint presidency. Other members of the committee include Andre Philip, Jean Monnet and Massigili.

* * * * *

- French Resistance -

The Michelin tire works at Clermont-Ferrand are soundly sabotaged.

* * * * *

- June Fourth -

- Free French -

General Henri Giraud takes up the post of Commander in Chief of the Free French forces.

* * * * *

- June Tenth -

- The *'Pointblank Directive'* -

The Allied Joint Chiefs of Staff issues the *'Pointblank directive'* to the commanders of the British and American heavy bomber forces in Europe. It authorized the initiation of *'Operation Pointblank'*.

'Pointblank' is the codename for the primary portion of the Allied combined bomber offensive, which is aimed at crippling or destroying the German aircraft fighter strength, in order to negate frontline German air operations during the planned future Allied invasion of Northwest Europe.

It directed the RAF Bomber Command and the U.S. Eighth Air

Force to bomb specific targets such as aircraft factories. The practice of these two forces acting independently as they had been up to this point in the war, the RAF and USAAF each attacking German industry in their own way was now over.

The operational execution of the Directive was left to the commanders of the forces and as such even after the directive the British continued in their previous night attacks and the majority of the attacks on German fighter production and combat with the fighters themselves was left to the USAAF.

The USAAF bombers began large scale daylight attacks on the factories involved in the production of fighter aircraft. The Luftwaffe was forced into defending against these raids, and its fighters were thereby drawn into battle with American bombers and their escorts. It was these ongoing battles of attrition that, over time, reduced the Luftwaffe's strength, despite a continued increase in German aircraft production.

* * * * *

- June Eleventh -

- Pantelleria -

The British First Division takes this Italian island situated between Tunisia and Sicily. They capture eleven thousand Italian prisoners.

* * * * *

- June Twelfth -

- Lampedusa -

A second island lying between Tunisia and Sicily surrenders to the Allied forces.

* * * * *

- June Sixteenth -

- *'Operation Husky'* -

The first of the invasion convoys leave the US headed for Sicily.

* * * * *

- June Seventeenth -

- Scapa Flow -

The first units of the British Home Fleet destined for the support of the invasion of Sicily sail from their home port.

* * * * *

- Sicily -

Both Sicily and the Italian mainland are hit by Allied bombers.

* * * * *

- June Twentieth -

- Friedrichshafen -

RAF bombers attack the industrial areas of the city.

* * * * *

- June Twenty-first -

- Solomon Islands -

'Operation Cartwheel' opens with the unopposed landings of the 4th Marine Raider Battalion at Segi Point on the southern tip of New Georgia.

* * * * *

- June Twenty-Second -

- Free French -

The Committee of National Liberation decides that Giraud will retain command of the Free French forces in North Africa and that De Gaulle will lead elsewhere.

* * * * *

- June Twenty-Third -

- Island Hopping -

The American strategy to drive up the Southwest Pacific by taking individual islands continues as they make landings on the Trobriand Islands.

* * * * *

- June Twenty-Eighth -

- New Guinea -

US forces occupy Kiriwina and Woodlark and begin immediate construction of an airfield.

* * * * *

- June Thirtieth -

- New Georgia -

American forces land on Rendova Island as part of the ongoing *'Operation Cartwheel'*.

Patrick Laughy

- Part 2 -

CHAPTER THIRTEEN

- July -

- Hitler -

- Wolfsschanze -

Time was running out.   Hitler's waffling on the decision for a new offensive on the Eastern Front against the Russians at Kursk had to be made.   This operation, code named *'Unternehmen Zitadelle'* (Operation Citadel), continued to worry the Fuhrer.

The Wehrmacht had been weakened by the loss of men and equipment in the battle of Stalingrad, but the army still could put more than three million troops into the field.   After months of delay, Hitler, eager to prove the German army was still formidable, finally made the decision to go ahead with it.

In so doing he determined to put his troops to the test in one great offensive that he said: *'will shine like a beacon around the world.'*

'Operation Citadel' was aimed at eliminating the Russian Army at Kursk. The town itself was of minor significance; it had been chosen simply because it was situated in a bulge between the fronts of Field Marshal Erich von Manstein's Army Group South and Field Marshal Hans Gunther von Kluge's Army Group Center.

Hitler was tentatively convinced by both Zeitzler and Kluge that the battle plan would destroy five Soviet armies and thereby prevent the Soviets from mounting any offensives for at least the remainder of the year. A German victory in this battle would also free Hitler up to direct more resources to the Mediterranean theater of war.

The Germans hoped to weaken the Russian's offensive potential for the summer of forty-three by cutting off a large number of forces that they anticipated would be in the Kursk salient, assembling for an upcoming offensive. By eliminating these enemy forces the Germans would also shorten their lines of defense and take the strain off of their overstretched forces.

The plan envisioned envelopment by a pair of pincers breaking through the northern and southern flanks of the salient. It was thought that a victory here would reassert Germany's strength and improve her prestige with allies who might be considering withdrawing from the war. It was also predicted that large numbers of Russian prisoners would be captured and could then be used as forced labour in the German armaments industries.

On July the first Hitler addressed his senior commanders. He told them:

'Germany must either tenaciously hold on to all conquered territory or fall. The German soldier has to realize he must stand and fight to the end.'

He admitted to them that *'Citadel'* was a gamble, but one he believed that Germany had to take, and:

'Hadn't he been right, against all military advice about Austria, Czechoslovakia, Poland and the Soviet Union?'

The Battle of Kursk began at the unusual hour of three P.M. on July fourth, nineteen forty-three.

For their attack, the Germans utilized three armies along with a large proportion of their total tank strength on the Eastern Front. The 9th Army, of Army Group Center, based north of the bulge, contained three hundred and thirty-five thousand men of which two hundred and twenty-three thousand were combat soldiers. In the south, the 4th Panzer Army and Army Detachment *'Kempf'*, of Army Group South, had two hundred and twenty-three thousand, nine hundred and seven men, one hundred and forty-nine thousand, two hundred and seventy-one of whom were combat soldiers and one hundred thousand men, sixty-six thousand being combat soldiers, respectively.

In total, these three armies had a strength of seven hundred and seventy-eight thousand men, consisting of five hundred and eighteen thousand, two hundred and seventy-one combat soldiers. Army Group South was equipped with the most armored vehicles, infantry and artillery when compared to the 9th Army. The 4th Panzer Army and Army Detachment *'Kempf'* had one thousand three hundred and seventy-seven tanks and assault guns, while the 9th Army possessed only nine hundred and eighty-eight tanks and assault guns.

Arriving just prior to the launch of the offensive, the two new Panther battalions, the 51st and 52nd, each equipped with one hundred tanks, were attached to the *'Grossdeutschland'* Division in the XLVIII Panzer Corps of Army Group South. As a result, these two units had little time to perform reconnaissance or to orientate themselves to the terrain they found themselves in. Such a decision was considered a breach of the methods of the *'panzerwaffe'* which was deemed essential for the successful use of amour.

Though led by experienced panzer commanders, many of the tank crews were new recruits and had little time to become familiar with their new tanks and their temperamental transmissions, let alone train together to function as a unit. The two battalions had arrived directly from the training grounds and lacked combat experience. In addition, the requirement to maintain radio silence until the start of the attack meant that the Panther units would have little training in radio procedures. These new Panthers were still experiencing problems with their transmissions, and were to prove mechanically unreliable.

By the morning of the fifth of July, the units had lost sixteen Panthers due to mechanical breakdown, leaving only one hundred and eighty-four available for the launch of the offensive.

Unbeknownst to the German planners, the Russians had complete intelligence of the German intentions. This information had been provided in part by the British intelligence service and Enigma intercepts.

Aware that the attack would fall on the neck of the Kursk salient months in advance, the Russians were able to build a defense in depth which was designed to wear down the German panzer spearheads.

The Germans had repeatedly delayed the start date of the offensive while they tried to build up their forces and amass new weapons, mainly the new Panther tanks but also to increase their numbers of the heavier Tigers.

These delays had given the Russians time to construct a series of deeply fortified lines. The defensive preparations included minefields, fortifications, pre-sighted artillery fire zones and anti-tank strong points, which extended to an approximate depth of one hundred and ninety miles. In addition, Russian mobile formations had been pulled back out of the salient to form a large reserve force which could then be used by the Russians in strategic counteroffensives.

In preparation for the German attack, the Russians used two *'Fronts'*, each the equivalent of an army group, for the defense of Kursk, and created a third *'Front'* behind the battle area which was held as a reserve.

The Central and Voronezh *'Fronts'* fielded twelve armies, with seven hundred and eleven thousand, five hundred and seventy-five men.

In reserve, the Steppe Front had an additional five hundred and seventy-three thousand, one hundred and ninety-five men, four hundred and forty-nine thousand, one hundred and thirty-three thousand being combat troops.

Thus the total size of the Russian defensive force was one million, nine hundred and ten thousand, three hundred and sixty one men of whom one million, four hundred and twenty-six thousand, three hundred and fifty-two were actually combat soldiers.

The battle began on a hot and sultry day with thunder rumbling ominously in the distance. Initially is seemed to the Germans that the Russians had been caught completely by surprise as their artillery did not respond to the German offensive until long after darkness had arrived; however, visions of a quick victory soon began to slip away as heavy rain began to fall.

When dawn broke, the ground had turned into a quagmire and as the morning slipped past, the streams grew into veritable roaring torrents and the German sappers found themselves working under horrific conditions as they struggled to bridge them for the heavy tanks.

The disastrous weather continued and by July ninth the leading German tank spearheads were still fifty-five miles away from Kursk. On July tenth Hitler received the news that an Anglo/American force had landed on Sicily and was meeting little opposition.

Although Manstein argued that failure to confine the Kursk operation would leave a long salient stretching all the way to the Black

Sea, a disillusioned Hitler could see no option but to order the offensive stopped in order to allow him to send reinforcements, which included the SS Panzer Corps, to Western Europe. He did so on July thirteenth of nineteen forty-three.

Hitler then turned his attention elsewhere.

Within a few days of the Allied landings on Sicily, it had become obvious to the Fuhrer that Mussolini's army was on the brink of collapse. Hitler summoned Mussolini to a meeting in northern Italy on the nineteenth of the month.

The conference was held at the imposing Villa Gaggia, near Feltre and began promptly at eleven in the morning with the two men seated facing each other in large armchairs, surrounded by their military and diplomatic entourages.

An initial period of uneasy silence filled the room as each waited for the other to speak first. Finally Hitler opened the conversation, speaking in subdued tones as he addressed the general military and political situation. Mussolini sat uncomfortably, cross-legged, on the very edge of his chair, which was too large and too deep for him, with his hands clasped on his knees.

'Il Duce', who listened with impassive patience, was so shaken from stress that he could no longer warm to Hitler's boasting. He began to fidget as Hitler abruptly began to assail the Italians for their defeatism. Mussolini's mood would latter darken even further, when the Allies chose to bomb Rome on the first day of the meeting. It was the first time the city had ever been the target of enemy bombing.

As the Fuhrer carried on with his tirade, Mussolini occasionally pressed a spot in his back that appeared to be paining him and would, from time to time, heave a deep resigned sigh as he grew more uncomfortable and the Fuhrer's monologue grew more strident.

Hitler was in no mood to humor the Italian leader. He carried on in the same vein as he drove home his point that the current situation could be overcome, if only Italy were to emulate Germany's fanatic determination to fight.

'Every German was imbued with the will to conquer. Lads of fifteen were manning anti-aircraft batteries. If anyone tells me that our task can be left for another generation, I reply that this is not the

case. No one can say that the future generation will be a generation of giants. Germany took thirty years to recover; Rome never rose again. This is the voice of history.'

On and on went the harangue.

At one in the afternoon an adjutant approached the Fuhrer from behind and whispered in his ear. Hitler's features registered his annoyance at being interrupted but he did not continue with his lecture. Instead he announced that the meeting was over and that luncheon was about to be served.

For two hours Hitler had berated the Italian leader for the performance of his troops and Mussolini had not once protested or interrupted to try to explain that his soldiers simply no longer had the means or the will to offer significant residence to the Allied attacks.

His entourage was aghast at his hopeless performance over the period of the conference.

* * * * *

- Mussolini -

Understandably, some prominent members of Mussolini's government turned against him after this meeting with Hitler.

Among these were Grandi and Ciano. With several of his closest colleagues close to revolt, Mussolini felt it necessary to summon the *'Grand Council of Fascism',* to reaffirm support for his leadership and he did so on the twenty-fourth of July. This was the first time that body had met since the start of the war.

When he announced that the Germans were thinking of evacuating the south, Grandi launched a blistering attack against the Italian dictator and moved a resolution asking the king to resume his full constitutional powers. This was, in effect, a *'vote of no confidence'* in Mussolini.

The motion was carried by a nineteen to seven, margin.

Despite this sharp rebuke, Mussolini showed up for work the next day as usual, allegedly viewing the Grand Council as *'merely an advisory body'* and he did not think the vote would have any substantive effect.

That afternoon, he was summoned to the royal palace by King Victor Emmanuel III, who had already been planning to oust Mussolini. *When 'Il Duce'* tried to tell the king about the meeting, Victor Emmanuel cut him off and told him that he was being replaced by Marshal Pietro Badoglio.

As an astonished Mussolini left the palace, he was arrested by Carabinieri at the direct order of the King.

Badoglio announced that *'the war continues at the side of our Germanic ally',* in the hopes that chaos and Nazi retaliation against the civilian population could be avoided. While keeping up the appearance of loyalty to the Axis, Badoglio dissolved the Fascist Party two days after taking over and his government immediately began negotiating an Armistice with the Allies.

* * * * *

- Hitler -

At the evening military conference that night the Fuhrer shocked his military advisors by announcing:

'The Duce has resigned. The government has been taken over by Badoglio.'

In response the gathering began to panic as they articulated what such a change could hold for the future. Hitler cut them off when Jodl suggested that they do nothing untoward until receiving a complete report from Rome. He told them:

'Certainly, but we have to plan ahead. Undoubtedly, in their treachery, they will proclaim that they will remain loyal to us; but this is treachery. Of course, they won't remain loyal. Anyway what's-his-name said straight away that the war would be continued - but that doesn't mean a thing. They have to say that. But we can play the same game; we'll get ready to grab the whole mess, all the rabble. I'll send a man down tomorrow with orders to the commandant of the third Panzer Grenadier Division to take a special detachment into Rome and arrest the whole government. The King - all that scum but

most of all the Crown Prince - to grab all that riffraff, particularly Badoglio and the entire gang. And then you watch them creep and crawl and in two or three days there'll be another coup.'

At his midnight conference the Fuhrer issued additional orders with regard to the 2nd parachute Division. They were to prepare to jump over Rome.

'Rome must be occupied. Nobody is to leave Rome and then the 3rd Panzer Grenadier Division moves in.'

He was then asked if the gateways leading into the Vatican were to be manned and responded.

'That doesn't matter. I'll go right into the Vatican. Do you think I worry about the Vatican? We'll take that right off. All the diplomatic corps will be hiding in there. I don't give a damn' if the entire crews in there, we'll get the whole lot of swine out. Afterward we can say we are sorry. We can easily do that. We've got a war on.'

* * * * *

- Ferdinand -

At the time of the competition for the design of the prototype of the Tiger I tank, Ferdinand Porsche's company, Porsche GmbH, had lost out to another manufacturer's design.

In preparation for the competition, Porsche GmbH had manufactured about one hundred chassis for their unsuccessful proposal for the *'Porsche Tiger'*. Both the successful Henschel proposal and the Porsche design had used the same Krupp-designed turret.

Once the competing Henschel Tiger design had been chosen for production, the prototype chassis Porsche had on hand were no longer needed, due to the company's loss of the successful bid for the Tiger tank project. It was then decided that the left over Porsche chassis could be used as the basis for a new heavy tank destroyer, which was to be named *'Ferdinand'* after its designer.

Two Porsche air cooled engines had already been placed in the middle of the hulls of the chassis to accommodate the Krupp-designed turret that both the Porsche and Henschel contenders had used for the initial Tiger tank contract, and that placement for the Porsche-designed contender gave room on the *'Ferdinand'* for the anti-tank main gun armament to be mounted at the rear.

The gun was mounted on top of this chassis in a simple box structure, with slightly sloped sides. Porsche intended to mount Krupp's newly developed 88 mm Pak 43/2 anti-tank gun on these remaining chassis. This would produce a long-range weapon capable of taking out enemy tanks before they were able to reach their own range of effective fire. Porsche hoped to see his new high-powered tank destroyer replace the German's previous light tank destroyers.

When Hitler was briefed on the project, he had high hopes for this weapon and rushed its production in order to have it ready for the Kursk battle, where it proved to be very effective in the initial push through Russian lines.

'Ferdinands' first saw combat in this armored battle. Eighty-nine were committed, representing the most concentrated usage of the vehicle in the war. It was optimized for destroying Soviet T-34 tanks and 76.2 mm anti-tank guns from behind the front lines, at a range of over three miles.

* * * * * *

- Amerika Bomber -

Long before the start of the war Hitler had demonstrated a fascination with the idea of New York City in flames.

In nineteen thirty-seven, Willy Messerschmitt picked up on the theme in the hope of winning a lucrative contract with the Nazis for a long distance heavy bomber that would be capable of delivering a payload to accomplish just such a feat. At that time, he showed Hitler a prototype of the ME 264 that was being designed by his firm to reach North America from Europe.

In July of nineteen thirty-eight, barely two years after the death of Germany's main strategic bombing advocate, *'Generalleutnant'* Walter Wever, and eight months after the Reich Air Ministry had awarded the contract for the design of Germany's only operational heavy bomber during the war years, Goering gave a speech during which he stated:

'I completely lack the bombers capable of round-trip flights to New York with a four-point five-ton bomb load. I would be extremely happy to possess such a bomber, which would at last stuff the mouth of arrogance across the sea.'

In both nineteen-forty and forty-one, when the German military was routinely accomplishing all its goals with relative ease, Hitler had raised the concept again and as a result, serious planning for such a craft began. In May of forty-one Hitler said, Germany needs to:

'...deploy long-range bombers against American cities from the Azores.'

Up until nineteen forty-three, Prime Minister Salazar, of the Portuguese Azores islands had authorized the refueling of German U-boats and warships in his territory. Hitler had believed that this location was the only practical landmass available to Germany from which he could bomb the Americans. He publicly stated then that due to their location, the Azores would provide the:

'...only possibility of carrying out aerial attacks from a land base against the United States.'

The concept of designing a long-range strategic bomber for the Luftwaffe that would be capable of striking the United States, a distance of about thirty-six hundred miles, was raised as early as nineteen thirty-eight. Requests for designs, made at various stages during the war regarding the need for such an aircraft, were put forward, including the proposed use of such a craft to deliver the atomic bomb, which the Nazis were working on.

These were sent to all the major German aircraft manufacturers. However, practical plans for such a long-range strategic bomber design, did not begin to appear in *'Reichsmarschall'* Goering's offices until the spring of forty-two, by which time they were all eventually abandoned as being too expensive, and potentially consuming far too much of Germany's steadily shrinking aviation production capacity after forty-two.

By nineteen forty-three much had changed. Germany was no

longer invincible; the Azores had transferred their loyalties and had begun leasing bases to the British, allowing the Allies to provide aerial coverage in the middle of the Atlantic.

* * * * *

- Focke-Wulf Ta 400 -

In response to the RLM guidelines of 22 January 1942, the Focke-Wulf company designed the Ta 400 as a combination bomber and long-range reconnaissance aircraft. This craft was a large six-engine bomber, designed as a serious contender for the Amerika Bomber project. It was one of the first aircraft to be developed using components from multiple countries and was one of the most advanced Focke-Wulf designs of World War II, though it never progressed beyond a wind tunnel model.

Designed as a bomber and long-range reconnaissance plane by Kurt Tank, the Ta 400 had a shoulder-mounted wing. One of the most striking features of the craft was its six BMW 81D radial engines and the two Jumo 004 jet engines which were added later.

Design work was begun in forty-three, much of it being carried out by French technicians who were working for Focke Wulf at Chatillon-sous Bagneux, near Paris, with the contracts for design and construction of the major components being awarded to German, French, and Italian companies. This outsourcing was done in an attempt to speed the process and bring about the construction of prototypes as soon as possible.

The Ta 400 had a shoulder-mounted wing with a long straight center section extending to the middle engine on each wing. The outer wing panels were highly tapered. It had twin vertical stabilizers mounted at the tips of the tail-plane. The craft sported a tricycle landing gear.

The Ta 400 had a pressurized crew compartment and tail turret, connected by a pressurized tunnel, as well as multiple remote-controlled turrets. It called for a nine man crew. It was provided with heavy defensive armament, which included ten 20 mm MG 151 cannons and used thirty-two separate fuel tanks.

Maximum bomb load was fifty-three thousand pounds. In the reconnaissance role and equipped with the radial engines, it had a range of seventy-five hundred miles and with the jet engines, eighty-seven hundred miles.

* * * * *

- Fritz X -

The first operational deployment of these radio-controlled bombs took place on July twenty-first in a raid on Augusta harbor in Sicily. Additional attacks with these weapons around Sicily and Messina followed. No confirmed hits were noted and the Allies had no idea that the large bombs being dropped were so guided.

* * * * *

- SS Expansion -

In July the 11th SS Volunteer Panzergrenadier Division Nordland was created from Norwegian and Danish Volunteers.

* * * * *

- Babi Yar -

By July of forty-three it appeared likely to the SS that the Russians were probably going to recapture Kiev. Himmler then ordered the undertaking of 'Aktion 1005', a directive that commanded all traces of the executions committed be eradicated. Prisoners were instructed to reopen the mass graves and cremate the bodies.

Once they had accomplished this task, these men were executed and suffered the same fate as those they had been forced to cremate.

* * * * *

- Einsatzgruppen -

As Russian forces threatened to recapture Kiev, the Germans also attempted to destroy all traces of the *'special handling'* that had occurred at Babi Yar. As part of *'Aktion 1005'*, Himmler's order to obliterate the evidence of mass murder all across Europe, prisoners were forced to reopen the mass graves and cremate the bodies. Once completed, as was the standard policy, they immediately met with their own *'special handling'*.

* * * * *

- Extermination Camps -

In July the Belzec camp, which had provided *'special handling'* for approximately six hundred thousand, the majority being Jews from the ghettos of southern Poland, was dismantled by the camp work force, after which, those prisoners were deported to Sobibor for liquidation.

Just prior to shipping the men out to Sobibor, the SS ordered the prisoners to establish a farm on the site, planting trees and crops to disguise the previous use of the area.

A Ukrainian, who had been a former guard at the camp, was then left to farm the land.

* * * * *

- The Family -

- Karl and Wilhelm -

Karl and Wilhelm had just finished spending over an hour going over the design updates for the *'Ferdinand'*, the ME 264 and Focke-Wulf Ta 400 with Hitler in his bunker at *'Wolfsschanze'*. It was two in the afternoon and the temperature had reached its peak for the day as they climbed into the open staff car for the trip back to the airport.

There wasn't the slightest breeze and the heat was oppressive.

Upon reaching the small airstrip the were informed that their flight back was going to be delayed due to some mechanical problems. They were assured that these were minor and would take no more than an hour to accomplish.

Due to the scheduling of their earlier flight from Berlin to the Fuhrer's forward compound, they had missed luncheon and Karl asked their Wehrmacht driver if it would be possible for him to find them something to tide them over while they waited for the aircraft to be made airworthy.

Shortly thereafter they were sitting under a large evergreen at the edge of the field, enjoying the shade it offered and taking advantage of the small folding table and chairs their military chauffer had managed to scrounge, finishing snacking on a large platter of cold meat and cheeses which the driver had been able to secure from the cookhouse that served the field crews.

Karl had thanked and dismissed the driver earlier and as he and Wilhelm were some distance from the building, they deemed it safe to talk freely as they waited for the work on the plane to be completed.

The contents being top secret, Wilhelm carried the tubular document case containing the top secret weapons designs they had just shown Hitler. As he spoke, he glanced down at the case, which was lying at his feet.

"I don't understand how can he still be so interested and involved in these new super weapons? He has to know better than anyone else, that we are losing the war now and that there is no way we can realistically manufacture any of these things in the numbers it would take to make any real difference. Our armaments factories are being bombed out of existence and even if they weren't, we no longer have enough people to fully staff them. Our raw materials are nearly exhausted..."

The count let out a soft sigh before responding.

"As isolated as he is and faced with bad news on all fronts; he has steadily cocooned himself against reality. He welcomes our visits because what we bring him is hope, help to fortify his resolve and make him more amenable to rational discussion. That's probably one of the reasons why that piggish bastard Bormann has taken no steps to prevent us from seeing him. Without Hitler, Bormann has no future and he knows it. He has to keep buoying him up in any way he can and offer relief from the steady flow of negative reports the Fuhrer is now receiving.

It's obvious that Hitler's frame of mind and depressed state have worsened over the past few months, you can see that. Unlike the past, now when we arrive, he is sullen and irritable but as soon as we begin our presentation to him, the relief offered by the thought of having new super weapons in the field gives him a real hope of a reversal. It overwhelms him and he rapidly becomes his old self, confident and animated. It's quite probable that by this point in the war, we provide him with the only good news he gets."

Wilhelm, who had been watching the ground crew work on their plane in the distance, shook his head slowly.

"I understand that, but he has to know that our ability to bring these weapons into the field of battle in sufficient numbers and in time to prevent the disastrous situation Germany now faces is pure fantasy. Even if we did have the industrial capacity left to manage it, which we don't, thanks to the continuous Allied bombing of our factories, we no longer have the manpower to complete the manufacture and if even if we could manage that, we've lost so many fighting men on the Russian front that we couldn't man the new machines coming off the production lines, if by some miracle that were to happen"

He raised his arm and pointed toward the aircraft.

"Looks like they're packing up their tools…"

The Count nodded and stood up, brushing a few crumbs off the front of his uniform as he rose.

"Hitler has surrounded himself with yes men, all of whom rely on him to keep them in the powerful positions they now hold. Individually these men are becoming aware of the dire situation in their specific areas of responsibility, but to varying degrees they, like the Fuhrer, prefer to live in a fantasy world rather than deliver bad news to Hitler. They lie to him and choose to believe that others around them will somehow come up with the miracles that will pull

Germany's feet from the fire, even at this stage of the war. No one in that group wants to even contemplate the loss of the war."

Wilhelm bent to pick up the document tube and stood. He looked over at his father as he spoke.

"We could tell him..."

Karl nodded and smiled.

"Yes we could but it is very unlikely that he would choose to believe us and the very act of us doing so would mean that we would lose our ability to lift his spirits, resulting in our being instantly barred from seeing him.

It is in the best interest of *'Operation Fatherland'* that we continue to play our role in this surreal world Germany's leaders now occupy. We want the flow of capital and the support of the Fuhrer to continue in all fields of new development and discovery.

If we intend to pick up the pieces after this war ends and help Germany rise from the ashes like a phoenix to retake its proper place in the world, we have to see to it that Germany continues to lead the world in research and development for as long as we can.

We will see to it that copies of those plans you carry, along with all the other advances now being made by German scientists and engineers, safely make their way to Brazil and once this insane war is over, they will be play an important part as negotiating tools in helping us to create the future foundation for the rebirth of our battered Fatherland."

* * * * *

- Eric -

Eric had settled into a monthly trip to the eastern coastal waters of North America ferrying expert art and gem teams and singles into both the US and Canada. The other two massive U-boats had now fictionally and officially suffered the same fate as his own, both having been supposedly lost at sea with their entire crews. As such, they too had begun to transport human cargo to the Northern hemisphere. To date each trip had been accomplished without serious incident and nearly sixty *'Operation Fatherland'* art, and raw gem and bullion experts, were now deeply imbedded into their newly adopted cities.

When not at sea, Eric spent his time in the new family mansion where he and Heidi had set up a very comfortable household. Although the couple regularly took part in family get-togethers, they spent a good deal of their free time on their own, getting to know each other better, and enjoying the bliss of new married life.

Although Heidi had only shared her suspicions with her husband and her mother so far, she was confident that the bliss of their joining had already resulted in her impregnation and it would soon be obvious to the other family members that this was indeed the case.

* * * * *

- Friedrichshafen -

The day-to-day activities at the castle had now firmly settled into a comfortable routine.

Erika was ensconced as the undisputed matriarch, around which all else revolved; Gabriella fully in charge of the running of the nursery and its staff and the oversight of the children; Konrad spending the vast majority of his time involved in his research, and Ursula, with Friedrich's support, fully absorbed in the organization and transportation of valuables to Switzerland for onward shipment to Brazil.

CHAPTER FOURTEEN

- July -

- Allied Air Operations-

- Europe -

RAF Bomber Command drops a total of sixteen thousand tons and the US Eighth Air Force thirty-six hundred. The British primarily hit Hamburg and send smaller missions to Essen and other Ruhr valley targets. The Americans strike at France, Norway and Germany.

* * * * *

- China -

The US Fourteenth Air Force targets Hankow, Pailochi, Hong Kong and Hainan.

* * * * *

- War at Sea -

The new British offensive in the Bay of Biscay is expanded and results in the sinking of twenty U-boats for the loss of only thirty-seven ships. US hunter-escort groups begin patrolling in the Gibraltar and Azores areas.

Total allied losses in all theatres amount to sixty-one ships with forty-six being sunk by submarines.

* * * * *

- July First -

- Rome -

Rumanian leader, Marshal Antonescu visits Mussolini. He suggests that Italy, Rumania and Hungary leave the war in unison. Mussolini would very much like to accept this plan but he is too frightened of Hitler's probable reaction to such a move to agree.

* * * * *

-New Guinea -

American Marines take Viru.

* * * * *

- July Fifth -

- Eastern Front -

The pivotal Battle of Kursk begins.

* * * * *

- July Seventh -

In the early morning hours Dr. Ernst Steinhoff flies Wernher von Braun and Major-General Dornberger in his Heinkel He -111 to Hitler's `*Führerhauptquartier Wolfsschanze'* headquarters. The next day Hitler views the film of the successful V-2 test launch, which von Braun narrates.

The Fuhrer is then shown scale models of the *'Watten bunker'*, a launching facility for the V-2 ballistic missile, which is being constructed near Saint-Omer in northern Pas-de-Calais, France, and launching-troop vehicles.

The bunker is designed to hold over one hundred missiles at a time and to launch up to thirty-six daily. The facility will have its own liquid oxygen factory and a bomb-proof train station to allow missiles and supplies to be received safely from production facilities in Germany. This massive structure is currently under construction, using the forced labour of thousands of prisoners of war and conscripted French workers.

An enthusiastic Hitler immediately approves this project and gives it a top priority.

* * * * *

- July Ninth -

- Sicily -

The Allied landing force for *'Operation Husky'* is being concentrated near Malta. Poor weather is causing slow organization. Allied deceptive moves are aimed at convincing the Axis powers that the invasion will take place in either Greece or Sardinia. They have proven successful and Hitler is convinced that the invasion point will be Sardinia. He has ordered an airborne corps to the south of France to guard against the move. Mussolini has not been fooled and he feels the invasion will take place in Sicily, but he does not have the balls to contradict the Fuhrer and will not ask for German help to strengthen the defenses there.

The allied invasion of Sicily begins in late evening.

* * * * *

- July Tenth -

- Eastern Front -

In the north, Model's forces grind to a halt in the Battle of Kursk. In the south the unrelenting German pressure has shaken the

Russians and reserves are sent in from the *'Steppe Front'*.

* * * * *

- Sicily -

The main allied landings begin.

US General Patton's Seventh Army lands in the Gulf of Gela between Licata and Scoglitti. They find little resistance and quickly take Gela, Vittoria and Licata.

British forces make landings between Syracuse and the southwest tip of the island. They are unopposed and take Syracuse before nightfall.

* * * * *

- New Guinea -

American and Australian forces link up, cutting the Japanese in Mubo off from Salamaua.

* * * * *

- July Eleventh -

- Eastern Front -

Kursk has become a war of opposing tanks. Air and other supporting units are unable to function due to the visibility on the battlefield, which has become negligible due to the dust and smoke caused by the vicious fighting. The advantage the Germans have in long-range gunnery is therefore negated.

* * * * *

- Volhynia Massacres -

The massacres of Poles in Volhynia and Eastern Galicia were part of an ethnic cleansing operation carried out in Nazi occupied Poland by members of the UPA (Ukrainian Insurgent Army). Their North Command took action in the regions of Volhynia which was located in the German occupied *'Reichskommissariat Ukraine'* and their South Command did the same in the Eastern Galicia region of the German controlled *'General Government'*.

The massacres began in March of nineteen forty-three and lasted until the end of forty-four. The peak of these atrocities took place in July and August of forty-three. Most of the victims were women and children.

The actions of the UPA resulted in the deaths of between thirty-five to sixty thousand Poles in Volhynia and twenty-five to forty thousand in Eastern Galicia.

The killings were directly linked with the policies of the Bandera faction of the Organization of Ukrainian Nationalists and its military arm, the UPA. This group had a specified a goal of purging all non-Ukrainians from the future Ukrainian state.

Not limiting its activities to the eradication of Polish civilians, the UPA was determined to erase all traces of sustained Polish presence in the area.

On this date, at the height of the massacres of the Poles in Volhynia, the village of Dominopol, an ethnic Polish village located in the Eastern regions of what was known as the Second Polish Republic before World War II and was currently governed by the Nazis under the *'Reichskommissariat Ukraine'*, was attacked by units of the UPA

All the Poles captured, regardless of their age, were tortured and murdered. Most sources report that sixty families, containing approximately four hundred and ninety persons, including several children were killed by those using axes and knives.

Afterward the slaughter; the possessions of the murdered Poles were looted by Ukrainian peasants, who had eagerly participated in the massacre. The village was then burned to the ground.

* * * * *

- July Twelfth -

- Eastern Front -

The Battle of Prokhorovka begins approximately fifty-four miles southeast of Kursk. The Russian Fifth Guards Tank Army attacks the II SS-Panzer Korps. This clash of armor is destined to be one of the largest tank battles in military history.

* * * * *

- July Thirteenth -

- Battle of Kolombangara -

On the night of July twelfth, a Japanese *'Tokyo Express'* reinforcement force under the command of Rear Admiral Shunii Izaki, made up of the light cruiser Jintsu, the destroyers *'Mikazuki'*, *'Yukikaze'*, *'Hamakaze'*, *'Kiyonami'* and *'Yueure'* with the destroyer transports *'Sasuki'*, *'Minazjki'*, *'Yunagi'* and *'Matsukcze'* begins a run, down *'The Slot'* from the upper Solomons to land troops at Vila on Kolombangara by way of Kula Gulf.

The U.S. had landed troops on New Georgia to attack Munda the week before and had just placed a force ashore at Rice Anchorage on New Georgia's northern shore with the intention of seizing Bairoko.

An Allied naval force commanded by Rear Admiral Walden Ainsworth comprised of the US light cruisers USS *'Honolulu'* and *'St Louis'* plus the Royal New Zealand Navy light cruiser HMNZS *'Leander'* and the destroyers USS *'Nicholas'*, *'O'Bannon'*, *'Taylor'*, *'Jenkins'*, *'Radford'*, *'Ralph Talbot'*, *'Buchanan'*, *'Maury'*, *'Woodworth'* and *'Gwin'* is in the vicinity. Admiral Ainsworth's mission is to protect the north shore beachhead from attack by the *'Tokyo Express'* and if possible to prevent Imperial reinforcements from landing. His ships re-deployed in a single column with five destroyers in the van followed by the light cruisers and then by five destroyers bringing up the rear.

Shortly after one in the morning on July thirteenth, the Allied ships established radar contact with the Japanese ships east of the northern tip of Kolombangara.

Ainsworth assumed he had complete surprise, but the Japanese had been aware of the Allied force for almost two hours. The Allied destroyers increased speed to engage the Japanese force while the cruisers turned to deploy their main batteries. Pre-warned, the Japanese destroyers had already launched torpedoes and turned away.

'Jintsu' engaged the Allied ships, while all Allied fire was concentrated on the largest ship. 'Jintsu' was rapidly reduced to a wreck while USS 'Leander' was struck by a torpedo and, severely damaged. She immediately retired from the battle, escorted by USS 'Radford' and 'Jenkins.'

'Jintsu' was finally broken in two by torpedo hits and sank at about one forty-five, with the loss of nearly her entire ships company, including Vice Admiral Izaki.

Ainsworth pursued the Imperial destroyers, but both USS 'St. Louis 'and 'Honolulu' were struck by torpedoes and damaged, while USS 'Gwin 'was struck amidships and scuttled at nine-thirty in the morning.

* * * * *

- New Guinea -

The Japanese positions at Mubo are virtually wiped out and occupied by Allied forces.

* * * * *

- Sicily -

The British take Augusta.

* * * * *

- Eastern Front -

Hitler calls off the German Kursk offensive. The Germans go over to the defensive and the Russians begin offensive thrusts.

* * * * *

- July Sixteenth -

- Sicily -

Despite strong resistance, the Canadian 1st Division takes Caltagirone and pushes on towards Piazza Armeroma.

* * * * *

- July Seventeenth -

- Sicily -

The Americans take Agrigento and Porto Empedocle.

* * * * *

- July Eighteenth -

- Sicily -

US troops capture Caltanisetta. The Canadians capture Valguarnerna.

* * * * *

- July Nineteenth -

- Italy -

Hitler and Mussolini meet. Hitler dominates the conversation, giving Mussolini little chance to speak while he berates the Italian dictator and demands more effort from Italian forces.

* * * * *

- Rome -

The Allies bomb the Italian capital for the first time in the war.

* * * * *

- July Twentieth -

- Quebec -

Roosevelt and Churchill meet to hash out the problems being experienced over the sharing of Atomic research information. They reach firm agreement over sharing of information and under what conditions atomic weapons may be used in the future and sign a formal agreement to that effect.

* * * * *

- Sicily -

Enna is taken by the Canadian forces.

* * * * *

- July Twenty-First -

- Friedrichshafen -

As part of 'Operation *Bellicose'*, the Wurzburg radar manufacturer factory is bombed.

* * * * *

- Sicily -

The British take Gerbini, the Canadians Leonforte and Americans Corleone and Castelvetrano.

* * * * *

- July Twenty-Second -

- Sicily -

US forces under Patton capture Palermo.

* * * * *

- July Twenty-Third -

- Sicily -

The Americans take Trapani.

* * * * *

- July Twenty-Fourth -

- Sicily -

US forces capture Cefalu.

* * * * *

- Germany -

In *'Operation Gomorrah'*, Hamburg is on the receiving end of one of the heaviest bombing raids so far in the war. The city receives a pounding for four consecutive nights.

* * * * *

- July Twenty-Fifth -

- Rome -

Mussolini is arrested.

* * * * *

- July Twenty-Eighth -

- Sicily -

The Canadians take Agira and US forces take Nicosia.

* * * * *

- July Thirtieth -

- Sicily -

British forces take Catenanouva and off the west coast the Egadi Islands surrender to the Allies.

CHAPTER FIFTEEN

- August -

- Hitler -

Hitler is doing his best to deal with his despair over the calamity in Italy resulting in Mussolini's arrest and the apparent collapse of Fascism.

He summons the two men he feels he can count on most in a major crisis. Goebbels who is always positive and upbeat and Goering, whom the Fuhrer describes to his military advisers in the following words,

'At such a time one can't have a better adviser than the Reichsmarschall. In time of crisis the Reichsmarschall is brutal and ice cold. I have always noticed that when it comes to the breaking point he is a man of iron without scruples.'

The two men are soon in attendance. Von Ribbentrop also joins them and when all are present, Hitler, now in control of himself after his initial fury, tells them he suspects that Mussolini has not willingly resigned; that he has been forcibly removed.

He goes on to suggest that the fascist movement in Italy is in mortal danger of collapse and outlines his plans to arrest the King and his family along with Badoglio and the other dissenters.

Not surprisingly, those present immediately support his conclusions without question.

This crisis is soon compounded by the devastating Allied carpet bombing of Hamburg.

The city is left a burning ruin. In excess of six thousand acres has been raised to the ground. Seventy thousand people have been killed.

Hitler is incensed. He rants on about the attack being Jewish, inspired, insinuating that the veins of the English RAF commanders contained Jewish blood.

* * * * *

- Inner Circle -

- Reichsmarschall and Propaganda Minister -

Hamburg is the straw that breaks the camel's back for both Goering and Goebbels.

Goering as head of the Luftwaffe knows Hitler will blame him for the German Air Forces failure to prevent the attack. In a panic, the Reichsmarschall immediately summons his commanders to his office.

Adolf Galland, one of those present at the meeting described the scene as follows.

'We were met with a shattering picture. Goering had completely broken down, His head buried in his arm on the table'

Goering moaned some indistinguishable words before telling them that they were:

'Witnessing his deepest moments of despair'. "The Fuhrer had lost faith in him.'

Goebbels inspected the area of destruction and was badly shaken. For the first time he began to doubt that Germany could go on to win the war. He quietly commented to one of his subordinates.

'What if we lose?'

From that day on, wherever he went, he carried a pistol.

* * * * *

- Speer -

Despite what others were saying, Albert knew all about the labour shortages and he was doing what he could to remedy them. He had tried to convince Hitler to allow women to work in the factories. The Fuhrer had dismissed that idea out of hand.

When he learned of Hitler's plan to order the SS to take no prisoners in the upcoming Battle of Kursk, in retaliation for reports he had received from SS sources that the Russians had killed their German prisoners in recent battles, Speer was able to convince the Fuhrer to instead use all Russian new prisoners as forced labour in the German armaments industries. Unfortunately, as the German forces would not been successful in this battle, this effort had done nothing to alleviate the worker shortage.

Speer had now formed good relations with both Generals, Zeitzler and Fromm and the three of them had quietly begun to discuss what they referred to as *'Germany's military leadership crisis'*.

* * * * *

- Heinz Guderian -

The Inspector General of the Tank Forces, Heinz Guderian, had also developed good relations with Speer and in the summer of forty-three he approached Albert with a request that he arrange a meeting for him with Zeitzler. Albert was aware that the two had recently had some minor jurisdictional disputes, and being on good terms with both, he was pleased to set up the meeting.

The three men met at Speer's home and it quickly became apparent that Guderian was not interested in solving some minor problems but was instead determined to discuss common tactics in regard to how they could arrange for a new Commander in Chief of the army.

Taken by surprise, both Albert and Zeitzler paused for breath and then they began to warm to the conversation as Guderian led the way into an in-depth discussion as to how they could solve the problem of Hitler assuming command of the army but then not using his power responsibly.

He belabored the fact that the interests of the army versus those of the other military branches and the ever growing SS forces needed to be individually represented more realistically. A military Commander in Chief had to remain nonpartisan in relation to all the participating military units.   Guderian expanded on that topic, suggesting that Hitler, in his position as Commander in Chief of the armed forces, had an obligation to maintain personal contact with all the army commanders. He should concentrate on the requirements of the troops and the fundamental concerns of supply.

The two men quickly came to agreement that the Fuhrer had clearly demonstrated that he had neither the time nor the inclination to act on this responsible level and instead tended to advocate for the special interests of a single branch of the service. They went further, decrying Hitler's tendency to appoint and dismiss generals whom he barely knew and his refusal to associate with his top ranking leaders on a personal basis.

Guderian openly admitted that it was common knowledge within the army that Hitler, rarely if ever, interfered in the personnel allocations of the commanders of the air force or the navy, and that the SS appeared sacrosanct in this regard and it was only the army who repeatedly faced this type of interference.

By the end of their meeting, the three men concluded that something had to be done about the current situation and it was decided that each of them would attempt to approach Hitler privately with the veiled suggestion that he appoint a new Commander in Chief.

At this point in the war, this need to have Hitler remove himself from the overall control of the German armed forces was generally accepted by his military advisors. Prior to Speer and Guderian making their moves to broach the topic with the Fuhrer, both Field Marshalls, von Kluge and von Manstein had tentatively raised the idea with Hitler and when the two of them made similar but separate suggestions to Hitler about such a move he cut them both off very sharply. In his paranoid state and sensing that his authority was being challenged from all sides, he was not about to entertain this repeated advice that he should give up the role of Commander in Chief.

At the time, he made it abundantly clear that he would allow no further discussion of it.

* * * * *

- Doenitz -

Speer played a part in an important shift in the leadership of the German Navy.

Albert had of necessity, as part of his responsibilities as Armaments Minister spent a good deal of time meeting with Doenitz during the period of the mass construction of U-boat pens for the protection of the German undersea fleet.

As a result a relationship of mutual respect had formed between the two men. Speer had then taken a page from Bormann's book.

When he'd been informed early on of serious dissension between the Berlin navy command and Doenitz and that the U-boat fleet was awash with reports that Admiral Raeder was planning to get rid of Doenitz, Albert had, whenever the opportunity arose, begun to plant little seeds of doubt in Hitler's mind about Raeder's abilities.

On once such occasion, Hitler, who was concerned about the numbers of U-boats being produced, asked Speer if it would be possible to assembly-line the production of the submarines. Speer took this opportunity to inform the Fuhrer that the concept was not only possible but should be immediately adopted. Taking it a step further, he added that although Doenitz was of the same mind. Raeder was against such a plan had ordered Speer to have no direct contact with Doenitz that involved any such discussion of technical matters.

Over time, this slow chipping away at Raeder's reputation took root and in January of this year in response to Hitler's growing disenchantment with Admiral Raeder and the growing public conflict between Raeder and Doenitz, the Fuhrer promoted Raeder to the position of Admiral Inspector of the navy. As a result, the man lost all authority overnight and became nothing more than a token figurehead.

Hitler then appointed Doenitz Grand Admiral to replace Raeder in his old command as Commander in Chief of the navy. Doenitz was now in full command of the German Navy.

He quickly moved to strengthen his relationship with Speer and was thereby provided with the expertise and technical arguments needed to convince Hitler to improve the U-boat fleet's equipment and numbers.

Nonetheless, Speer was taken by surprise when Hitler suddenly raised the production of naval armament to the highest priority. This, as was typical of Hitler's approach to such things, caused an immediate conflict in that the Fuhrer had already stipulated that the expanded tank program was to have that production designation.

Speer suggested to Doenitz that, in order to circumvent any conflict with the army, the responsibility for the construction of U-boats should be transferred to his own organization. As such he could guarantee to carry out the naval program as Doenitz had envisioned.

This was done and Doenitz made it clear to Albert that what he wanted was a new U-boat to replace the current model. He indicated that this was necessary to ensure German mastery of the oceans. He wanted to replace what was basically a surface ship that had the ability to submerge for short periods, with a new type, one that spent the majority of its patrol safely underwater.

This would require an entirely new design, a design that would provide a brand new U-boat with the best possible streamlining. This new craft was to be provided with a higher underwater speed and offer a greater underwater range by doubling the power of the electric motors as well as encompassing a more simplified system for the storage batteries.

* * * * *

- Hs 293 -

The Hs 293 project had begun in nineteen-forty, and was based on the *'Gustav Schwartz Propellerwerke'* pure glide bomb designed in thirty-nine. The initial concept strove to supply a bomb that could be launched from a bomber at a sufficient distance to allow the bomber to remain out of range of anti-aircraft fire during its mission.

The Henschel Hs 293, designed by Herbert A Wagner, was an anti-ship radio-controlled glide bomb (guided missile), with a rocket engine slung underneath it. The original Schwartz design from which it was developed had a terminal guidance system while the rehashed design for the Hs 293 used an autopilot to hold it on course.

A Henschel team, under Dr. Herbert Wagner, had further developed the Schwartz by adding an HWK 109-507 rocket motor underneath, which provided thirteen hundred pounds of thrust for ten seconds or alternatively, the BMW 109 -511, for thirteen hundred and twenty-three pounds.

The first test flights of the new weapon took place between May and September of nineteen-forty and consisted of unpowered drops made from Heinkel He111 medium bombers. The first test using a motor-powered *'Walter'* rocket, took place toward the end of nineteen-forty.

The weapon tested consisted of a modified standard SC 500, five hundred kilogram bomb with an added *'kopfring'*, on the nose for maritime use. This was a triangular section steel ring fitted around the nose of some SC bombs in order to reduce the bomb surface penetration so as to maximize the bomb's blast effect. The bomb itself had a thin metal shell with a high explosive charge inside.

A rocket engine was affixed under the bomb which had been given a pair of wings, and fitted with an MCLOS guidance and control system. This system incorporated an eighteen frequency *'Funk-Gerat'* (FuG) 230 *'Strassburg'* radio receiver. A FuG 203 *'Kehl'* transmitting set, located in the carrier aircraft, provided the required signals.

Unlike the unpowered, armor-piercing *'Fritz X'*, the Hs 293 was designed to destroy commercial unarmored ships. Five colored flares were attached to the rear of the weapon to make it visible at a distance to the operator and when used in darkness flashing lights were used rather than flares.

Once the Hs 293 had been launched, the bomber needed to fly in a straight and level path at a set altitude and speed parallel to the target in order to maintain a line of sight and as such could not maneuver if had to contend with attacking fighters.

The Allied forces began to work on jamming devices to defeat the Hs 293 shortly after the first of these guided missiles were used and over time this effort became relatively effective.

To improve control of the weapon and reduce vulnerability of the launching aircraft, wire-guided Hs 293B and television-guided Hs 293D variants were in the planning stages. The first of these guided missiles went into production in nineteen forty-two and over one thousand were built during the war.

On August the twenty-fifth of nineteen forty-three, an Hs 293 was used in the first successful attack by a guided missile, against the sloop HMS *'Bideford'*.   In this application, the warhead failed to detonate and the damage was minimal.

Two days later, the British sloop HMS *'Egret'* was successfully sunk by a squadron of eighteen Do 217's equipped with Hs 293s. This sinking led to the anti-U boat patrols in the Bay of Biscay being temporarily suspended.

* * * * *

- Peenemunde -

Early in the year, two Polish slave janitors from Peenemunde's camp Trassenheide had provided maps, rough sketches and reports to Polish Home Army Intelligence on the V2 complex. In June British intelligence had been forwarded two such reports which clearly identified the *'rocket assembly hall'*, *'experimental pit'*, and *'launching tower'*.

By midsummer of forty-three, the first trial runs of the assembly-line in the Production Works at *'Werke Sud'* had been made.

The first Allied response to deal with the rocket complex was an air raid codenamed *'Operation Hydra'*. Carried out on the night of August seventeenth, it was made up of three hundred and twenty-four Lancasters, two hundred and eighteen Halifaxes and fifty four Sterlings. The attack was primarily targeted to hit the *'Sleeping & Living Quarters'* with a view to killing the scientists. Secondary targets were the *'Factory Workshops'*, and the *'Experimental Station'*.

The enormous hangar *'Fertigungshalle 1'* (Mass Production Plant No. 1) was just days away from going into operation when the air raid struck.

As a result of the attack, Speer, on the twenty-sixth of August, chaired a meeting with Hans Kammler, Dornberger, Gerhard Degenkolb and Karl Otto Saur, to arrange to move the V-2 production to an underground factory located in the Harz Mountains.

* * * * *

- Special Handling -

On August second two hundred Jews escaped from Treblinka during a revolt. All were recaptured.

On the sixteenth of August the Bialystok ghetto was liquidated.

Toward the end of the month, after an estimated eight hundred and seventy thousand deaths, exterminations ceased at Treblinka.

* * * * *

- Concentration Camps -

- Auschwitz -

As the camp began to run out of candidates for *'special handling'*, the remaining prisoners realized that the camp would soon be dismantled which would mean that they would be subject to the same treatment as their predecessors. With no hope left, these men decided to revolt against their guards and attempt an escape. On August second they seized weapons from the camp armory and stormed the main gate.

The guards opened up with machine guns and were able to kill many before they could break free but just over three hundred made it out. The majority who reached freedom were soon mopped up by German police and troops.

A good portion of the camp was destroyed by fire in the uprising and those who survived the revolt were soon put to work removing all traces of the compound and were then shot.

* * * * *

- Natzweiler-Struthof -

In the summer of forty-three the Germans had begun to use this camp, which was located in occupied France, to house what they referred to as the *'Nacht und Nebel'* (Night and Fog) prisoners. These individuals were being picked up in an attempt to subdue the growing anti-German resistance that was forming throughout Western Europe. Under this program, suspected resistance fighters, primarily French, were suddenly arrested without warning. Their families were not notified of these arrests and those who were swept up simply vanished without trace into the *'Night and Fog'*.

In August a gas chamber was constructed at this camp in one of the buildings that had formed part of the original hotel compound. The bodies of eighty Jewish prisons who were gassed here were sent on to the Strasbourg University Institute of Anatomy. The Germans also used gypsies, who had been transferred from Auschwitz, in the new gas chamber for medical experiments which involved the testing of poison gases. Additional prisoners were used in experiments involving treatment for typhus and yellow fever.

* * * * *

- Ghettos -

The Germans began the final destruction of the Bialystok ghetto and started the systematic round up of Jews for onward deportation to Treblinka. One thousand Jewish children were sent to the Theresienstadt ghetto in Bohemia, prior to being loaded onto trains headed for Auschwitz Birkenau where they were immediately processed. Twenty thousand Jews were concentrated in a central transit camp in the city before they were shipped on to Treblinka.

Others were sent on to Majdanek extermination camp. Once they arrived there, those considered fit for forced labour were transported to the camps at Poniatowa, Blizyn or Auschwitz. The remainder was provided with *'special treatment'*.

During these transports, it became apparent that German intent was to empty the ghetto and shut the camp down and as a result, a small uprising took place. Armed Jews attacked German forces near the ghetto fence along Smolna Street. Fighting lasted for several days, and fewer than one hundred of the internees managed to escape but the vast majority was killed.

* * * * *

- The Family -
- Karl and Wilhelm -

Those involved in the leadership of *'Operation Fatherland'* had now taken the next step in their planning.

Both the Count and Wilhelm were spending the majority of their time in advancing preparedness for the anticipated end of the war.

The ratlines had been tested and found to be secure.

By this point, a streamlined method for the selection and freeing up of additional experts in all fields of advanced German research and development for onward shipment to the family holdings in South America had been put into place. The rapidly growing compound in Brazil was bristling with new refugees settling into to the new safe, state of the art facilities.

Due to the prevalence of air raids and the desperate state of the military conflict, there was little in the way of leisure activities and political events that they might have, in the past, been expected to attend in the German capital. Subsequently, although they were obliged to take great care to maintain their good standing with both Himmler and Hitler, there were few other outside demands on their time.

* * * * *

- Eric -

Heidi's pregnancy had been confirmed and along with a delivery of art treasures and bullion, Eric had received a letter from his father in which the Count forbade him to make further trips to sea unless he personally ordered him to do so. As Karl's successor to the family title, Eric was now to keep himself safe from harm in order to ensure the unbroken future of the von Stauffer line.

While Eric understood his father's position on the matter, he was of two minds over this change in his responsibilities.

While he appreciated the fact that this would mean more time with Heidi and looked forward to tackling the new responsibilities of expanding the family compound and the research and development laboratories, tucked safely beneath the mining operation, he knew he would miss his time at sea.

For her part, Heidi made no secret of her delight over the changed

The phase of the operations at sea that had been necessary for the delivery of deeply imbedded art, bullion and gem experts into cities in North America had reached its final stages. Eric had already determined that, as of the end of the month, two of the big U-boats were to remain within their secure pens below the mountain for the foreseeable future. While he had intended to personally captain the remaining craft until the job had been completed, he would now leave this job to one of his other captains.

* * * * *

- Friedrichshafen -

To the delight of all, on August eighteenth Gabriella gave birth to her second child, a girl.

The air raid on the industrial section of the city had served to unnerve those living nearby but fears that it might become a regular event proved to be unfounded.

Life within the walls of castle von Stauffer changed little, although for Ursula and Friedrich the workload had lessened. With the military situation having turned against the continued German advancement into new areas, shipments of art treasures and other booty looted from the occupied territories had begun to decline over the month and what had previously been daily trains had dropped to weekly.

The booty currently held in the secret sub-basement vault deep below the castle now held far more riches than *'Operation Fatherland'* would require to fulfill its goals and Karl went about doing his best to distance both the castle and his family from any link with seized treasures.

The fact that the castle was on official record as being a facility for holding such material was acceptable to him. He was after all, simply helping his country by providing safe storage facilities to protect art treasures in a time of war. From now till the end of the war he would do his best to play no further part in dealing with looted booty, with the hope that by the time the war was over there would be little record of, and little interest in, the amount that he had managed to set aside for the future financing of *'Operation Fatherland'*.

With that in mind, the count had informed Ursula that, by months end, he would advise his superiors that castle von Staffer had reached capacity and was no longer able to accept further consignments.

CHAPTER SIXTEEN

- August -

- Allied Air Operations Europe -

The combined forces of the Allied air forces concentrate their raids on German targets. They fly thirty major raids of fourteen thousand, five hundred sorties, bomber command delivering nineteen thousand tons and the American Eighth Air force three thousand, six hundred tons of bombs. Nuremberg, Bochum, Milan, Berlin, Turin and Genoa are hit. Milan is specifically targeted on four occasions for a total of four thousand tons. Peenemunde and Schweinfurt receive special attention. In addition, fighter aircraft deliver raids to several airfields and communication centers.

* * * * *

- Mediterranean -

Major raids target Rome and Foggia.   Ploesti in Rumania it hit by the Americans who suffer heavy losses during the attack.

* * * * *

- Battle of the Atlantic -

U-boat activity is at a low level; however twenty-five German subs go to the bottom. Ten U-tankers are also sunk. Total allied loses amount to just over one hundred thousand tons.

* * * * *

- August First -

- Romania -

The Ploiesti Oil fields are bombed by American aircraft in a costly daylight raid.

* * * * *

- Free French -

Leadership is reorganized with De Gaulle appointed as President of the new National Liberation Committee where all matters other than military are discussed. Giraud presides over the Committee in those specific instances when only military matters are being conducted.

* * * * *

- Burma -

The Japanese declare that the country is now independent under the leadership of Ba Maw. Maw has signed a secret protocol with the Japanese who have subsequently appointed him as a puppet.

* * * * *

- August Second -

- Sicily -

The Canadians capture Regalbuto and the British Centuripe.

* * * * *

- Eastern Front -

The Russians take Znamenskaya.

* * * * *

- Auschwitz -

Two thousand eight hundred and ninety-seven gypsies go to the gas chambers as the camp is being liquidated.

* * * * *

- August Fourth -

- Eastern Front -

The Russians take Orel.

* * * * *

- The Solomons -

American forces take Munda and its airfield.

* * * * *

- August Fifth -

- Stockholm -

The Swedish government announces that it will no longer allow German troops and war material to transit Swedish railways.

* * * * *

- Eastern Front -

Russian troops take Belgorod.

* * * * *

- August Sixth -

- Solomons -

Overnight the Americans win the *'Battle of Vella Gulf'* off Kolombangara.

* * * * *

- Sicily -

The Americans take Troina.

* * * * *

- Eastern Front -

Russian forces take Zolochev to the northwest of Kharkov.

* * * * *

- Italy -

German troops begin to pour into the country to take over defensive positions.

* * * * *

- August Seventh -

- Sicily -

The British take Adrana.

* * * * *

- August Eighth -

- Sicily-

The Americans land a small amphibious group east of Sant Agata and the Germans retreat as they take it. The main US force captures Cesaro.

British forces take Bronte and Acireale.

* * * * *

- August Ninth -

- Denmark -

The Danish government takes a stand as the Prime Minister refuses to accept a German demand that saboteurs be tried in German courts.

* * * * *

- August Tenth -

- Eastern Front -

The Russians capture Khotinets, east of Orel.

* * * * *

- August Eleventh -

- Eastern Front -

The Russians cut the Poltava-Kharkov railroad thirty miles west of Kharkov.

* * * * *

- Sicily -

German and Italian forces begin to evacuate the island.

* * * * *

- August Twelfth -

- Eastern Front -

Chuguyev is taken by the Russians and their troops are now offering a real threat to the strategically important Ukrainian city of Poltava.

* * * * *

- August Thirteenth -

- Eastern Front -

Closing in on Kharkov, the Russians take Bolshaya and Danilovka.

* * * * *

- Quebec -

Roosevelt and Churchill head up a meeting of the British and American military leaders held in the Canadian city. Over the next twelve days, plans for the invasion of Europe are discussed.

The British commit to the construction of the Mulberry Harbors

(Artificial ports) which will be required adjacent to the French beaches. They accept the position that an American will fulfil the position of Supreme Commander of the invasion when it comes. The Americans agree to a British position that a continued push for the defeat of Italy must continue.

* * * * *

- August Fourteenth -

- Sicily -

A combined American and British force captures Randazzo.

* * * * *

- August Fifteenth -

- Aleutians -

Japanese troops abandon Kiska Island before Canadian and US forces invade to retake it.

* * * * *

- Solomons -

The Battle of *'Vella Lavella Island'* commences.

* * * * *

- Eastern Front -

Karachev is taken by the Russians.

* * * * *

- August Sixteenth -

- Bialystok Ghetto -

With few weapons, Polish Jews attempt a revolt. It is quickly put down by the Germans and the leaders commit suicide after running out of ammunition.

* * * * *

- Sicily -

British forces enter Taormina and advance American units enter Messina.

* * * * *

- Eastern Front -

Russian forces take Zhidra.

* * * * *

- August Seventeenth -

- Sicily -

The Allies are now in control of the Island. In excess of one hundred thousand Italian troops have been captured. The Germans have lost ten thousand men killed or captured and suffer many wounded.

The British and American losses are considerable. They have seven thousand killed and fifteen thousand wounded. While the invasion has been a success from a political standpoint, the Germans have been highly successful in the evacuation of their troops.

Incredibly, forty thousand Germans, fifty tanks, one hundred guns and a vast quantity of supplies have been successfully transported across the Messina Strait along with a force of sixty-two thousand Italians, who will now be in a position to fight another day.

* * * * *

- Germany -

The Americans carry out a large daylight air raid on the ball-bearing manufacturing centers located in Schweinfurt and Regensburg. They lose fifty-one aircraft, a full one-fifth of the attacking force, a clear indication that this type of bombing raid is unsustainable.

In the evening, in the opening of *'Operation Hydra'*, close to six hundred RAF bombers hit the rocket research and manufacturing compound at Peenemunde. Forty-one aircraft are lost but a great deal of damage is done to the site.

* * * * *

- August Nineteenth -

- Canada -

Churchill and Roosevelt sign the *'Quebec Agreement'* in Quebec.

* * * * *

- Italy -

The Italians open tentative surrender negotiations with the Allies.

* * * * *

- Germany -

'Gerneraloberst' Hans Jeschonnek, the Chief of the General staff of the Luftwaffe, commits suicide after being soundly criticized for failure to prevent the Allied attacks on Peenemunde and Schweinfurt.

* * * * *

- August Twentieth -

- Eastern Front -

The Russians capture Libedin, west of Kharkov.

* * * * *

- New Guinea -

The Allies take Babdubi Ridge located southwest of Salamaua.

* * * * *

- August Twenty-Second -

- Eastern Front -

In the face of the advancing superior Russian forces, Manstein convinces Hitler to allow him to pull the German troops out of Kharkov.

* * * * *

- Central Pacific -

US forces begin their occupation of several islands in the Ellice group. Namumea and Nukufetau are taken without opposition and work is immediately begun on the building of airfields.

* * * * *

- August Twenty-Third -

- Eastern Front -

The Russians take Kharkov. The Battle of Kursk becomes the first successful major Russian summer offensive of the war.

* * * * *

- August Twenty-Fourth -

- Berlin -

Himmler is appointed by Hitler to the post of Minister of the Interior. The former Interior Minister, Wilhelm Frick, an antagonist of Himmler's, replaces Konstantin von Neurath as Protector of Bohemia.

* * * * *

- Denmark -

Growing resistance to the Nazi occupation leads to several bomb incidents in Copenhagen and causes shipyard strikes.

* * * * *

- Augusta Twenty-Fifth -

- Atlantic -

An escort vessel hunting U-boats in the Bay of Biscay is struck by the first Hs 293 guided missile.

* * * * *

- Eastern Front -

The Russians take Zenkov and Akhtyrka.

* * * * *

- August Twenty-Seventh -

- Solomon Islands -

Unchallenged, the Americans land on Arundel and occupy the island.

* * * * *

- Eastern Front -

The Russians capture Kotleva and Sevsk.

* * * * *

- August Twenty-Eighth -

- Denmark -

Up to this point in the war the Danes have been relatively successful in mitigating the effects of the Nazi occupational force and avoiding any impression of collaboration. In the face of a German ultimatum, the Danish government resigns. The German Commander immediately proclaims martial law. The Germans move to capture the small Danish Navy but succeed in taking only a few ships while the others are successfully scuttled by their crews or sailed to the safety of neutral Swedish ports.

* * * * *

- August Twenty-Ninth -

- Eastern Front -

Russian forces take Lyubotin.

* * * * *

- August Thirtieth -

- Eastern Front -

The Russians capture Yelena and Taganrog.

* * * * *

- August Thirty-First -

- Pisa -

The Northwest African Air Forces carry out an air raid on the Italian City.

* * * * *

- Eastern Front -

Russian forces take Glukhov and Rylsk.

CHAPTER SEVENTEEN

- September -

- Hitler -

A peace-feeler had been received from Stalin shortly after the Russian success at Stalingrad. Although at the time, it was staunchly rejected by Hitler, it had stimulated a good deal of discussion at the German Foreign Office.

Admiral Canaris, who had been covertly and unsuccessfully attempting to deal secretly with Roosevelt for a separate peace, was so convinced as to the authenticity of the Russian move when it was made, that he'd managed to convince von Ribbentrop to present it to Hitler. The Fuhrer's response to the resulting memorandum forwarded from Joachim was swift and unequivocal.

Hitler had ripped the document into shreds and threatened to execute anyone attempting to mediate on his own. There were to be no negotiations until such time as the Wehrmacht had regained the initiative and terms could be dictated by Germany. He forbade his Foreign Minister to raise the matter again.

In response to Hitler's statement, von Ribbentrop had faintheartedly suggested that perhaps a reduction in the scope of the Nazi conquest in Europe might make it more acceptable to the Allies.

Hitler was furious.

"Believe me, we shall win. The blow that has fallen is a sign telling me to grow harder and harder and risk all we have. If we do, we shall win in the end."

In March, von Ribbentrop had shared his frustration at Hitler's reaction with the head of the Fuhrer's Press Office, Fritz Hesse while the two men took a private walk through a forest at *'Wolfsschanze'*, in the falling snow.

"All we can hope for now is that at least one of our opponents will grow sensible. Surely the English must realize that it would be

madness to deliver us into the hands of the Russians."

A few days later the two men found the opportunity for a second walk in the snow. Von Ribbentrop picked up on his theme again on that occasion.

"There must be some way of persuading the British and the Americans of the insanity of the war they are waging against us. Can't we somehow make the British and the Americans see that the victory of the Russians is the opposite of what they want?

Hesse, who had spent several years in England, doubted that western Allies were particularly worried about the Russians and he shared this view with von Ribbentrop. This only served to increase the Foreign Minister's determination that Germany must then seek a negotiated peace with the Russians.

Even the Fuhrer was beginning to realize that fighting an extended two-front war was an unhappy situation, one unlikely to improve as time went by.

* * * * *

- Inner Circle -

- Von Ribbentrop -

While keeping his thoughts to himself, von Ribbentrop turned a blind eye to the activities of Bruno Perter Kleist, a German Foreign Office diplomat who acted as his expert on the east and the Russians.

Kleist had been dabbling in opening peace discussions for some time with Madame Kollontai, the Russian ambassador to Sweden, by way of a middle man named Edgar Clauss. Clauss had met both Trotsky and Stalin before the revolution and had connections with the Russian Embassy in Stockholm.

In June, Clauss had reported to Kleist that after two long meetings with embassy members, he was convinced that the Russians were determined *'not to fight for a day or even a minute longer than necessary on behalf of British and American interests'.*

He went on to explain that the Russians were of the opinion that

Hitler had been blinded by ideology and had allowed himself to be pushed into the war by the intrigues of the capitalist powers. He said the Russians believed that they could beat the Germans, however were very concerned that after doing so their current Allies would promptly turn on them and they would then find themselves on the receiving end of a strong combined Anglo-American attack directed against them when they were at their weakest.

He went a step further by suggesting that Stalin was unhappy with the British and American refusal to come up with any definite statements about war aims and the territorial boundaries which would be put into place after the Germans had been beaten in the east and not as yet come up with a solid plan for what they suggested would be a *'Second-Front'* in Europe. He went on to indicate that the Russian leader was of the opinion that his Allies landings in Africa appeared more an attempt to protect their own flank from the Russians than a serious move to weaken Axis powers overall. He firmly believed that Stalin did not trust Roosevelt and Churchill to fulfil their promises and indicated that it was only common sense that this would be a good time to use the vast Russian areas currently held by the Germans as a basis for discussion along with an offer of a guaranteed peace and economic aid as negotiating chips for a separate peace deal with the Russians.

Clauss had convinced Kleist, who took the next flight to Berlin to pass on this information. When the plane landed he was immediately arrested on the charge that he had been; *'conniving with the Jew Clauss'.*

* * * * *

- Ernst Kaltenbrunner -

It fell to Kaltenbrunner of the SS, Heydrich's replacement, to interrogate Kleist with regard to the charge. Despite the risk, Kleist was convinced that it was his duty to go against Hitler's last position on any outside negotiations for a peace treaty with the Russians, in an attempt to end the folly of a two front war. He threw caution aside and poured out an honest and straight-forward account of what he had been told.

Kaltenbrunner was convinced that Kleist was providing sound intelligence and accepted the man's denial that Clauss was a Jew. He placed Kleist under house arrest briefly but then allowed him to return to his responsibilities for the resettlement of Estonian Swedes.

* * * * *

- Von Ribbentrop -

Von Ribbentrop had of course been apprised of Kleist's report and after the defeat at Kursk the Foreign minister was convinced that the Russians were going to be victorious on the Eastern Front. He had then summoned Kleist to *'Wolfsschanze' on* August the sixteenth and when he arrived, said to him:

"I have asked you here because I want to hear that absurd story again of what went on up north. I mean your meeting with the Jew in Stockholm...before it's finally filed and put away."

Kleist did as he was bid and a two hour discussion of what had taken place ensued before the Foreign Minister dismissed him.

Never a particularly brave sole, Joachim dithered for a short time over what to do and then decided that, despite Hitler's last word on negotiations with the Russians, he had to act. He summoned up enough courage to provide the Fuhrer with the gist of what Kleist had told him.

To his relief, Hitler did not fly off the handle. Instead he simply repeated that there would be no negations with the Russians. The war was to continue until Germany was victorious.

Surprisingly, however, the Fuhrer could see not see any harm in allowing Kleist to keep his contact with Clauss active and in the event that the Russians had any kind of concrete offer, it was to be forwarded to Berlin for his consideration without delay.

Clauss, by this point frustrated with his inability to convince the German's to take some positive steps toward negotiations with the Russians, bit his tongue and did as he was told. A few weeks later he returned to Berlin to provide a hopeful Kleist with a requested update.

It was with some satisfaction that he was able to inform him that, in view of their success at Kursk, the Russians had indicated that they were now only prepared to have discussions if the Nazis provided some indication of sincere interest in peace. For example: the dismissal of Rosenberg and Ribbentrop from their current positions would be considered a step in the right direction.

Kleist had some difficulty restraining the grin that threatened to break out on his face, before pointing out that at the moment, the Fuhrer had no intention of negotiating. Clauss let out a sigh and shook his head then responded with the opinion that the Germans understood nothing about negotiating and pointed out that in order to do so, one needed both patience and a solid understanding of one's foe, which in this case, Hitler was demonstrating neither.

Kleist made no comment about this observation but instructed Clauss to keep his ear to the ground and report any new information, if and when it arose.

Kleist was surprised nonetheless when an excited Clauss eagerly sought him out to inform him that his source at the Russian embassy had just informed him that Moscow had initiated another contact. He had been advised that the Vice-Commissar for Foreign Affairs, Vladimir Georgievich Dekanozov, who was a former ambassador to Berlin, planned a trip to Stockholm in the near future and would arrive with authorization to speak directly to Kleist.

There were preconditions to such a meeting. Kleist must return to Stockholm prior to Dekanozov's arrival and the Germans had to meet the previously outlined plan requiring the resignation of both von Ribbentrop and Rosenberg, this to demonstrate that Kleist had been officially authorized to represent the Nazis in the talks.

* * * * *

- Goebbels -

On September eighth, shortly after the Allies had breached the channel between Sicily and the toe of the Italian boot, the new Italian government under Marshal Badoglio's leadership announced that it had signed and armistice with the West.

Although Hitler had predicted that this would happen, he was seriously shaken by the event and immediately summoned Goebbels to *'Wolfsschanze'* for a conference.

Hitler outlined his concerns over the Italian decision. Not only were the fifty-four odd thousand German troops in Corsica and Sardinia at risk, but there was a very good likelihood that, in view of the recent heavy bombing raids, the Allies would now launch their long-planned second front. That, coupled with the latest Russian successes on the Easter Front, which had necessitated the withdrawal of German troops to the Dnieper, was extremely alarming.

Goebbels agreed that the situation was very serious and suggested that perhaps something could be done with the Russians. Hitler's reaction was predictable.

"Not for a moment. It would be easier to make a deal with the British. At any given moment they would come to their senses."

Goebbels took a different view. He believed that Stalin was the more practical of the two leaders. He told Hitler that while the Russian leader was more realistic in his approaches, Churchill was more of a romantic adventurer type who would be hard pressed to consider any sensible approach from the Germans.

He then bravely took the next logical step.

"Sooner or later, we shall have to face the question of inclining toward one enemy side or the other. Germany has never yet had luck with a two-front war; it won't be able to stand this one in the long run either."

When Hitler did not comment on this suggestion, an emboldened Goebbels expanded his concept, offering the opinion that concessions would have to be made.

"We did not come to power in thirty-three by making unqualified demands."

He paused and then continued.

"We did present absolute demands on August of thirteenth of nineteen thirty-two, but we failed because of them."

He then summed up by advising Hitler to publicly accept the fact that Italy was lost, by way of addressing the people in a public speech, offering them a frank view of this turn of events coupled with both comfort and reassurance as to the future of the war.

* * * * *

- Kleist -

On September Tenth, with the overall situation worsening, Kleist felt obligated to take Clauss's most recent intelligence from Moscow to von Ribbentrop. Needless to say, the Foreign Minister was not pleased with the report, which called for both he and Rosenberg to resign.

He made light of the whole suggestion and dismissed it out of hand.

Displeased by it or not, he could not fail to report the matter to Hitler. He would of course argue against accepting any such plan, but he would nonetheless deliver it.

Hitler told von Ribbentrop to instruct Kleist to delay matters for the time being, but to hold onto the thread and see what the Russians would do in response. Von Ribbentrop returned to Berlin and passed on that message. The next day, after receiving a message from Hitler, von Ribbentrop called Kleist back in and told him that after reconsideration, the Fuhrer had decided to avoid any additional direct contact with the Russians.

After all he had accomplished, Kleist was flabbergasted and completely disenchanted about any further attempts on his part to pull the German fat from the fire.

* * * * *

- Goebbels -

Hitler had reluctantly agreed with the Propaganda Minister's evaluation of the current situation and his suggestion that he make a public broadcast. On the evening of September tenth the Fuhrer recorded a twenty-page speech in his bunker at *'Wolfsschanze'*, which was taped and then delivered to the nation.

During the broadcast he said.

"My right to believe unconditionally in success is founded not only on my own life but also on the destiny of our people."

* * * * *

- Mussolini -

During tea after the speech had been broadcast, Hitler appeared rejuvenated to those around him. But the Fuhrer had privately conceded to himself that in the face of the pounding Germany was taking from the air, the speech alone could not shore up his people's morale.

He decided that to do that he would have to rescue Mussolini and return him to power.

'Il Duce' was being held prisoner one hundred miles from Rome in a hotel near the top of Gran Sasso which was the highest peak in the Apennines mountain range.

At Himmler's urging, the Fuhrer chose SS Captain Otto Skorzeny to lead the airborne assault on the mountain top and on Sunday September twelfth at one in the afternoon Skorzeny and one hundred and seven men boarded gliders for the trip to a grassy meadow adjacent to the hotel where the Italian Fascist leader was being held.

The Germans quickly overpowered the Italian soldiers and police holding Mussolini, who was quickly bundled off to a small Fiesler-Storch single engine plane which had managed to land on the sloping meadow. At three in the afternoon Skorzeny, Mussolini and the pilot took off and within the hour they landed in Rome where they were transferred to a large trimotor Heinkel and took off headed for Vienna.

Upon getting the news directly from Skorzeny by telephone, a relieved Hitler said:

"You have performed a military feat which will become part of history. You have given me back my friend Mussolini."

A stopover was made in Munich so Mussolini could be briefly reunited with his family and then early on the fourteenth of September he and Skorzeny left for East Prussia.

Hitler eagerly awaited the flight at the airstrip at *'Wolfsschanze'* and warmly embraced his old ally the moment he came off the plane.

Once the two men had completed their greetings, Skorzeny deplaned and was heartily received by Hitler. The rescue had been an audacious act which had been carried out with panache and it would forever endear the SS-Captain to his Fuhrer who lavished upon him a promotion to *'Sturmbannfuhrer'*, and the Knight's Cross of the Iron Cross.

As a Propaganda exercise it had been an absolutely astounding accomplishment, widely acclaimed, not only among the Axis members, but throughout the world.

Hitler was buoyant and invigorated by the accomplishment and looked forward to a renewed Mussolini who would join him in his plans to take vengeance on Badoglio and the others involved in *'Il Duce's'* fall. In short order the beaten Italian dictator disabused the Fuhrer of that expectation, telling Hitler that he wanted only to retire from political life.

Hitler was incensed. In private, he belittled *'Il Duce'* to his face, saying:

"What is this sort of Fascism which melts like snow before the sun? For years I have explained to my generals that Fascism was the soundest alliance for the German people. I have never concealed my distrust of the Italian monarch; at you insistence, however, I did nothing to obstruct the work which you carried out to the advantage of your King. But I must confess to you that we Germans have never understood your attitude in this respect."

His eyes coldly flashing, he paused for a few seconds and then continued, advising Mussolini that he would treat Italy well despite Badoglio's treachery, but only, "IF" *'Il Duce'* would first agree to reassume his role in a new German occupied Italian Social Republic.

He then sighed and softened the delivery of his remaining words somewhat.

"The war must be won and once it is won Italy will be restored to

her rights. The fundamental condition is that Fascism be reborn and that the traitors be brought to justice."

He then mused, suggesting that the only other option would be his having to treat Italy as an enemy, in which case after the war the country would have to be occupied and governed by Germans.

At the best of times, Mussolini had never been one to seriously spar verbally with Hitler, and now, down trodden, ill and tired, he obediently accepted his fate.

He renounced his plan to retire, issued an official communique announcing that he had assumed the supreme direction of Fascism in Italy and immediately issued four orders of the day which served to reinstate those authorities dismissed by Badoglio, reconstitute the Fascists militia and instructed the party to support the Wehrmacht and investigate the conduct of members involved in the coup d'état carried out on the twenty-fifth of July.

Hitler had gotten what he wanted but from this point on he considered Mussolini as, at best, nothing more than a figurehead. That evening, while chatting with his tight family circle he made his feeling known.

"I admit that I was deceived. It has turned out that Mussolini is only a little man."

* * * * *

- V-2 Production -

In early September, von Braun promised the Long-Range Bombardment Commission that the design development of the A-4 was near completion.

As a result of the earlier bombing of Peenemunde, Speer had ordered that all manufacturing of this important super weapon was to be relocated to a bombproof production line and in early September, machinery and personnel required for production of the V-2 rocket was moved to a new site along with machinery and personnel from the two other previously planned A-4 assembly sites.

* * * * *

- SS Expansion -

In September, the 12th Panzer Davison *'Hitlerjugend'* was formed using volunteers for the Hitler Youth. Himmler then convinced Hitler to allow him to form a Bosnian Muslim division and the 13th Waffen Mountain Division of the SS Handschar (1st Croatian), the first non-Germanic division was formed for service against Tito's Yugoslav Partisans. Next was the formation of the 14th Waffen Grenadier Division of the SS (1st Latvian) created from compulsory military service initiated in the *'Ostland'*.

* * * * *

- Sturmgewehr 44 -

At the start of the Second World War, the German infantry was equipped with weapons comparable to those of most other military forces. A typical infantry unit was equipped with a mix of bolt action rifles and some form of light or medium machine guns. A better weapon design was underway at that time with the intent of improving infantry firepower and led to the eventual production of the *'Sturmgewehr 44'*.

The StG 44 (Sturmgewehr 44, assault rifle 44), was also known under the designations MP 43 (Maschinenpistole 43) and MP 44 (Maschinenpistole 44), respectively. The weapon is considered to be the world's first modern assault rifle. The different models denote earlier development versions of the same weapon which were manufactured with minor updates in production including the butt end, muzzle nut, shape of the front sight base and an unstepped barrel. The differences in each are only visible after close inspection.

The various models were developed from the Mkb 42(H) (machine carbine) and combined the characteristics of a carbine, submachine gun and automatic rifle. The gun's name was chosen personally by Hitler for propaganda reasons and means *'storm rifle'*.

The rifle was chambered for the 7.92 x 33 mm Kurz cartridge, a shorter version of the German standard 7.92 x 57 mm rifle round. The ammunition, in combination with the weapon's selective-fire design, provided a compromise between the controllable firepower of a submachine gun at close quarters with the accuracy and power of a Karabiner 98 k bolt action rifle at intermediate ranges. The end result produced a weapon that had less range and power than the more powerful infantry rifles of the day and was designed to fulfil a need to respond to German army studies which had shown that few combat engagements occurred at more than three hundred meters and the majority took place within two hundred meters. Fifty rifles were to be delivered for field testing in early nineteen forty-two.

The resulting accuracy was excellent for a weapon of its type. It was the first successful weapon of its class, and the concept was to have a major impact on modern infantry small arms development.

Production soon began with the first batches of the new rifle being shipped to troops fighting in Russia. The assault rifle proved a valuable weapon, especially on the Eastern front, where it was first deployed. A properly trained soldier with a StG 44 had an improved tactical repertoire, in that he could effectively engage targets at longer ranges than with an MP 40, but be much more useful than the Kar 98k in close combat, as well as provide covering fire like a light machine gun.

It was also found to be exceptionally reliable in the extreme cold of the Russian winter. The StG 44's rate of fire varied between five hundred and fifty and six hundred rounds per minute.

The 1st Infantry Division of Army Group South and the 32nd Infantry Division of Army Group North, both being refitted from heavy losses on the Eastern Front, were selected to be issued the rifle. Ammunition shortages meant the 1st was the only division fully equipped.

It was intended that the MP44/StG44 would effectively counter the Russian PPS and PPSh-41 submachine guns. These cheap, mass-produced weapons had proven themselves effective weapons in close-quarter engagements with the Germans. The StG 44, while lacking the range of the old standard Kar 98k, had a considerably longer range than the Russian submachine guns, a comparable rate of fire, an ability to switch between a fully automatic, a default semi-automatic fire mode and surprising accuracy.

The StG 44's inline design gave it controllability even on full-auto. It provided the individual German infantryman with unparalleled firepower compared to that of all earlier handheld firearms.

Unfortunately for the Germans however, it was to be yet another one of their extraordinary design developments, which came too late in the war to provide a significant effect on the outcome.

* * * * *

- Fritz X -

After Badoglio had publicly announced the Italian armistice with the Allies on September the eighth, the Italian fleet had steamed out from La Spezia for Malta.

On September ninth, the *Luftwaffe* achieved their greatest success to date with the new radio guided anti-ship glide bomb. To prevent the ships from falling into Allied hands, six Dornier 217K-2s took off, each carrying a single Fritz X. The Italian battleship *'Roma'*, flagship of the Italian fleet, received two hits and a near miss, and sank shortly after her magazines exploded.

One thousand, two hundred and twenty-five members of her crew, including Admiral Carlo Bergamini went down with the ship. Her sister ship, the *'Italia'*, was also damaged but managed to complete the trip to Malta.

At ten in the morning of September the eleventh, during the invasion of Salerno, the American light cruiser USS *'Savannah'* was hit by Fritz-Xs and damaged seriously enough to force it to return to the US for repairs. One of the bombs had passed through the roof of *'C'* turret and killed the turret crew and a damage control party when it exploded in the lower ammunition handling room. The blast tore a large hole in the ship's bottom, opened a seam in her side, and blew out all fires in her boiler rooms. The *'Savannah'* lay dead in the water.

It took eight hours to relight her boilers and get underway. Her sister ship, the USS *'Philadelphia'*, had been targeted earlier that same morning, but in that case the bomb just missed the ship, exploding some eighteen feet away and damage to the ship was minimal.

On September thirteenth at two-forty in the afternoon, the British light cruiser HMS *'Uganda'* was hit by a Fritz-X off Salerno. The bomb passed through seven decks and straight out through the bottom, exploding just under the keel. The concussive shock of the explosion killed sixteen men and extinguished all her boiler fires. She had to be towed to Malta for repairs.

On September sixteenth, the battleship HMS *'Warspite'*, which was providing long-range gunfire support for troops off Salerno, was hit by a Fritz. The bomb penetrated six decks before exploding in number four boiler room. This explosion put out all fires and blew out the double bottom. A second near-missed *Warspite*, holing her at the waterline. Although casualties were light, she lost all power and was towed to Malta.

The last Fritz-X attack at Salerno took place on September seventeenth. It caused minor damage to the light cruiser USS *'Philadelphia'* with two near misses. The Dutch sloop *'Flores'* and the destroyer, HMS *'Loyal'* were also damaged in this attack.

* * * * *

- Ferdinand -

In September all surviving *'Ferdinands'* were recalled to be modified based on battle experience gained in the Battle of Kursk. Over the next two months, forty-eight of the remaining fifty surviving vehicles were scheduled to be modified by adding a ball-mounted MG-34 machine gun in the hull front. This change was intended to improve anti-infantry ability.

A commander's cupola for improved vision and the application of *'Zimmer'* paste, a non-magnetic coating used for the purpose of combating magnetically attached anti-tank mines was also added. The frontal armor was also thickened and the tracks widened. The changes increased the weight of the beast from sixty-five to seventy tons.

Later, at Hitler's order, these upgraded vehicles went through a name change to become the *'Elefant'* (Elephant).

* * * * *

- Special Handling -

During the month the Vilna Ghetto is liquidated.

On September eleventh, after occupying northern and central Italy, the Germans move into Rome. They have now become the occupying force in an area containing approximately thirty-five thousand Jews.

On the same date Jewish transports to Auschwitz begin from the Nazis Theresienstadt concentration camp in Czechoslovakia.

* * * * *

- Concentration Camps -

- Sobibor -

On September twenty-third a consignment of Russian military prisoners of war, all of Jewish extraction arrives by transport.

* * * * *

- Ghettos -

- Vilna -

No mass killings had taken place at Vilna since the spring of forty-two. The final liquidation of ghetto number one began in late September with all children, elderly and sick to be transported to Sobibor extermination camp or shot at Ponary. The remaining men were to be transported to labour camps in Estonia and the women to labour camps in Latvia.

Earlier in the month, when the Germans had entered the camp to prepare for the shutdown, the inmates had realized that the ghetto was to be closed. At that time there were some minor confrontations but in the end the Jewish council agreed to co-operate in the transports, in the hopes of minimizing bloodshed.

After the Ghetto had been emptied, a small force of labourers was held back and forced to open the mass graves and burn the corpses before attempts were made to obliterate all traces of its existence.

* * * * *

- The Viannos Massacres -

On September the fourteenth, the Germans launch a mass extermination campaign against the civilian residents of around approximately twenty villages located in the areas of east Viannos and west Ierapetra provinces on the Greek island of Crete. The killings, with a death toll in excess of five hundred, were carried out over the next ten days by Wehrmacht units. Most of the villages were looted and then burned to the ground. There was a wholesale destruction of pending harvests. The operation was ordered by *'Generalleutnant'* Friedrich-Wilhelm Muller, in retaliation for the support and involvement of the local population in the Cretan resistance.

* * * * *

- The Family -

- Karl and Wilhelm -

Father and son had settled into a routine wherein they divided the majority of their time between *'Wolfsschanze'* and Berlin ensuring that they maintained good standing with both Hitler and Himmler, and whenever time allowed, escaped to the family castle.

Hitler's paranoia and Himmler's growing influence meant that they had to take increasing care in managing their covert *'Operation Fatherland'* activities. The Gestapo was diligently looking for anyone who appeared disloyal and Karl and Wilhelm kept themselves well out of any conversations or alliances that could lend it to this type of risk.

Thanks to earlier endeavors and careful planning, their actual direct involvement with *'Operation Fatherland'* had begun to wind down and had settled into a relatively static endeavor, where, if all went to plan, it would hopefully remain until the end of the war was imminent.

Recruitment for Brazil, if slowed to a trickle now, was continuing, while the heavy allied bombing and the resulting decision to evacuate civilians from Berlin was providing cover for the final stages of the brain-drain of research scientists and engineers needed to complete the research compliment for Brazil. People were on the move and civilian casualties were high. Karl and his group were finding that, amid the confusion, arranging the disappearance of the people they wanted and quietly slipping them into the ratlines, was relatively easy to achieve.

* * * * *

- Eric -

Supplied with new identity papers, Eric easily blended in with his large Brazilian extended family and had quickly assumed the management of both the mining operation and the covert research facilities it served to camouflage.

Sufficient staff and equipment was now in place to fulfil the predetermined *'Operation Fatherland'* needs until the war had ended and the shipments of new materials and manpower by neutral ship had dropped off to almost nothing.

Although Eric's responsibilities had risen overall, he had a dedicated and efficient workforce already in place and he found himself enjoying his new challenge. The war seemed to be a long way off. He and Heidi found themselves able to lead a very satisfying lifestyle, surrounded by a substantial number of von Stauffer relations, while they awaited the birth of their first child.

As was the case with the rest of his immediate family back in Germany, they were now in a holding pattern and were set up very comfortably to wait out the war while they planned and looked forward to the part they would play in the resurgence of the German race which, for them, the war's end would bring.

* * * * *

- Friedrichshafen -

The isolated location of castle von Stauffer meant that they were well buffered from the destruction of the more populated industrial areas of Germany. The day to day existence for the family housed within the battlements was serene and due to their wealth and position, they experienced little of the sufferings of their fellow citizens.

Trains arriving at the castle were few and far between now and by month end, would cease. Konrad and the Baron were busy with their research, Gabriella now had two children to watch over and Ursula's workload was grinding to a halt in step with the declining arrival of the railcars from shrinking occupied territory.

As summer began to wane, outdoor activities centered around the pool and tennis courts lessened but the new members of the family had added a good measure of entertainment and absorbed a great deal of the adults' time as they settled in to patiently await war's end.

CHAPTER EIGHTEEN

- September -

- Allied Air Operations -

- Europe -

RAF Bomber Command delivers fourteen thousand tons of bombs on targets which include Hanover, Mannheim and Berlin. US heavy bombers drop five thousand four hundred tons, primarily on Nantes, Paris and Stuttgart.

* * * * *

- Mediterranean -

Allied bombers take part in over fifteen thousand sorties over Italy concentrating on communications facilities and airfields.

* * * * *

- Maritime Warfare -

- Atlantic -

An upgraded fleet of U-boats sporting new radar search receivers, improved anti-aircraft armament and acoustic homing torpedoes; sails back into the North Atlantic convoy routes. They have new orders from Donitz to target convoy escort ships rather than the merchant ships. Nine U-boats go to the bottom and twenty-nine ships go down for a total of one hundred and fifty-six thousand, four hundred tons.

* * * * *

- Pacific -

American subs sink one hundred and sixty thousand tons of Japanese shipping.

* * * * *

- September First -

- Eastern Front -

The Russians take Dorogobuzh between Smolensk and Vyazma.

* * * * *

- Central Pacific -

American troops land on Baker Island and immediately begin the construction of an airfield.

* * * * *

- Solomons -

US troops are on the offensive and reach Orete Cove.

* * * * *

- September Second -

- Eastern Front -

Russian forces take Lisichansk, Kommunarsk, Glushkovo and Sumy.

* * * * *

- September Third -

- Italy -

The Italians sign an armistice and the mainland is invaded with the first landing by the British at Reggio Calabria.

* * * * *

- Berlin -

The evacuation of the civilian population begins.

* * * * *

- Eastern Front -

Russian troops take Putivl, cutting the Bryansk/Konotop railway line.

* * * * *

- September Fourth -

- Moscow -

Russia declares war on Bulgaria.

* * * * *

- New Guinea -

American forces land and take Nadzab which lies just west of the port city of Lae. Lae is taken by the Australians, who also take

Salamaua.

* * * * *

- September Sixth -

- Eastern Front -

The Russians take Makeyevka, Kromatorsk, Slavyansk and the rail yards at Konotop.

* * * * *

- Italy -

Advancing up the toe of the boot, the British Eighth Army takes Palmi and Delianuova.

* * * * *

- September Seventh -

- Eastern Front -

Russian forces capture Baturin and Zvenkov in the Kharkov sector and the Germans begin to pull out of Stalino.

* * * * *

- Italy -

British forces take Bova Marina.

* * * * *

- September Eighth -

- Italy -

Eisenhower publicly announces Italy's surrender to Allied Forces.

The Germans immediately enact *'Operation Achse'*, the disarmament of the Italian armed forces. Badoglio confirms the Italian surrender and the main body of the Italian fleet, consisting of three battleships, six cruisers and nine destroyers, sets sail from La Spezia and Genoa to Allied ports.

The Americans bomb Frascati, the German General Headquarters for the Mediterranean zone.

The British take Locri and land forces at Pizzo.

* * * * *

- Eastern Front -

The Russians occupy Stalino and take Yasinovataya and Krasnoarmeisk.

* * * * *

- September Ninth -

- Italy -

Allied forces land at Salerno. The British take Taranto.

* * * * *

- Iran -

Iran declares war on Germany.

* * * * *

- Italy -

The Italian battleship *'Roma'* is sunk by a Fritz X bomb.

* * * * *

- Eastern Front -

The Russians capture Bakhmach.

* * * * *

- September Tenth -

- Italy -

German forces occupy Rome.

* * * * *

- Malta -

The Italian fleet arrives to surrender.

* * * * *

- Aegean -

The British occupy Castelrosso.

* * * * *

- Eastern Front -

In a seaborne attack in the Sea of Azov, Russian forces take

Mariupol.
The Russians capture Barvenkovo, Volnovakha and Chaplino.

* * * * *

- September Eleventh -

- Italy -

The British First Airborne takes Brindisi without opposition.

* * * * *

- New Guinea -

Australian forces take the airfield and occupy the town of Salamaua.

* * * * *

- September Twelfth -

- Italy -

The British take Crotone.
German forces rescue Mussolini from captivity.

* * * * *

- Eastern Front -

The Russians capture Stary Kermenchick.

* * * * *

- New Guinea -

The Australians take Salamaua.

* * * * *

- September Thirteenth -

- Italy -

Serious German counter attacks threaten to drive a wedge between the British and American forces on the Salerno beachhead. The Allies move quickly to shift reinforcements to the beach.

* * * * *

- Greece -

Over the next ten days the Italians resist the Germans in Cephalonia. Fifteen hundred are killed before they surrender and the infuriated Germans promptly execute an additional five thousand and deport the remainder to labour camps.

* * * * *

- September the Fourteenth -

- Crete -

The *'Viannos Massacres'* begins. General Müller earns the nickname *'the Butcher of Crete'*.

* * * * *

- September Fifteenth -

- Italy -

Mussolini issues a proclamation to the effect that he is resuming leadership. In fact he has now become the puppet of German occupied Italy.

* * * * *

- Aegean -

Cos in Dodecanese is taken by British paratroops and as soon as it is secured they fly in a squadron of Spitfires.

* * * * *

- Eastern Front -

The Russians take Nezhin on the rail line between Konotop and Kiev. In the north they take Dyatkovo.

* * * * *

- September Sixteenth -

- Aegean -

The British take Leros and Samos.

* * * * *

- Eastern Front -

On their advance toward Kiev, Russian forces capture Novgorod, Seversky and Romny. They also take a railroad junction located northeast of Pavlograd, called Lozovaya and Novorossiysk in the Kuban.

* * * * *

- September Seventeenth -

- Eastern Front -

The Russians take Bryansk, Bezhitsa and Trubchvsk and in the south on the Sea of Azov, Berdyansk.

* * * * *

- September Eighteenth -

- Eastern Front -

Priluki, Luny and Romodan are taken by the Russians as the drive toward Kiev. In the south, they capture Pavlograd, Krasnograd, Pologi and Nogaysk.

* * * * *

- Aegean -

The British occupy Simi, Stampalia and Icaria.

* * * * *

- September Nineteenth -

- Italy -

The Germans evacuate Sardinia.
British forces take Auletta.

* * * * *

- Eastern Front -

The Russians capture Yartsevo and Dukovschina.

* * * * *

- September Twentieth -

- Eastern Front -

The Russians overrun Velizh and Kholm.

* * * * *

- Italy -

Canadian troops take Potenza.

* * * * *

- September Twenty-First -

- Eastern Front -

Demidov, Cherinigov and Sinelnikova fall to the Russians.

* * * * *

- September Twenty-Second -

- Norway -

British midget submarines attack the German battleship *'Tirpitz'* while she is riding at anchor in a Norwegian fjord. The massive ship is significantly damaged and will be out of service for six months.

* * * * *

- Eastern Front -

The Russian troops take Anapa in the Kuban and Novomoskovosk just north of Dnepropetrovsk. The Germans begin to pull out of Poltava.

* * * * *

- September Twenty-Third -

- Eastern Front -

Russian forces take Poltava and enter Unecha was lies just east of Klinsy.

* * * * *

- Corsica -

The Free French occupy Bonifaccio.

* * * * *

- Italy -

Mussolini founds the Italian Social Republic and decrees that part of northern Italy will now fall under German control and administration.

* * * * *

- September Twenty-Fourth -

- New Guinea -

Australian forces smash through Japanese defenders at the River Bumi and Finschhafen airfield is captured.

* * * * *

- Eastern Front -

The Russians capture Borispol just east of Kiev and in the north the Germans begin to evacuate their forces from Smolensk and Roslavl.

* * * * *

- September Twenty-Fifth -

- Eastern Front -

Smolensk is occupied by the Russians.

* * * * *

- September Twenty-Sixth -

- Corsica -

Free French forces occupy Ghisonaccia airfield.

* * * * *

- September Twenty-Seventh -

- Corfu -

After all but annihilating the Italian defenders, the Germans take full control of the island.

* * * * *

- Eastern Front -

The Russians take Temryuk, removing the last port under German occupation.

* * * * *

- Italy -

British troops capture Foggia and its airfield without a fight. Canadian forces take Melfi.

* * * * *

- September Twenty-Ninth -

- Eastern Front -

The Russians take Kremenchug, and in the north, Rudnya situated on the Smolensk/Vitebsk rail line, is occupied.

* * * * *

- September Thirtieth -

- Italy -

American forces take Avellino.

* * * * *

- Eastern Front -

Russian troops take Krichev on the River Sozh.

* * * * *

- Denmark -

As the Gestapo starts to round up the Danish Jews, a resistance effort begins to ferry Jews to Sweden by private boat.

CHAPTER NINETEEN

-October -

- Hitler -

On June nineteenth of forty-three, Hitler and Himmler have a private meeting at Berchtesgaden, the Fuhrer's home in the Bavarian compound. The topic of conversation at that time covered the examination of the various Nazi security policies, which Himmler was moving to organize and fully absorb under the SS umbrella, something for which he would require Hitler's authorization.

Himmler's intent was to tie the extermination of the Jews, for which the SS already held responsibility, to the eradication of insurgency in occupied territories, which was a growing problem and currently being done haphazardly by various organizations, including the Wehrmacht.

If he could convince Hitler that the SS could do a much better job of dealing with resistance problems than a mishmash of other agencies, then the strength and influence of the SS would increase yet again.

Himmler presented Hitler with a memo on the subject. This document was made up of two sections.

The first listed a number of radio signals that he had earlier presented to the Fuhrer. These included reports from the General Government of Poland, Reichskommissar Seyss-Inquart of Holland and Dr. Rainer who was Gauleiter Carinthia. All referred to the *'Bandenverhaltnisse'* (Bandit situation), in Poland, Russia, Slovenia, Croatia and Yugoslavia. It also contained a copy of Himmler's June eleventh order which dealt with the liquidating of Jewish ghettos in the east.

Accompanying this first section was a *'Bandenkarte'* (Bandit map) which illustrated the *'Bandit'* situation in the General Government as of the end of May. Himmler then accepted full responsibility for a failure to eradicate the *'Bandits'* over the previous winter, explaining that having his SS forces pulled away from his control in order to plug the gaps in the front for the Wehrmacht had negated their ability to carry out their normal activities in occupied territory. He then promised Hitler that he would eliminate the entire 'Bandit' problem within the year and properly pacify the areas presently experiencing such activist activity, 'IF' the Fuhrer could see his way clear to giving him sole control of the forces under SS command, including the SS-Cavalry Division, the 1st SS Infantry Brigade, and the numerous police formations, in addition to the returning police formations that had been serving in the army's security divisions.

The second section of the memorandum listed seven decisions that had already been made by the Fuhrer and that Himmler now requested be recorded as the Fuhrer's personal commands.

1. The 'Bandenkampf' (Bandit-fight) remained the business of the Reichsfuhrer-SS, the SS and police.

2. He (The Fuhrer) clearly confirmed that no reproach is held against the SS and police because of the growing bandit danger after the transfer of forces to the front.

3. He (The Fuhrer) promised to check if the two police regiments, 'Griese', based in Marseilles and ' Franz', based in Finland, could be returned to the SS.

4. His order of June 11, 1943, was completely correct and gave the order to inform the General-Governor it will remain in force.

5. The Fuhrer declared, after my report, the evacuation of the Jews, despite the unrest that would thereby still arise in the next 3 to 4 months, was to be radically carried out and had to be seen through.

6. The Fuhrer stated clearly that Badenbekampfung and questions of security were solely the matter and authority of the Reichsfuhrer-SS even in the General-Government.

7. The Fuhrer declined all suggestion to raise Polish formations, following the Katyn propaganda, as some on the German side have suggested. The formation of Galician units from the area of Galician White Ruthenia is

acceptable, as this had been part of Austria over the last one hundred and fifty years.

Himmler managed to successfully tie the 'final solution of the Jewish question' to that of the *'Bandenverhaltnisse'* in the Fuhrer's mind and Hitler readily agreed to the correctness of the second part of the document, saying:

"Regardless of any unrest it might cause during the next three of four months, it must be carried out...in an all-embracing way."

With one fell swoop, Himmler had made an end run around both the army and General Governor Hans Frank of Poland and both his influence and power had increased considerably.

By October, Himmler was making good use of the new authority Hitler had given him in June.

* * * * *

The Inner Circle -

- Heinrich Himmler -

By October, the *'Reichsfuhrer of the Schutzstaffel'* has arguably become the second most powerful man in the Nazi Reich and there was no more contradictory figure in the higher reaches of National Socialism than Himmler.

As complete an understanding as is possible is necessary to reach an informed understanding of what made this pivotal figure in the Nazi hierarchy tick if one intends to fully encapsulate the mindset of the leadership of the Third Reich.

Heinrich Leopold Himmler was born in Munich on October seventh, nineteen hundred. He had two brothers. His family was middle-class and conservative Roman Catholic.

Himmler's first name, *Heinrich*, was the same as that of his godfather, Prince Heinrich of Bavaria of the royal family of Bavaria. The Prince had been tutored by Gebhard Himmler, Heinrich's father.

Heinrich attended a grammar school in Landshut where his

father was deputy principal. He did well in his schoolwork, but struggled in athletic endeavors. His health was poor. He lived with lifelong stomach complaints and other ailments.

In his youth he trained daily and exercised regularly in an attempt to build himself up physically. His peers at that time remembered him as studious, and awkward in social situations.

Himmler intermittently kept a diary from age ten and it reflected the fact that he took a keen interest in current events, dueling, and *'the serious discussion of religion and sex'*.

Heinrich began training with the Landshut Cadet Corps in nineteen-fifteen. His father used his connections with the royal family to get him accepted as an officer candidate, and he enlisted with the reserve battalion of the 11th Bavarian Regiment in December of nineteen-seventeen.

His older brother, Gebhard had served on the western front and saw combat. He received the Iron Cross and was eventually promoted to lieutenant. The war ended with Germany's defeat in November of nineteen-eighteen, while Himmler was still in training, removing the opportunity for him to become an officer or see combat. After his discharge from the Corps on December the eighteenth, he returned to Landshut.

After the Great War, Himmler completed his grammar-school education. From nineteen-nineteen to nineteen-twenty-two, he studied agronomy (the science and technology of producing and using plants for food, fuel fiber and land reclamation) at Munich's *'Technische Hochschule'* following a brief apprenticeship on a farm and a subsequent period of illness.

Although many regulations discriminating against non-Christians, including Jews and other minority groups, had been eliminated during the German unification in eighteen seventy-one, anti-Semitism had continued to exist and thrive in Germany as it had in other parts of Europe. Himmler did lean toward anti-Semitism by the time he went to university, but no more than the others at his school, where students generally avoid their Jewish classmates.

Heinrich remained a devoted Catholic while a student, and spent most of his free time with members of his fencing fraternity, the

'League of Apollo', the president of which was Jewish. In spite of his growing anti-Semitism, Himmler maintained a polite demeanor with this individual and with the other Jewish members of the fraternity.

From a young age Himmler had been enthralled with the idea of pursuing a military career. During his second year at university, he redoubled his attempts to pursue this goal. Although he was not successful, he was able to extend his involvement in the paramilitary scene in Munich. While doing so he first met Ernst Rohm, an early member of the Nazi Party and co-founder of the *'Sturmabteilung'* (Storm Battalion or SA). Himmler admired Rohm because he was a decorated combat soldier, and at his suggestion, Himmler joined his anti-Semitic nationalist group, the *'Reichskriegsflagge'*.

By nineteen twenty-two, Himmler had become more interested in the *'Jewish Question'*. From that point on his diary entries contained an increasing number of anti-Semitic remarks and recorded a number of discussions about Jews he'd had with his classmates. His reading lists, as recorded in his diary, were dominated by anti-Semitic pamphlets, German myths, and occult tracts

After the June twenty-fourth murder of Foreign Minister Walther Ruthenium, Himmler's political views veered towards the radical right, and he took part in demonstrations against the Treaty of Versailles. Hyperinflation raged that summer, and as a result his parents could no longer afford to keep all three sons in school. Disappointed by his failure to make a career in the military and his family's inability to finance his doctoral studies, Heinrich was forced to take a low-paying office job once he had obtained his agricultural diploma. He remained in this position until September of nineteen twenty-three.

Himmler joined the Nazi Party (NSDAP) in August of that year and as a member of Rohm's paramilitary unit, Himmler took part in the Beer Hall Putsch. This event would set Himmler on his path into politics. He was questioned by the police about his role in the putsch, but was not charged because of insufficient evidence. He did however, lose his job and was unable to find other employment as an agronomist.

As a result he was forced to move back in with his parents in Munich.

Frustrated by these failures, he became more irritable, aggressive, and opinionated and began to alienate both friends and family.

In twenty-three and twenty-four, while struggling to find his purpose in life, Himmler moved away from Catholicism and dove deeper into his interests, both in the occult and in anti-Semitism.

Over time, Germanic mythology, reinforced by occult ideas, became a substitute religion for him and he found his membership in the NSDAP appealing due to its political positions, which tended to fall into step with his own views.

He was not initially swept up by Hitler's charisma or the blossoming cult of Führer worship. As he learned more about Hitler through his reading, he did however begin to regard him as a useful face of the party and over time he came to not only admire, but eventually worship him.

To consolidate and advance his own position within the NSDAP, Himmler took advantage of the disarray in the party which followed Hitler's arrest in the wake of the Beer Hall Putsch.

From mid nineteen twenty-four he worked under Gregor Strasser as a party secretary and propaganda assistant. In that position he began to travel all over Bavaria, agitating for the party, making speeches and distributing party literature.

In late nineteen twenty-four Strasser placed him in charge of the party office in Lower Bavaria. Here, he became responsible for integrating the area's membership within the NSDAP under Hitler when the party was re-founded in February of twenty-five. In that year, he joined the 'Schutzstaffel' (SS) as an SS-Fuhrer (SS-Leader). His SS number was one hundred and sixty-eight.

The SS was initially part of the much larger SA. It had been formed in twenty-three to provide a personal protection unit for Hitler and was re-formed in twenty-five as an elite unit of the SA.

Himmler's first leadership position in the SS was that of 'SS-Gauführer' (district leader) in Lower Bavaria in nineteen twenty-six. Pleased with Himmler's dedication and bureaucratic efficiency, Strasser appointed him as deputy propaganda chief in January of twenty-seven. As was typical in the NSDAP, he had considerable freedom of action in his post and this was to increase over time.

Himmler began to collect statistics on the number of Jews, Freemasons, and enemies of the party, and following his strong need for control, over time he developed an elaborate bureaucracy. In September of twenty-seven, Himmler told Hitler of his vision to transform the SS into a loyal, powerful, racially-pure elite unit.

Convinced that Himmler was just the man for the job, Hitler appointed him Deputy *'Reichsführer-SS'*, with the rank of *'SS-Oberführer'*.

At this point, Himmler joined the *'Artaman League'*, a *'Volkisch'* youth group.

Here he met Rudolf Höss, who was later commandant of Auschwitz concentration camp, and Walther Darre, whose book, *'The Peasantry as the Life Source of the Nordic Race'*, had caught Hitler's attention. Hitler appointed Darre, who was a firm believer in the superiority of the *'Nordic race'*, as Reich Minister of Food and Agriculture.

Himmler, who was by this time enthralled with Hitler' found Darre and his philosophy impossible to resist.

Upon the resignation of SS commander Erhard Heiden in twenty-nine, Himmler, while still maintaining his duties at propaganda headquarters and with Hitler's approval, assumed the position of *'Reichsführer-SS'*.

One of his first responsibilities was to organize SS participants at the Nuremberg Rally in September. Over the next year, Himmler grew the SS from a force of about two hundred and ninety men to approximately three thousand. By nineteen-thirty, Himmler had persuaded Hitler to turn the SS into a separate organization, although it was still to be subordinate to the SA.

The Nazi Party's rapid political rise to power provided Himmler and the SS an unfettered opportunity to thrive. By thirty-three, the SS numbered fifty-two thousand members.

Himmler saw to it that strict membership requirements ensured that all members of the SS were of Hitler's *'Aryan Herrenvolk'* (Aryan master race). Applicants were vetted for Nordic qualities.

Himmler said that: *'like a nursery gardener trying to reproduce a good old strain which has been adulterated and debased; we started from the principles of plant selection and then proceeded quite unashamedly to weed out the men whom we did not think we could use for the build-up of the SS'.*

Ironically, neither he nor those around him appeared to recognize that he himself came nowhere near his own ideals as far as this selection process went.

Himmler's organized, bookish intellect served him well as he began setting up different SS departments. In thirty-one, he appointed Reinhard Heydrich as chief of the new intelligence service, which was renamed the *'Sicherheitsaienst '*(SD: Security Service) in thirty-two. He later officially appointed Heydrich as his deputy.

The two men had a good working relationship and a mutual respect. In thirty-three, they began to remove the SS from SA control. Along with Interior Minister Frick, they aimed at creating a unified German police force.

In March of thirty-three, the Reich Governor of Bavaria, Franz Ritter von Epp appointed Himmler to the position of chief of the Munich Police, and Himmler appointed Heydrich to the post of commander of Department IV, the political police. That same year, Hitler promoted Himmler to the rank of *'SS-Obergruppenführer'* which now made him equal in rank to the senior SA commanders.

Thereafter, Himmler and Heydrich working in lock-step, determinedly took over the political police of state after state until only the Prussian police were left under Goering's control.

Himmler then established the *'Rasse- und Siedlungshauptamt or RuSHA'* (SS Race and Settlement Main Office), a racist and anti-Semitic organization. He appointed Darre as its first chief, with the rank *of 'SS-Gruppenführer'.*

This department implemented racial policies and began to monitor the *'racial integrity'* of the entire SS membership. SS men were now to be carefully vetted for their racial background.

On December the thirty-first of nineteen thirty-one, Himmler introduced the *'marriage order'*, which required SS men wishing to marry to produce family trees proving that both families were of Aryan descent all the way back to eighteen hundred. If any non-

Aryan forebears were found in either family tree during the resulting in-depth racial investigation, the person concerned was excluded from the SS. After the vetting, each man was issued a *'Sippenbuch'*, which was a genealogical record detailing his genetic history Himmler specified that each SS marriage should produce at least four children, which would then create a pool of genetically superior prospective SS members.

In March thirty-three, less than three months after the Nazis seized power, Himmler set up the first concentration camp at Dachau. Hitler had told him that he did not want this to be just another prison or detention camp. In June of that year, Himmler appointed Theodor Eicke, a convicted felon and ardent Nazi, as the camp Commandant.

As previously discussed, Eicke then devised a system that was used as a model for future camps throughout Germany. Its features included isolation of victims from the outside world, elaborate roll calls and work details and the use of force and executions was initiated in order to extract obedience. There was a strict disciplinary code for the guards. Uniforms were issued for prisoners and guards alike; the guard's uniforms had a special *'Totenkopf'* (death's head) insignia on their collars. By the end of thirty-four, Himmler had taken full control of the camps under the aegis of the SS and created a separate division, the *'SS-Totenkopfverbände'*.

Initially the camps had housed only political opponents, but over time, undesirable members of German society; criminals, vagrants and deviants were placed there as well. A Hitler decree issued in December of thirty-seven allowed for the incarceration of anyone deemed by the regime to be an undesirable member of society. This group was to include Jews, Gypsies, communists, and persons of any other cultural, racial, political, or religious affiliation deemed by the Nazis to be *'Untermensch'* (sub-human).

Thus, the camps had now become a mechanism for social and racial engineering. By the outbreak of World War II in the autumn of thirty-nine, there were six camps housing approximately twenty-seven thousand inmates.

In early thirty-four, when Hitler and other Nazi leaders became concerned that Rohm, who had socialist and populist views and believed that the real revolution had not yet begun, might be considering a coup d'état, he took action. Rohm had made no secret of the fact that he felt the SA, which now numbered some three million men, should become the sole arms-bearing corps of the state. He had openly lobbied that the army should be absorbed into the SA under his leadership and that Hitler should appoint him to the position of Minister of Defense, a position then held by conservative General, Werner von Blomberg.

Goering had created a Prussian secret police force, the 'Geheime Staatspolizei' or Gestapo in November of thirty-three, appointing Rudolf Diels as its head. In short order, Goering came to the conclusion that Diels was not ruthless enough to use the Gestapo effectively in its new role to counteract the power of the SA.

In order to deal with the situation, he handed over its control to Himmler on April twentieth of thirty-four. On that same day, Hitler appointed Himmler chief of all German police outside Prussia. Heydrich, who had been named chief of the Gestapo by Himmler on April twenty-second of the same year, also continued in his position as head of the SD.

On the twenty-first of June, Hitler came to the determination that Rohm and the SA leadership had to be eliminated. He sent Goering to Berlin on the twenty-ninth, to meet with Himmler and Heydrich to plan the move against the SA. Hitler took personal charge in Munich, where Rohm was arrested. He gave Rohm the choice to commit suicide or be shot. When Rohm had refused to kill himself, he was shot dead by two SS officers. Some where between eighty and two hundred members of the SA leadership and other political adversaries, including Gregor Strasser, were consequently summarily executed between June thirtieth and July second in what later referred to as the Night of the Long Knives.

The SA was then converted into a sports and training organization.

With the SA thus neutralized, the SS became an independent organization as of July thirtieth nineteen thirty-four and Himmler's title of 'Reichsführer-SS', the highest formal SS rank making him answerable to no one but Hitler.

On the seventeenth of June, nineteen thirty-six, with Himmler's urging, Hitler decreed the unification of all police forces in the Reich, and named Himmler Chief of the German Police. The police now effectively became a division of the SS, and hence independent of anyone but Himmler's control. This move gave Himmler operational control over Germany's entire detective force and authority over all of Germany's uniformed law enforcement agencies.

He promptly amalgamated these into the new *'Ordnungspolizei'* (order police), which then became a branch of the SS under Daluege. Shortly thereafter, Himmler created the *'Kriminalpolizei'* (Kripo) or criminal police and joined it to the Gestapo to become the *'Sicherheitspolizei'* (SiPo), the new security police; which now came under Heydrich's command.

Following the outbreak of the war, Himmler formed the *'SS-Reichssicherheitshauptamt'* (RSHA: Reich Main Security Office) to bring the Gestapo, Kripo and the SD together under one umbrella commanded by Heydrich.

Himmler believed that the SS needed its own military branch, and created the *'SS-Verfügungstruppe'* (SS-VT), which later evolved into the *'Waffen-SS'*.

Nominally under the authority of Himmler, the *Waffen-SS* went on to develop a fully militarized structure of command and operations. This force would grow from three regiments to over thirty-eight divisions during the war and fought alongside the regular army but never formally became a part of it.

In addition to his military ambitions, Himmler established the beginnings of a separate SS economic empire.

In nineteen forty he instructed Oswald Pohl to set up the *'Deutsche Wirtschaftsbetriebe'* (German Economic Enterprise) under the auspices of the SS Economy and Administration Head Office. Among other things, this holding company held title to housing corporations, factories, and publishing houses.

When Hitler asked for some pretext to justify the invasion of Poland in thirty-nine, it was Himmler, Heydrich, and Heinrich Müller who masterminded and carried out the false-flag plan which they code-named *'Operation Himmler'*.

German soldiers wearing Polish uniforms took part in border incursions intended to demonstrate Polish aggression against Germany. These incidents were then used by the Nazi propaganda machine to justify the German invasion of Poland which led to war.

Hitler had pre-authorized the killing of Polish civilians, including Jews and ethnic Poles before his troops crossed the frontier. The *'Einsatzgruppen'* which had been originally formed by Heydrich to secure government papers and offices in areas taken over by Germany prior to the war, had been now been transformed. With the advent of war it would, under SS control, morph into death squads, who would follow the army into Poland, and eliminate approximately sixty-five thousand intellectuals and other civilians. In addition, these squads were also tasked with rounding up Jews and other undesirables for confinement in ghettos and concentration camps.

On June twenty-first, the day before invasion of Russia, Himmler commissioned the preparation of the *'Generalplan Ost'* (General Plan for the East). The plan called for the Baltic States, Poland, western Ukraine, and Byelorussia to be conquered and resettled by ten million German citizens. The current thirty-one million residents were be expelled further east where they would be starved, or used for forced labour. The plan would have extended the border of Germany one thousand kilometers to the east. Himmler predicted that it would take twenty to thirty years to complete the plan, at a cost of sixty-seven billion Reichsmarks.

When presenting the plan, Himmler calmly explained it as follows:

"It is a question of existence, thus it will be a racial struggle of pitiless severity, in the course of which twenty to thirty million Slavs and Jews will perish through military actions and crises of food supply."

Himmler, who considered the war in the east to be a pan-European crusade to defend the traditional values of old Europe from the *'godless Bolshevik hordes'*, searched for and found SS volunteers across northern and western Europe. They came from Scandinavia, Liechtenstein, Luxembourg, Flanders, the Netherlands, and Switzerland. Only those deemed to be racially close to German blood were accepted into the elite organization. Spain and Italy also provided men for Waffen-SS units.

Hitler named Heydrich Deputy Reich Protector of the newly established *'Protectorate of Bohemia and Moravia'* in nineteen forty-one. A staunch believer in SS doctrine, Heydrich immediately began to racially classify the Czech population. Sub-humans were deported to concentration camps, while members of the growing resistance were summarily shot.

Himmler was tickled to death to have absolute SS control over a state and this new appointment served to strengthen the collaboration between himself and Heydrich, who although now had direct access to Hitler, remained absolutely loyal to his old boss.

With Hitler's approval, Himmler, who had experienced some push back from the regular army during the invasion of Poland, moved to strengthen the autonomy of the *'Einsatzgruppen'* prior to the lead-up to the invasion of Russia.

In support of this move, the Fuhrer issued a special directive, the *'Guidelines in Special Spheres re Directive No. 21 (Operation Barbarossa)'*. It was his intent to put paid to any non-SS interference with the *'Einsatzgruppen'* as they carried out their duties during the Russian campaign. In this directive Hitler said:

"In the operations area of the army, the Reichsführer-SS has been given special tasks on the orders of the Führer, in order to prepare the political administration. These tasks arise from the forthcoming final struggle of two opposing political systems. Within the framework of these tasks, the Reichsführer-SS acts independently and on his own responsibility."

Nazi racial policies, including the notion that people who were racially inferior would have no long-term part to play in the new German Reich, dated back to the earliest days of the party and Hitler had made no bones about the fact that the Jews of Europe were to be *'eliminated'* and in early forty-two he had come to the conclusion that this meant *'special handling"*. He had now chosen to have the SS do the job.

Heydrich arranged the Wannsee meeting for those Nazi officials who would be involved and there outlined the plans for the *'final solution to the Jewish question'.*

When Hedrick was assassinated, Himmler took over personal leadership of the RSHA and stepped up the pace of the *'special treatment'* of Jews, in what was codenamed *'Aktion Reinhard'* (Operation Reinhard), named in Heydrich's honor. He ordered the construction of *'Aktion Reinhard'* camps, the first specifically designated extermination camps, to be constructed at Belzec, Sobibor, and Treblinka.

Himmler believed unconditionally in the racist Nazi ideology. Sub-humans had no value to him unless they could act as slave labour for the new Reich. He had no hesitation in issuing the orders to eliminate Polish intellectuals and restrict non-Germans in the General Government and conquered territories to a fourth-grade education. He firmly believed that he could breed a German master race of racially pure Nordic Aryans. His education as an agronomist and farmer left him confident that he had a good grasp on the principles of selective breeding, which he was sure could be successfully applied to humans.

He acknowledged that it would take time but was sure he could engineer the German populace to be Nordic in appearance within several decades of the end of the war, by using eugenics.

So what was this relatively small, insignificant looking little man like?

We now have some idea of what type of environment surrounded him in his early days and what policies and peer influence he was subjected to, but the question remains, what did those around him think of him?

Despite his growing power to the point that he now literally held the power of life and death in his hands, to those closest to him he demonstrated charm and politeness, was modest when in meetings, prepared to listen attentively to others and be reasonable whenever possible.

Diplomats of the time thought of him as a man of sober judgment. He was according to all reports a warm and loving father to his children. The vast majority of his subordinates and staff thought of him as an earnest, thoughtful and fair employer who had a deep sense of the need to maintain democracy in the workplace. He took the time to play board and card games with his secretaries and soccer with aides and adjutants and went out of his way to include those who performed the menial tasks in his office, even his charwomen, on special occasions and dinners.

His dress was impeccable.

He was a tidy and organized individual, a proven bureaucrat, meticulous in carrying out his duties and demonstrating self-control that often caused others to suggest that he, at times, appeared almost robotic.

Unpretentious and conscientious, no task was below him, and he would often concentrate upon the little things that others could easily have handled for him. He worked diligently to create his SS, using basic Jesuit principles, which he knew well and valued.

He was a sentimental and honest man, indifferent to material objects, unlike some of his subordinates and the majority of his peers in Hitler's inner circle. He had no desire to feather his own nest and would never have even considered using his powerful position for personal profit.

He detested any form of corruption on the part of others and did not hesitate to take immediate and fatal remedial action if he became aware of it, and this was carried out with absolutely no consideration given to an individual's position or power.

A man who had suffered from stomach and gastric-related complaints for most of his life, he lived in frugal simplicity, ate moderately, imbibed alcohol sparingly and restricted himself to no more than two cigars a day.

His interests were wide and many of his beliefs were unusual to say the least.

He believed in *'Glazial-Kosmogonie'*, the concept that ice was the basic substance of all cosmic process and that it had determined the entire development of the universe and in the power of magnetism, homeopathy, mesmerism, natural eugenics, clairvoyance, faith healing and sorcery.

He was loyal to a fault, believing in, and supporting Hitler till the end. He once commented to a subordinate that when speaking to Hitler, he often:

'Felt like a schoolboy who hadn't done his homework.'

Hitler did not like Himmler and fostered no personal relationship with him. While he respected the man's abilities and used him, he spent no unnecessary time with him. Himmler was forever trying to wangle an invitation to Berchtesgaden as a guest, in addition to those official summonses that resulted due to his duties in his official capacity.

Hitler stymied all such attempts and once commented:

'I need such policemen, but I don't like them.'

The Fuhrer had even gone so far as to order his personal adjutant, an SS-Captain, to not inform Himmler as to the content of the daily military meetings.

Despite this strange, non-personal relationship, Hitler did not hesitate to put the *'Reichsfuhrer'* in absolute charge of the operation that was closest to his heart, that of *'The final Solution to the Jewish Question.'*

How could he not? From the very start, Himmler had been completely enamored with the Fuhrer and he remained indisputably Hitler's disciple and loyal subordinate.

The strange little man represented the epitome of National Socialism, a committed and extremely professional party worker who had overcome his social shortcomings to become Hitler's faithful right hand man. Despite his queasiness at the sight of blood or cruelty he had become the competent manager of a mass murder machine that would commit extermination on a scale that the world had never seen before. He never doubted that what Hitler had asked of him was absolutely necessary to the future of the new Reich, that it was a righteous and just cause, one that was without question, both distasteful and difficult, but one that had to be taken on and was something the SS could and would do with a sense of responsibility, pride, and efficiency.

Because of who he was, Himmler expected this job to be done competently and without personal individual artifice. He saw it as a difficult job that needed to be dispassionately and professionally done. Early on, he forbade independent action against the Jews, by any member of his organization.

"The SS commander must be hard but not hardened. If, during your work, you come across cases in which some commander exceeds his duty or shows signs that his restraint is becoming blurred, intervene at once."

When reviewing one such situation involving an unauthorized shooting of Jews, he sent down this directive to the SS legal department.

"If the motive is selfish, sadistic or sexual, judicial punishment should be imposed for murder or manslaughter as the case may be."

Himmler's understanding was that it was a dirty job, but it had to be done and the Fuhrer had chosen the SS to do it. The SS, the elite of Germany, would do as ordered, but there were going to be rules and they would be steadfastly followed. If not, proper and severe justice would be brought to bear.

Heinrich Himmler was by any standard, a complex and unique man

* * * * *

- The Posen Speeches -

In October of nineteen forty-three, Himmler gave two speeches in the city of Posen. These were secret meetings and those forming the audience were there by invitation only.

Of the SS's management, thirty-three Obergruppenführers, fifty-one Gruppenführers and eight Brigadeführers from over the Reich were present. Many of these came from areas of occupied Eastern Europe. Large parts of the speech were therefore concerned the precarious situation on the Eastern Front. War and resistance successes by the supposedly sub-human Slavs required an explanation in order for the SS officers to agree to the imminent and arduous battles in the third winter of the Russian campaign.

Only around two minutes of the speech directly concern the destruction of the Jews. During this time Himmler postulates his audience's experiences with mass shootings, ghetto liquidations and extermination camps, and accordingly, their knowledge of them. This part of his speech is aimed at justifying the crimes already perpetrated, and to commit its listeners to the *'higher purpose'* bestowed upon them. Approximately fifty officers could not be present.

They were sent a copy of the speech and had to confirm, in writing, their acknowledgment of it.

This first meeting was held in the town hall on October fourth, and the audience was made up of the senior SS commanders. The second took place two days later on October sixth. In this instance, the audience was composed of both *'Gau'* (regional administrators) and Reich leaders.

Historically, Himmler had eagerly broadcast the construction of his first concentration camp to the German public as it was intended to act as a *'stick'* to discourage those who were not committed party followers. At that time those individuals being rounded up and sent to this camp were primarily political in nature. Hitler believed that the general population would accept this situation without much concern and he was right.

Once the political enemies of the party had been locked behind barbed wire and the Nazis had begun to round up those they considered as sub-human, which included the Jews, the existence of the camps, of necessity, had become restricted and *'out of sight, out of mind'*. Knowledge of all new camps had then become a closely held secret, shared with only those who had a need to know.

The recently constructed, dedicated *'special handling'* camps, which had been designed for the sole purpose of exterminating humans, took the consideration of public knowledge up a notch. Knowledge of these camps had to be extremely restricted and was to be considered top secret.

Due to the reversal in the direction of the war, Hitler had decided that it was now important that the existence of these camps and their true purpose be shared with a slightly larger audience. He had therefore instructed Himmler to make his two speeches in Posen.

The Fuhrer had a couple of good reasons for doing this.

The Allies had indicated that they were going to pursue criminal charges for German war crimes and Hitler hoped to strengthen the loyalty and silence of his subordinates by making them all parties to the ongoing genocide of the Jews.

He believed that in ensuring that all party leaders were made aware of these plans and actions, it would be impossible for them to later deny knowledge and support for the plan. He felt that by making them co-conspirators in the *'final solution'* he would oblige them to fight to win the war with more determination, in view of the personal consequences of a loss.

Additionally, the existence of these camps and the knowledge of what was now taking place had, over time, begun to leak out and by enlarging the circle of those privy to the extermination of the Jews to include the leading members of the party and the military in the *'final solution'*, he hoped to stem the spread of information. He strove to drive home the seriousness of the situation with the need to keep information flow in check and away from the general population until it was a *'fait accompli'*.

The first speech Himmler gave to the SS leadership took three hours to deliver.

There have been many translations of this speech undertaken and they are worth reading in their entirety. Because of the document's length, it makes sense to summarize and quote only specific sections, in order to understand the core information the speech provides. In so doing, it is only sensible that one be very much aware of the old saying *'lost in translation'* and also of the fact that certain translated words can often have more than one meaning.

Additionally it is worth noting that there have been excerpts from this speech that have been translated with a definite bias and a careful selection of the connotation to create a biased meaning of some of these multi-meaning words, in order to reflect a chosen point of view.

Suffice to say however, there is little doubt that any of those who sat in the audience of these two speeches, who had not been fully aware of what had gone on in the camps up to this point, knew exactly what *'special handling'* meant, before they left the room.

In His first speech, which was made to the commanding officers of Himmler's own SS, the *'Reichsfuhrer'* faced what he considered to be his hardest sell. While many in the room were only generally aware of some of the activities of the new camps, some were completely in the picture and knew exactly what was going on.

Himmler's problem was that he had to convince the entire SS leadership that the implementation of this necessary, but distasteful crusade which had been assigned to his men, was not at variance with the highest principles of their order, which he had laboriously laid out for them.

The *'Reichsfuhrer'* began the speech on the fourth by honoring the fallen. He then provided an overview of the difficult situation facing them in the fifth year of the war, commented on the Russian leadership, the invasion of Russia, the winter of forty-one/ two, the events of forty-two and what had taken place so far in forty-three.

He then moved on to addressing the human potential of the Russians, spending a good deal of time on the subject to set the stage for his conclusion suggesting that they were near collapse. He then touched on the partisan war and the ability of a superior minority to successfully rule over conquered masses. A lecture on the phycology of the slaves followed and then an evaluation of how a good SS member could hold to his superior view of life, while dealing with the realities of conquering sub-human races. He touched on how the overrun Russians could eventually be used as soldiers by the Germans in a minority formation, after being provided indoctrination and under the direction and control of German officers.

He shifted from there to offer his evaluation on the war theaters, Russian, and Italian and then denounced the Italians for their hopelessness as an Ally. He applauded the successful rescue of *'Il Duce'*. He touched on the situation in the Balkans and other occupied territories and the new war against sabotage.

Next, he touched on the air war, the naval war and the domestic front. He frankly admitted recent failures but painted a bright future for each, to be brought about by better equipment and organization.

He discussed the problems of dealing with the masses of people now brought under German occupation but suggested that over time a firm hand would check this difficulty and turn these sub-humans into slave workers for the betterment of the new Reich.

He then turned to an evaluation of the Allied side in the war. Individually he gave his overview of the Russians, the English and the

Americans and their political problems. Although honest in many ways, this assessment was delivered through *'rose colored'* glasses.

Himmler now moved to the part the SS had and would play in the war, lauding their growth and accomplishments and covering the personal changes to date and the general expansion of the organization. Now he went into specifics of the different arms of the SS and the part each would play in the future steps needed to win the war.

He then outlined his own responsibility for the remainder of the war.

"In addition to all else we've achieved in this time, I cannot keep silent about the fact that I have become Reichminister of the Interior. I have a little more work. I view my responsibilities as falling into the following general groups:

Restoration of the authority of the Reich, which to a great extent has been lost.

Decentralization of tasks not of importance to the Reich. To keep the Reich in hand, while calling upon all the creative powers slumbering in the German people under German self-government.

Radical elimination of corruption or misconduct through this entire apparatus and in every case.

I will proceed ruthlessly. If somebody has done something wrong and if I catch him, he's coming before the Khadi, big or little, since such a case exorcised and carried out in public, does not harm respect for the state and party, but strengthens it, because then everybody says 'All kinds of respect. Decent. If somebody's a rascal, throw him out.'

That applies just as much to us within the SS. I am now coming to a few things which, as is my custom, I will state clearly. It is quite clear that human shortcomings are found everywhere. Organizations distinguish themselves only through the following:

One organization conceals them and thinks it has to cover them up with three famous blanket of Christian brotherly love, so as not to hurt its prestige. Another organization cleanses itself brutally. It says 'He was a swine, we've shot him' or 'we've locked him up' or in any case, 'We threw him out'. Then it says 'Now, get busy and blabber about it or do something else'. That gives it the right to sway 'If anybody else among you is a swine, then he's going to get the same'.

As Reichsfuhrer SS, as Chief of the German Police, and now as Reichminister of the Interior, I would have no moral right to proceed against any racial comrade, nor could we bring forth the strength to do so, if we did not take care to cleanse our own ranks brutally.

You can be sure that I will do this as Reichminister of the Interior. You can also be sure that I will not go off at a madman's clip and then maybe pull the bridle so hard that the nag falls down on his hindquarters; rather, the bit will be pulled slowly and gradually, so the horse will be brought to a decent pace again."

Himmler then lectured them on the need to work hard on making a success of the individual personal SS economic commercial operations.

That done, he shifted gears and made his move to carry out Hitler's instructions to widen the extent of those in the know, about the *'Final Solution to the Jewish Question'.*

Here is the crucial part of what he told them.

"I also want to refer here very frankly to a very difficult matter. We can now very openly talk about this among ourselves, and yet we will never discuss this publicly. Just as we did not hesitate on (referring to the night of the long knives), to perform our duty as ordered and put comrades who had failed up against the wall and execute them, we also never spoke about it, nor will we ever speak about it. Let us thank God that we had within us enough self-evident fortitude never to discuss it among us, and we never talked about it. Every one of us was horrified, and yet every one clearly understood that we would do it next time, when the order is given and when it becomes necessary

I am now referring to the evacuation of the Jews, to the extermination of the Jewish People. This is something that is easily said: 'The Jewish People will be exterminated', says every party member, 'this is very obvious, it is in our program - elimination of the Jews, extermination, a small matter.' And then they turn up, the upstanding eighty million Germans, and each one has his decent Jew. They say the others are all 'swine', but this particular one is a splendid

Jew. But none has observed it, endured it. Most of you here know what it means when one hundred corpses lie next to each other, when there are five hundred or when there are one thousand. To have endured this and at the same time to have remained a decent person - with exceptions due to human weaknesses - has made us tough, and is a glorious chapter that has not and will not be spoken of. Because we know how difficult it would be for us if we still had Jews as secret saboteurs, agitators and rabble-rousers in every city, what with the bombings, with the burden and with the hardships of the war. If the Jews were still part of the German nation, we would most likely arrive now at the state we were at in nineteen sixteen and seventeen.

The riches they had, we've taken away from them. I have given a strict order, which the SS Group Leader Pohl has carried out, that these riches shall, of course, be diverted to the Reich without exception. We have taken none of it. Individuals who failed were punished according to an order given by me at the beginning, which threatened: he who takes even one mark of it, that's his death.

A number of SS men, not very many, have violated that order and that will be their death. Without Mercy! We had the moral right, we had the duty to our own people, to kill this people which wanted to kill us. That doesn't mean, that in so doing, we want to be infected by that bacillus and die. I will never permit even one little spot of corruption to arise or become established here. Wherever it may form, we shall burn it out together. In general, however, we can say that we have carried out this most difficult task out of love for our own people and we have suffered no harm to our inner self, our soul, our character, in so doing."

Himmler then turned his attention toward driving home his vision of what strict principles and actions were necessary to make an SS man. He extolled their superiority in all things good and the elite position in which the organization was held in its service to the new German Reich and made it more than clear, in great detail, that he would accept no lesser behavior on the part of any man wearing an SS uniform.

The second speech, which Himmler gave to the Reichsleiters and Gauleiters on the sixth, had been adjusted to fit his new audience. The pivotal topic had not been adjusted. He told them.

"The sentence 'The Jews must be exterminated' with its few words gentleman, can be uttered easily. But what that sentence demands of the man who must execute it is the hardest and toughest thing in existence."

The captive audience had to know what was coming, the confirmation of what many of them had been choosing to ignore for several months. Himmler continued.

"I ask you only to hear and never talk about what I tell you in this circle. When the question arose, 'What should be done with the women and children?' I decided here also to adopt a clear solution. I did not deem myself justified in exterminating the men, which is to say to kill them or let them be killed, while allowing their children to grow up to avenge themselves on our sons and grandchildren. The hard decision had to be taken...this people must disappear from the face of the earth."

He told them that this assignment had been the most arduous ever given the SS.

"It was carried out - I think I can say - without our men and our leaders suffering the slightest damage to spirt or soul."

In closing, he said.

"You now know what is what and you must keep it to yourself. Perhaps at a much later time we shall consider whether something about it can be told to the German people. But it is probably better to bear the responsibility on behalf of our people - a responsibility for the deed as well as for the idea - and take the secret with us into our graves."

One of those in attendance, Baldur von Schirach, once the leader of the Hitler Youth and at this time holing the position of *'Gauleiter'* or *'Reichsstatthalter'* of Vienna, later commented:

"He spoke with such icy coldness of the extermination of men, women and children, as a businessman speaks of his balance sheet. There was nothing emotional in the speech, nothing that suggested an inner involvement."

The indisputable facts of *'The final Solution to the Jewish Question'* had now been clearly shared with those in the audience. A larger group was now in the know and as Hitler had intended, the idea of losing the war was no longer something any of them wished in the slightest to contemplate.

* * * * *

- V-2 Rocket -

On October nineteenth, the German limited company *'Mittelwerk'* (GmbH) was issued War Contract No. 0011-5565/43 by General Emil Leeb, head of the Army Weapons Office, for twelve thousand of the latest designed A-4 missiles, at a cost of forty thousand Reichsmarks each.

* * * * *

- *'Jagdpanther'* -

In October of forty-three, the prototype for what would become the tank destroyer, using the 8.8 cm Pak gun and the Panther tank chassis, was demonstrated for Hitler.

* * * * *

- Deportations -

The Danish underground assists in the transport by sea of seven thousand, two hundred and twenty Danish Jews to safety in Sweden.

On October fourteenth, knowing the camp is about to be closed, the inmates of Sobibor, with assistance from Russian POW's, stage a revolt. Three hundred escape. Of these only fifty survive. All traces of the extermination camp are then removed and trees are planted over the site.

On October sixteenth the Germans begin to round up the Jews in Rome. One thousand are put aboard rail cars, destination Auschwitz.

* * * * *

- Ghettos -

- Minsk -

The Germans liquidate the ghetto on October twenty-first. The remaining Jews are sent to the Sobibor and Maly Trosetenets extermination camps for *'special handling'*.

* * * * *

- Kovno -

The ghetto in Kovno provided slave labor for the German military. Jews were employed primarily as forced laborers at various sites outside the ghetto, especially in the construction of a military airbase in *'Aleksotas'*.

The Jewish Council running the camp believed the Germans would not kill Jews who were producing for the army and had also created workshops inside the ghetto for those women, children, and elderly who could not participate in the labor brigades. These workshops employed almost sixty-five hundred people.

In the autumn of forty-three, the SS assumed control of the ghetto and converted it into the Kovno concentration camp. Immediately the Jewish Council's role in day to day affairs was drastically curtailed. Thirty-five hundred inmates were then dispersed to sub-camps, where strict discipline governed all aspects of daily life. On October twenty-sixth, the SS deported in excess of twenty-seven hundred people from the main camp, sending those deemed fit to work to the Vaivara concentration camp in Estonia, and transporting the surviving children and the elderly to Auschwitz for *'special handling'*.

* * * * *

- Concentration Camps -

- Treblinka -

On October nineteenth, *'Operation Reinhard'* was terminated by a letter from Odilo Globocnik. The following day, a large group of Jewish *'Arbeitskommandos'* who had worked on dismantling the camp structures over the past several weeks were loaded onto the train and transported to Sobibor for *'special handling'* on October twentieth. Cleanup operations continued over the winter.

* * * * *

- Majdanek -

Until nineteen forty-three the camp was officially classified as a POW camp run by the Waffen-SS, but in mid-February it had been reclassified as a concentration camp. *'Special handling'* operations had begun here in October of forty-two and continued into the fall of forty-three.

* * * * *

- The Family -

- Karl and Wilhelm -

'Operation Fatherland', due to the strict diligence in planning its initial structure by its handful of creators, was now functioning like a well-oiled machine. At this advanced stage of development, each of its individual operational cells, using the experience it had developed since inception, was functioning independently with very little need for supervision and incidents that required higher decision making.

Demand for information about new super weapon designs on the part of both Hitler and Himmler had in no way lessened; however the free time of both men to languish over such items had definitely decreased. Thus, without the risk of initiating the situation himself,

Karl's intent to do his best to distance him and his family, as well as the leaders of the separate `Operation Fatherland's'` cells, from the Nazi leadership, was given a boost by the increased work demands now placed upon the two powerful German leaders.

Less time spent in Berlin and *'Wolfsschanze',* meant more time for the Count and Wilhelm with the rest of the family at castle von Stauffer.

There had been one incident of serious concern however, that had come up during the month.

Both Karl and Wilhelm had received an invitation to hear Himmler's upcoming speech which was to be given at Posen on the sixth of October.

Upon receipt of this invitation, which was very clearly a thinly-veiled command, the Count's initial response was to accept. Obviously, with things not going well on all fronts, he expected the speech would be nothing more than a morale-building exercise, aimed at garnering a stronger war effort. Given a moment of sober second thought however, he decided to contact General Dieter Bichler in order to ascertain what the upcoming speech was all about.

Two days later they arranged to meet at the family's Berlin mansion for dinner and after trading innocuous banter during the meal, the two men, Wilhelm having begged off to spend the night with his current girlfriend, had retired to the Count's library for brandy and cigars and to discuss the real reason for the get-together.

Once the cigars had been lit and without preamble, Karl handed the invitations to the General.

Dieter glanced at them briefly and then handed them back to him.

"I've one of my own, so I don't have to read them, but I am somewhat surprised that you and Wilhelm have received them. I would have thought that, thanks to the Fuhrer, you had been able to distance yourself enough from the Reichsfuhrer-SS to slip under the radar for this particular type of treatment."

Intrigued, the Count raised an eyebrow and spread his hands out before him in an *'elucidate please'* gesture.

The General continued.

"There are to be two meetings scheduled one on the fourth and this one on the sixth. The first is to be presented to SS commanders only and the second, the one to which you and Wilhelm have been directed to attend, is intended for Reichsleiters and Gauleiters..."

The General paused, pursed his lips and then shook his head slowly before continuing.

"This is not good. I am cognizant of the content and purpose of these two speeches."

The count raised a hand and opened his mouth to interject, but Bichler cut him off.

"Just bear with me for a moment, while I consider the ramifications of this situation Karl and hear me out on this before we discuss it further."

Karl nodded his assent, dropped his hand into his lap and sat back in his chair to listen.

Both men lifted their glasses and drank and as the General set his glass down on the table between them he began to speak again.

"The central topic of these two speeches is something that, in view of what you will be called on to do to advance the objectives of *'Operation Fatherland'* once this damned war is over, is one that neither you nor Wilhelm should be in any way linked to at war's end.

You are going to have to accept my assessment of this situation as correct, as a matter of faith I'm afraid, in that a discussion about it here and now would be just as damning to you as would your attendance at Himmler's meeting itself. I can tell you this. The central topic has to do with a subject that will have serious repercussions after the war ends, for those who had knowledge of its occurrence or were involved in carrying it out. You have no current awareness of it, and to the best of my knowledge neither does Wilhelm. For the sake of everything we have done so far for *'Operation Fatherland'*, neither of you can attend this meeting."

The Count, as a matter of curiosity, was tempted to probe more deeply but the look on the SS-General's face was enough to convince him to keep silent. For his part, Bichler's mind was struggling to find a way out of the problem. He raised his drink, drained it and Karl stood up and took their glasses over to the sideboard to refresh them.

He then set the refills on the table and resumed his seat.

The General, deep in thought, drummed his fingers on the table and then let out a sigh.

"You no doubt noted the rider in the so called *'invitation'* to the meeting, the proviso that those who were not able to attend would be receiving a copy of the speech which was then to be initialed as read and returned to the office of the Reichsfuhrer. A list of those so doing will no doubt be on file somewhere after the war and you do not want to have your names on that list either.

Therefore you will not only have to find an acceptable excuse for not attending, but also avoid the proviso itself."

Bichler looked over at Karl.

"Is there some way that you can get Hitler to intervene and order Himmler to remove you from the list of invitees? At this stage, anything else will be insufficient to keep you out of this thing."

Karl pursed his lips and thought for a second before responding.

"There is perhaps one possibility. I have been instructed to arrange for Hitler to observe the testing of the *'Jagdpanther'*, the prototype for the new heavy, self-propelled tank destroyer. I could probably manage to arrange it for the morning of the sixth without raising any questions. Then I could inform Bormann of the date and he would add it to Hitler's agenda. Once it was there I could then raise the matter of it now conflicts with Himmler's recent invitation to the speech and let Bormann make the decision on his own. He will refer it to Hitler and knowing the Fuhrer as I do, he will not allow anything to interfere with an opportunity to make his own assessment of, and to comment on, a new weapon. He will instruct Bormann accordingly and when Bormann contacts me with his answer, I will ask him to notify Himmler's staff of the Fuhrer's decision, which is that both Wilhelm and I be removed from the list of those invited to the speech."

The General rolled his head slightly from side to side as he considered the idea and then nodded.

"That would do it and I doubt that Himmler will even be made personally aware of the change. Will Hitler let you include Wilhelm in this though?"

Kart smiled as he reached for his glass.

"Oh yes, the Fuhrer seems to be of the opinion that Wilhelm is an expert in super weapons. He is at my side whenever we see the Fuhrer in that regard. Thank you General, for your guidance in this matter."

Bichler simply waved his hand in a dismissive gesture.

* * * * *

- Eric -

Their existence now one of peaceful contentment, Eric and Heidi, who was now definitely showing and reflecting the best aspects of her advancing pregnancy, had settled in to a very comfortable routine; Heidi as head of a growing household staff and Eric deeply involved with the day to day responsibilities of overseeing the operation of both the family owned mining enterprise and that of the research and development facility's nestled deep below the mountain.

* * * * *

- Friedrichshafen -

Karl and Wilhelm were able to spend more of their time at the castle, where day to day activities were flowing very smoothly, under the ever watchful eye of the Countess, Erika. Despite some wartime shortages, the war itself seemed to be happening far away and was of little concern to those who lived in Friedrichshafen.

Ursula, who was no longer needed to the previous degree for the task of cataloguing arriving treasures, had been complaining for several weeks about being bored. The Countess, who had readily picked up her daughter's need for labour of some sort, had promptly done something to solve the problem.

At her mother's urging, Ursula was now organizing the set up for a spring leap into plans for the castle to become self-sufficient in relation to its food supplies. In the works there were preparations for vegetable gardens and the other components of a working farm, which a strong-minded Ursula had determined would include chickens, cows and pigs among other strange things.

A bundled up Ursula could be regularly seen trudging about outside as she selected specific areas for future seeding, or ensconced in the library researching animal husbandry among and bizarre topics, that Erika had neither the desire nor patience to comprehend.

The Countess, who had been the one to push the idea in the first place was by this point not quite sure if she had created a monster; however Ursula was now being kept very busy with her plans and so her Mother was content to let things go, at least for the time being.

Although the Countess made no comment, she admitted to herself that cows aside, the thought of hoards of chickens and pigs running about the grounds did alarm her to a degree.

CHAPTER TWENTY

- October -

- Allied Air Operations -

- Europe -

Targets for Bomber Command include Frankfurt, Kassel and Munich. Light aircraft strike both railroads and airfields. They drop thirteen thousand tons of explosives.

The heavy bombers of the American Eighth Air Force hit Anklam, Bremen and Emden with four thousand, seven hundred tons. The Americans also hit Schweinfurt, targeting the bearing manufactures, causing heavy damage but with a great loss of aircraft. Additionally they attacked French airfields with eight hundred and fifty tons.

* * * * *

- Pacific -

Air missions are frequent and delivered in many geographical locations. Rabaul is most heavily hit, being targeted on five occasions.

* * * * *

- Maritime Warfare -

- Atlantic -

The operational distances of Allied air patrols have been extended by the use of airfields in the Azores. The newly equipped U-boat strength has increased to one hundred and seventy-five operational vessels with two hundred and thirty-seven in training or on sea trials.   They have little success and twenty-six are sent to the bottom.

* * * * *

- October First -

- Italy -

The citizens of Naples successfully complete their uprising against the Germans as the Nazi occupiers pull out of the city.

* * * * *

- October Second -

- New Guinea -

Finschhafen is taken by the Australians.

* * * * *

- October Third -

- Aegean -

The Germans land on island of Kos. Over the next twenty-four hours they capture it and take fourteen hundred British and three thousand, one hundred and fifty Italians, prisoner.

* * * * *

- October Fourth -

- Corsica -

Free French forces liberate the island.

* * * * *

- New Guinea -

Australian forces capture Kumpu.

* * * * *

- October Fifth -

- Italy -

The invading Allies cross the Volturno Line.

* * * * *

- October Sixth -

- Italy -

As the British on the east coast begin to gain the upper hand around Termoli, the American Fifth Army takes Caserta and Capua.

* * * * *

- October Seventh -

- Eastern Front -

In the north, the Russians take Nevel and at the western end of the Kuban Peninsula, Taman is captured.

* * * * *

- October Eighth -

- Italy -

The British Eighth Army takes Larino and Guglionesi Island.

* * * * *

- October Tenth -

- Eastern Front -

Russian troops take Dobrush.

* * * * *

- Italy -

The US Fifth takes Portelandalfo.

* * * * *

- October Eleventh -

- Eastern Front -

Russian forces capture Novobelista which is situated on the outskirts of Gomel.

* * * * *

- October Twelfth -

- New Britain -

In the opening salvo of *'Operation Cartwheel'*, three hundred and forty-nine planes from the US Fifth Air Forces drop three hundred and fifty tons on Rabaul in a surprise attack.

* * * * *

- October Thirteenth -

- Rome -

Italy declares war on Germany.

* * * * *

- October Fourteenth -

- Sobibor Camp -

Inmates initiate an attack against their Ukrainian guards and their SS masters. They kill eleven members of the SS and several guards but the revolt is uncovered quickly and many of the inmates are killed while the remainder is forced to run for their lives under heavy fire.

* * * * *

- Eastern Front -

Russian forces take Zaporozhye and cut the rail line leading to the Crimea from Melitopol.

* * * * *

- Italy -

The First Canadian Division takes Campobasso.

* * * * *

- October Fifteenth -

- Italy -

The Canadians take Vinchiaturo.

* * * * *

- October Seventeenth -

- Eastern Front -

Russian forces take Loyev.

* * * * *

- Italy -

US troops take Liberi and Alvignano.

* * * * *

- October Eighteenth -

- Italy -

The Americans take Gioia.

* * * * *

- October Nineteenth -

- Berlin -

A contract is signed by the Nazi War Office ordering twelve

thousand V-2 rockets.

* * * * *

- Eastern Front -

Russian troops capture Vishgorod.

* * * * *

- October Twentieth -

- Italy -

US troops take Piedimonte d'Alife.

* * * * *

- October Twenty-Second -

- Germany -

An overnight Allied air raid on Kassel causes a firestorm which lasts for a week.

* * * * *

- October Twenty-Third -

- Eastern Front -

After a hard-fought ten day battle, the Russians take Melitopol.

* * * * *

- English Channel -

The British cruiser HMS *'Charybdis'* is sunk and the destroyer *'Limboure'* is damaged by German torpedo boats.

* * * * *

- Italy -

British troops take Sparanise.

* * * * *

- October Twenty-Fourth -

- Italy -

US forces take Sant Angelo.

* * * * *

- October Twenty-Fifth -

- Eastern Front -

The Russians take Dnepropetrovsk and Dneprodzerzhinsk.

* * * * *

- October Twenty-Seventh -

- Italy -

The British capture Montefalcone.

* * * * *

- October Twenty-Ninth -

- Italy -

The British take Cantalupo.

* * * * *

- October Thirtieth -

- Italy -

US forces take Mondragone.

* * * * *

- October Thirty-First -

- Italy -

Heavy rains begin to slow the Allied advance. The British take Teano.

* * * * *

- Eastern Front -

Russian forces take Chaplinka and are now in control of all the railroad lines leading out of the Crimea. In so doing they have cut off the movement of all German supplies to that front.

CHAPTER TWENTY-ONE

- November -

- Hitler -

Despite, or perhaps because of, the worsening military situation now apparent, the Fuhrer is spending a good deal of his time fantasizing about his concept for the future of the world.

Among his subordinates, he has begun to expand and articulate on his intentions with regard to his *'New Order in Western Europe'*.

It became apparent that what he had initially described quite simply as an *'amalgamation of states for the common good'* was, after many months of German occupation, in reality an euphemism for his plan to use his newly conquered territories by plundering their economies and using their citizens as forced labour for the betterment of the German Reich.

Exactly how this goal was to be accomplished hadn't been outlined in any detail prior to the start of the war. Planning for the upcoming war itself had taken priority then, but German bureaucratic efficiency being what it is, there had been in the works an expanding preparation for accomplishing the task, based on the experience gained after each of the territories had fallen to the German war machine.

Not surprisingly, millions of those who had been overrun were not particularly pleased at the thought of willingly becoming vassals of the German state. As this became apparent to those responsible for bringing Hitler's plans for the *'New Order'* to fruition, gentle persuasion had understandably given way to the efficient use of brute force.

By this point, the day to day function of ensuring that those individuals who now found themselves to be part of the *'New Reich'* were expected to properly fulfill their new responsibilities to the Reich. Acts of work stoppage and sabotage in occupied territory were swiftly responded to with enforced labour and execution of hostages. Legalized pillaging, rail cars packed with food, clothing, machinery, vehicles and art treasures moving in a steady stream to Germany from Denmark, Norway, France, Belgium, and Luxembourg, was an accepted fact of life. This on top of the fact that each conquered country was obliged to pay huge *'occupation assessments'* to their new masters. This, for enjoying the privilege of the provision of appropriate German oversight for the betterment of their daily lives.

Hitler involved himself directly in the planning and implementation of his *'New Order'*. He kept up to date on new policy implementations his bureaucracy had come up with as he deemed changes were required. At a party leadership meeting in Berlin, he began to flesh out this concept for the *'New Order in Western Europe'*. He told those in attendance the following:

"All that rubbish of small states still existing in Europe must be liquidated as fast as possible. The aim of our struggle must be to create a unified Europe: the Germans alone can really organize Europe".

Amazingly, despite the oppressive conditions now in place, the vast majority of those living in occupied territory accepted their fate. In order for them to live somewhat ordinary lives, they were prepared to accede and make the best of what they felt as the inevitable long-term reality.

Hitler had additional ideas for the future, of course: a new *'European Order'* was to eventually morph into a new *'World Order"*, but he did not, as yet, share these outside his inner circle.

There was no limit to what part Germany was to play in this new world.

Some of Hitler's musings on the topic:

Once Germany had won the war England would be allowed to remain in its current form. The King would be removed and replaced with the Duke of Windsor and then Germany would arrange a permanent treaty of friendship with England.

The Iberian Peninsula would be joined with Scandinavia.

The US was to be sidelined from world politics and its Jewish community was to be destroyed. Goebbels would act as Governor there and undertake the re-education of the racially mixed and inferior population. Goering would be responsible for mobilizing all those who had German blood. The men in the US could then be educated militarily and regenerated nationalistically.

* * * * *

- Inner Circle -

- Reality Shunned -

Hitler was not alone in his increasing shift from reality to fantasy with regard to the world around him. In varying degrees, all the members of the *'Inner Circle'* were following the same course.

In normal times and under normal conditions, an individual who turns his back on reality is quickly brought out of their reverie by a loss of credibility brought on by the ridicule and reproach of those who surround them. Among the leaders of Nazi Germany at this time there was no longer any such sounding board available. Rose colored glasses were now the *'dress of the day'* in this limited group and to some extent they all lived within a dream-world that offered very few and heavily draped windows into the real world.

* * * * *

- Goering -

The Reichsmarschall was in denial.

Still the official number two man in Germany, Goering's influence with Hitler was in a downhill spiral. In addition to his inability to effectively manage his offices, he was very aware of Hitler's dislike of bad news, which, in view of the increased Allied bombing, was all that was currently available.

Goering retreated into hiding whenever possible but in order to make the best of things he was unable to fade completely into the background. When cornered on specific topics he did not wish to discuss, the corpulent Reichsmarschall did his best to put some positive spin on it and then move quickly onto another subject.

An example of how he dealt with a current situation he found himself in, was indicative.

General Galland, the man in charge of the Luftwaffe fighter squadrons, which were mainly held responsible for stopping the Allied bombing had told Hitler that several US fighters had been shot down in a recent bombing run made over Aachen. He went on to tell the Fuhrer that obviously the Americans had developed improved fuel capacity for their fighters and this meant that they were now able to increase their protective coverage of the American daytime bombing raids much deeper into German territory.

Hitler had shared Galland's concern over this development and quickly brought the matter up with Goering, who had promptly dismissed such comments as Allied propaganda. A short while later Galland ran into Goering who soundly ripped into him for making any such suggestion to the Fuhrer.

Galland held his ground, firmly stating that in fact American fighters had been shot down over Aachen during the raid and despite Goering's alternating pleas and possible explanations as to how some mistake had probably been made in such a report, he simply repeated that it was a fact.

Galland would not budge on the point and in the end, a furious Goering, told him that he himself had told Hitler that no American fighters had been shot down over Aachen. He then issued the General a direct order to the effect that if asked again, he was to answer that *'no American fighters had been over the target'*.

Messy facts which put him in a bad light were no longer to be entertained in Goering's world. They were now simply untrue or enemy propaganda

* * * * *

- Speer -

As did the others in the Nazi hierarchy, Speer had unconsciously begun choosing to concentrate his thoughts on the few positive things happening around him and to view the reality of the overall situation through another set of those tinted glasses.

Speer owed his auspicious position to Hitler and like most men at the pinnacle of their power, had no desire to allow his conscious thought to examine or even accept the increasing reality of the growing collapse of his immediate world. Having been soundly thwarted again and again, he had all but given up the battles to bring about positive change in a system which had man-made barriers ensconced at every twist and turn.

He was now, more often than not, satisfied to go with the flow and hope for the best.

* * * * *

- Goebbels -

Of all those in the *'inner circle'*, Goebbels was probably the least likely to ignore reality. It was not in his nature.

That did not however, make him any less susceptible to the domino effect that had resulted from Hitler's new outlook on the situation facing Germany. Hitler was committed to the path he had chosen. Privately he was no longer absolutely convinced that he would succeed in gaining all his goals, but he was resolved to see the fight to achieve them play out, whatever the end result.

There could be no turning back.

Goebbels was just as human as the others in the Nazi hierarchy. He was at the panicle of his power. Hitler had put him there and kept him there. He still believed in Hitler's vision and had no desire to see the regime crumble.

Goebbels was not a military man, nor was he directly involved in the *'Final Solution to the Jewish* Question'. Those areas fell under the expertise of others and he had neither the ability nor the desire to actively involve himself in them.

He was the Minister of Propaganda, Hitler's supporter and Hitler's voice to the German people. He was the Protector of Nazi culture.

Goebbels worshiped Hitler. He existed only to please his master.

If need be, he would willingly die for the Fuhrer. He could not afford to even consider losing this war.

The reality of the current situation was something Hitler had chosen to put on the back burner and Goebbels, who did not want to upset or disappoint his Fuhrer, had no intention of venturing there, unless specifically asked by the Fuhrer to do so. If and when Hitler did ask for his advice on a certain matter, he responded, but did so with great care and an eye to keeping within the new boundaries deemed acceptable to his leader.

When he was around the Fuhrer, Goebbels now wore his own pair of those rosy glasses.

* * * * *

- Himmler -

Despite the worsening military situation, the SS-Reichsfuhrer was riding high in his beloved Fuhrer's esteem.

His expanded and excellently equipped armed SS military units had demonstrated much better fighting capabilities than those of the battered and under-equipped Wehrmacht. Even more importantly, Himmler was the man who was delivering on Hitler's need to fulfill his obsession of `The final Solution to the Jewish Question`.

Hitler might be frustrated by the progress of his military, but he had no complaints when it came to how the Jews were being dealt with.

Himmler's progress in this regard was intoxicating for Hitler and his God-given mission was rapidly reaching its culmination.

Hitler may not have liked Himmler, and it was common knowledge that he kept him at a distance in a social sense, but the Fuhrer could certainly find no fault with the man, who never disagreed with him and always had good news to deliver.

Himmler didn't need the colored glasses. He was at the top of his form and everything around him was coming up roses and would continue to do so, as long as Hitler remained at the helm and Germany had any chance of winning the war.

Himmler was definitely going to do his best to see that that happened.

* * * * *

- Bormann -

Not in it, but always on the periphery of the inner circle, Bormann nevertheless spent more time with Hitler than any of the others. Over time he had made himself indispensable to the Fuhrer and he maintained that position by taking great care to be always aware of what Hitler wanted, believed and needed at any given moment in time and providing exactly that.

Those in the inner circle could afford to drift in and out of Hitler's immediate circle, depending on the situation. For example, if Hitler became angry with Goering, the Reichsmarschall would simply fade into the background for a while and await an opportune moment to reenter the scene. He might be somewhat tarnished when he did so, but by carefully stroking the Fuhrer the previous unhappy situation could usually be pushed to the back of Hitler's mind and if not forgotten, at least forgiven.

Bormann could not afford any such luxury.

If Hitler was to become angry with him and as a result Bormann fell out of favor, there would be no coming back for him. He had far too many enemies for that to happen.

Additionally, if Bormann had no other option but to deliver bad news to Hitler, which he carefully worked to avoid, you can be sure that someone else was going to take the blame for whatever had gone wrong and it was going to be very effectively laid at their door.

It certainly wasn't going to have anything to do with Bormann.

Bormann controlled Hitler's calendar. If Bormann did not want someone to see Hitler, it was generally the case that it didn't happen. It followed that if someone wanted to get to the Fuhrer, he had to satisfy Bormann first. An end run around Bormann to see Hitler was an option of course, but it would immediately put you on Bormann's blacklist and experience had soundly demonstrated that that did no bode well for an individual's future prospects.

Bormann did not to begin to wear rose colored glasses at this point in the war. He had taken out the patent on them a very long time ago.

* * * * *

- SS Expansion -

The *'16th SS Panzergrenadier Division Reichsführer-SS'* was a *'Panzergrenadier'* is formed in November by adding *'Volksdeutsche'* recruits to the *'Sturmbrigade Reichsführer SS'*, which was used as the cadre for this new division.

The Waffen-SS has increased in size from eight divisions and some brigades to sixteen divisions.

* * * * *

- FSSF -

The *'1st Special Service Force'* (also referred to as *The Devil's Brigade*, *The Black Devils*, and *The Black Devils' Brigade*) was an elite, joint Canadian and American commando unit. This unit was organized in forty-two and trained in the US at Fort William Henry Harrison near Helena, Montana.

The initial concept for such a fighting unit had come from scientist Geoffrey Pyke, of the British Combined Operations Command, who envisioned the creation of a small, elite British military force capable of fighting behind enemy lines in winter conditions.

He envisioned that such a unit would then be landed, by sea or air, into occupied Norway, Romania, and the Italian Alps, on sabotage missions against hydroelectric plants and oil fields.

In Norway, for the Allies, the chief industrial threat was the creation of the heavy water required for the German atomic weapon research being conducted at Rjukan. In Romania, there were the strategically important Ploesti oil fields that met one quarter of the German consumption, and the Italian hydroelectric plants, which powered most of south German industry.

Pyke suggested that a tracked vehicle be developed especially for the unit, one which was capable of carrying the men and their equipment at high speed across snow-covered terrain.

In March forty-two, Pyke had proposed the idea, to Lord Louis Mountbatten, Chief of Combined Operations Headquarters (COHQ), that these commandos could be parachuted into the Norwegian mountains to establish a base on the Jostedalsbreen. From that base they would then conduct guerrilla actions against the German army of occupation. Pyke was able to persuade Mountbatten that such a force would be invulnerable in its glacier strongholds and could reasonably be expected to tie up large numbers of German troops trying to dislodge it.

While Mountbatten liked the idea he could not see his way to creating it. He lacked both the manpower and equipment required. Instead, he chose to pass on the idea on to the US and did so at the Chequers Conference which was held in March of forty-two.

General George Marshall, Chief of Staff of the United States Army, readily embraced the concept of such a unit. The Allies had no vehicle which would meet the needs for this unit so in April of that year, the American government asked automobile manufacturers to look into designing one and Studebaker subsequently created the T-15 cargo carrier, which later became the M29 Weasel.

This accomplished, in May, the concept papers for deploying this new type of fighting force in Norway was forwarded to US Lieutenant Colonel Robert T. Frederick for evaluation. Frederick was a young officer working at the Operations Division of the U.S. General Staff.

Frederick was not impressed with the material he read.

He predicted it would be a military fiasco on the following grounds. The idea had unrealistic objectives in consideration of the small number of troops that the plan called for. Similarly, he argued that such a small, elite division would be outnumbered and overtaken in any defensive attempts to hold an area once it was captured. He concluded that there would be no way to evacuate such troops after a mission.

He pointed out that the plan called for troops to be dropped by airplane to their targets, which was impossible at the moment, since there were no planes available to fly these men into Norway.

Despite this scathing assessment, the idea went ahead as proposed, primarily because General Marshall and General Eisenhower had already agreed to the operation with the British High Command and both men were eager for an opportunity to open an American front of some type in Europe.

The first officer picked to lead the unit, was kicked off the project for arguing with Mountbatten and Eisenhower about the feasibility of the plan. His replacement, as suggested by Mountbatten and assigned by Eisenhower was Frederick himself. He was promoted to full colonel to command it.

In accepting the assignment, Colonel Frederick had negotiated a very high priority in obtaining equipment and training areas. Originally, due to its winter warfare mission, it had been intended that the unit should be equally created from American, Canadian, and Norwegian troops. However, a lack of suitable Norwegians led to the decision to use equal numbers of Americans and Canadians. In the end it was agreed that a Canadian would serve as second in command of the Force and that half of the officers and one third of the enlisted men would be Canadian.

The Canadians would be paid by the Canadian government and remain subject to their own army's code of discipline, but be supplied with uniforms, equipment, food, shelter and travel expenses by the US.

Thus agreed, letters of recruitment were posted. These called for single men, aged twenty-one to thirty-five with three or more years of grammar school. Preferred prewar occupations were listed as: Rangers, lumberjacks, north-woodsmen, hunters, prospectors, explorers and game wardens

Owing to the secrecy of the mission, those chosen were often told that they had been selected to undergo training for a parachute unit. Indeed the unit was so secretive that the windows of the trains carrying the troops were painted black and many soldiers did not know where they were headed until they arrived in Helena for training.

The combat force was to be made up of three regiments. Each regiment was led by a lieutenant-colonel and thirty-two officers and boasted a force of three hundred and eighty-five men. The regiments were divided into two battalions with three companies in each battalion and three platoons in each company. The platoon was then broken up into two sections.

American members of the Force arrived for training in Helena in standard US Army attire: green twill coveralls, some wearing khaki pants and fatigue hats. Others were dressed in trousers and green uniform jackets and wore green caps. Ultimately, however, the American uniforms did not differ widely from one another.

The Canadian troops, however, arrived in all different manners of uniform: some wore kilts, others plaid trousers and others Bermuda shorts. Headgear differed just as widely, depending on where the soldier was from. Wedge caps for some, black berets for troops taken from armored regiments and large khaki Tam o' Shanters for soldiers from Canadian Scottish regiments.

In order to help this diversified group of men to morph into an elite, tightknit fighting unit, Frederick decided that a unique uniform had to be designed for them.

Once designed, the uniform was sourced from an American supplier and the resulting olive drab trousers and blouses were issued. Force men also wore a red, white and blue aiguillette. For mountain warfare, the men were given baggy ski pants, parkas and a helmet. From that point on, the only thing that differentiated an American Force member from a Canadian one, was the blood type identity disk worn by the soldier, Americans wore American disks and Canadians wore Canadian disks.

Standard boots were originally the same as those issued to parachuting regiments, but these were substituted for infantry combat boots during the Italian champagne.

The unit was unofficially first known as the *'Braves'* and their spearhead shoulder insignia was chosen with this name in mind. The formation patch was a red spearhead with the words USA written horizontally and CANADA written vertically. The branch of service insignia was the crossed arrows formerly worn by the U.S. Army

Indian Scouts. The unit wore red, white, and blue piping on their garrison cap and on the breast an oval (or trimming) behind their Parachutist Wings.

Colonel Frederick had been concerned from the outset that the soldiers from both countries would have trouble forming a single cohesive unit. On a base level, the techniques and commands used by either army were confusing to the other. Commands for marching, for example, had to be homogenized in order for the unit to operate in the field effectively. In order to satisfy the men from both countries, compromises were made. Canadian bagpipers were put into American unit marching bands to play *'Reveille'* every morning. The marching styles and commands of the American and Canadian armies were amicably balanced and uniforms were made identical.

It turned out that Frederick's initial fears about the possibility of creating a cohesive force out of the members of the two different armies, was unfounded. In short order, through training and dedication to itself, the Force bonded and formed itself into a strong self-protective unit.

Training for this new unit began in August of forty-two.

The men were on a strict and physically demanding three phase training schedule. From August to October they participated in parachute, weapons and demolitions usage and small unit tactics. From November to July they perfected skiing, rock climbing, adaptation to cold climates and practiced in the operation of the M29 Weasel.

The weekly training schedule was intense. Reveille at 04:30 from Monday to Saturday, followed by breakfast at 06:30. The obstacle course was run by 08:00 four times a week followed by the day's training, which differed depending on the month. Soldiers had no option but to march double time between training exercises in order to adhere to their strict schedule. Training lectures were given by veterans of overseas wars in the evenings from Monday to Friday. Soldiers were given Saturday evenings and Sundays off.

Marches were conducted on a sixty-mile course; the record time for its completion was twenty hours. In addition to their own weapons training, the Force trained with enemy weapons, taking them apart, reassembling and shooting them until they were as proficient with them as with their own.

The hand-to-hand combat instructor was Dermot (Pat) O'Neill, an ex-Shanghai International Police Officer, who was an expert at unarmed combat. O'Neill, who was well-versed in several forms of martial arts, taught the men to attack the eyes, throat, groin and knees. He also taught knife fighting tactics and showed the men how to quick-draw their pistols. During this training the men attacked one another with unsheathed bayonets, and injuries were common

Ski training was taught by Norwegian instructors and commenced in December. The men received lectures and demonstrations on skiing techniques and most had mastered the basics within two weeks. At this point the men were made to ski cross-country in formation from dawn until dusk carrying their full equipment, until they had reached or bettered Norwegian army standards.

As a light infantry unit destined for alpine or winter combat the Force was issued various items of non-standard clothing, equipment and rations. These included skis, parkas, haversacks and the Mountain ration, which was the US military ration developed for use by troops operating in the high-altitude or mountainous regions of the European theater of operations (ETO).

The 1st Special Service Force (FSSF) was armed with a variety of non-standard or limited-issue weapons, such as the M1941 Johnson machine gun. This gun in particular helped greatly increase the firepower of the unit and was highly regarded by those who used it in combat. Frederick became involved in the design of a unique fighting knife for the Force which developed into the V-42 combat knife, which was made exclusively for members of the Force.

On July tenth of forty-three the Force took part in its first action. It sailed for the Aleutian Islands off Alaska and on August fifteenth took part in the invasion force that landed on the island of Kiska. This island had already been evacuated by the Japanese troops and, unneeded, the disappointed members of the Force returned to Fort Ethan Allen, in Arlington Virginia; arriving there on September ninth.

Patrick Laughy

* * * * *

- Sonderaktion 1005 -

The German *'Sonderaktion 1005'* (Special Action 1005), also called *'Aktion 1005'*, had begun in May of nineteen forty-two when it had been deemed to be precipitous to have used mass graves for those in receipt of *'special 'handling'*. By this point it seemed prudent to attempt to correct this situation and permanently destroy any evidence of the mass killings that had occurred in occupied Poland.

The operation to accomplish this was to be conducted in strict secrecy from forty-two to forty-four, by using prisoners to exhume mass graves and burn the bodies. These work groups were officially called *'Leichenkommandos'* (corpse units) and were all part of *'Sonderkommando 1005'*. Inmates forced into performing this work were often put in chains in order to prevent escape.

In May forty-three this operation had moved into the occupied territories in Eastern Europe to destroy evidence of the mass killing perpetrated by the *'SS-Einsatzgruppen'* squads that had massacred hundreds of thousands of Jews, as well as Roma and local civilians in occupied territories of Eastern Europe.

The *'Aktion'* was to be overseen by selected squads from the *'Sicherheitsdienst'* (the intelligence agency of the SS and the Nazi party) and the *'Ordnungspolizei'* (order police).

In June of forty-three, *SS-Gruppenführer* Heinrich Müller, head of the Gestapo gave *'SS-Standartenführer'* (Colonel) Paul Blobel his orders to begin the action. Its principal aim was to erase evidence of Jewish exterminations; however, the *'Aktion'* would also include non-Jewish victims of the Nazi *'Einsatzgruppen'* units.

Blobel had been born in Potsdam, and he had participated in the Great War. He'd served well and was decorated with the Iron Cross first class. After the war, Blobel studied architecture and practiced this profession from twenty-four to thirty-one, when upon losing his job he'd joined the Nazi Party, the SA and then the SS.

In thirty-three he joined the police force in Düsseldorf and in June of thirty-three he was recruited into the SD. In June of forty-one he became the commanding officer of *'Sonderkommando 4a'* of *'Einsatzgruppe C'* that was active in Ukraine. Following Wehrmacht troops into Ukraine, the *'Einsatzgruppen'* had liquidated political and racial undesirables. In August of forty-one Blobel had decided to create a ghetto in Zhytomyr to hold three thousand Jews until they could be liquidated. On the tenth of August in forty-one, he'd received the order from Friedrich Jeckeln, on behalf of Hitler, to kill the whole Jewish population. On the twenty-second of August the *'Sonderkommando'* murdered Jewish prisoners at Bila Tserkva, with the consent of Field Marshal Walther von Reichenau, who commanded the 6th Army.

Blobel, in conjunction with von Reichenau and Friedrich Jeckeln's units, had organized the Babi Yar massacre in late September of forty-one in Kiev. In November of forty-one Blobel had received and activated the first gas vans at Poltava.

Blobel had been relieved of his command on January thirteenth of forty-two, supposedly for medical reasons, but in fact for his rampant alcoholism.

In June of forty-two he was put in charge of *'Aktion 1005'*, and given the task of destroying the evidence of all Nazi atrocities in Eastern Europe. This entailed exhumation of all mass graves, then incinerating the bodies and disposing of the ashes. It was Blobel who developed efficient incineration disposal techniques through experimentation, such as alternating layers of bodies with firewood on a frame of iron rails. To prepare for his ask, Blobel began his work by experimenting at Chełmno.

Attempts to use incendiary bombs to destroy exhumed bodies were unsuccessful as the weapons tended to set fire to nearby forests. The most effective way was eventually found to be the use of giant pyres over iron grills. The method involved building alternating layers of corpses and firewood on railway tracks. Afterwards remaining bone fragments could be crushed by pounding with heavy dowels or in a grinding machine and then re-buried in pits.

The operation itself officially began at Sobibor extermination camp. The *'Leichenkommando'* exhumed the bodies from mass graves around the camp and then burned them, after which the workers were executed. The process had then moved to Belzec in November of forty-two. Because the Auschwitz and Belsen camps had crematoria with furnace rooms on site to dispose of the bodies, *'Aktion 1005'* commandos were not required there.

The corpses that had been buried at Treblinka with the use of a crawler excavator were dug up and cremated on the orders of Himmler himself, who visited the camp in March of forty-three. The bodies were placed on cremation pyres that were ninety-eight feet long, with rails laid across the pits on concrete blocks. They were splashed with gasoline over wood, and burned in one massive blaze, tended by roughly three hundred prisoners who operated the pyres. At Belzec, the round-the-clock operation lasted till March of forty-three. At Treblinka, it went twenty-four hours a day until the end of July.

The operation also returned to the scenes of earlier mass killings such as Babi Yar, Ponary, the Ninth Fort, as well as Bronna Góra. By the end of forty-three, with Soviet armies advancing, *'SS-Obergruppenführer'* Wilhelm Koppe, head of the *'Reichsgau Wartheland'* ordered that each of the five districts of the *'General Government'* territory set up its own *'Aktion 1005'* commando to begin *'cleaning'* mass graves. These operations were not to be entirely successful as the advancing Russian troops would reach some of the sites before they could be cleared.

* * * * *

- Camp X -

Camp X was the unofficial name of a Second World War paramilitary and commando training installation, located on the northwestern shore of Lake Ontario between Whitby and Oshawa, in Ontario, Canada.

It had been established on December sixth, nineteen forty-one by the chief of British Security Coordination (BSC), Sir William Stephenson, who was a Canadian from Ajax, Ontario. Stephenson was a close confidante of both Winston Churchill and Franklin Delano Roosevelt.

The camp was originally designed to link the British and Americans at a time when the US was forbidden by the Neutrality Act to be directly involved in World War II. Before the attack on Pearl Harbor and America's entry into the war, Camp X opened for the purpose of training Allied agents from the Special Operations Executive, Federal Bureau of Investigation, and American Office of Strategic Services (OSS) intended to be dropped behind enemy lines as saboteurs and spies.

However, prior to the United States entering the war on December seventh of forty-one, agents from America's intelligence services expressed an interest in sending personnel for training at the soon to be opened Camp X. Agents from the FBI and the Office of Strategic Services (forerunner of the CIA) secretly attended Camp X. Most notable was Colonel William *'Wild Bill'* Donovan, war-time head of the OSS, who credited Sir William Stephenson with teaching the Americans about foreign intelligence gathering. Once formed, the CIA named their recruit training facility *'The Farm'*, in a nod to the original farm that had existed at the original Camp X site.

Camp X trained over five hundred Allied units, of which 273 graduated and moved on to London for further training. Many secret agents were also trained here. The Camp X pupils were schooled in a wide variety of special techniques including silent killing, sabotage, partisan support and recruitment methods for resistance movements, demolition, map reading, use of various weapons, and Morse code.

One of the unique features of Camp X was *'Hydra'*, a highly sophisticated telecommunications centre. Given the name by the Camp X operators, *'Hydra'* was invaluable for both coding and decoding information in relative safety from the prying ears of German radio observers. The camp was an excellent location for the safe transfer of code due to the topography of the land; Lake Ontario made it perfect site for picking up radio signals from the United Kingdom. *'Hydra'* also had direct access via land lines to Ottawa, New York and Washington, D.C. for telegraph and telephone communications.

* * * * *

- Deportations -

The Riga Ghetto is liquidated.

The US Congress holds hearings regarding the State Departments inaction regarding European Jews, despite mounting reports of mass extermination.

On November third the Germans carry out *'Operation Harvest Festival'* in occupied Poland. Forty two thousand Jews are transported for *'special treatment'*.

A quote from the weekly Nazi newspaper *'Der Sturmer'*, published by Julius Streicher dated November fourth reads: "It is actually true that the Jews have, so to speak, disappeared from Europe and that the Jewish *'Reservoir of the East'* from which the Jewish pestilence has for centuries beset the peoples of Europe has ceased to exist. But the Fuhrer of the German people at the beginning of the war prophesized what has now come to pass."

On November the eleventh *'Auschwitz Kommandant'*, Rudolf Hoss, is promoted to chief inspector of concentration camps. His replacement, Arthur Liebehenschel, decides to concentrate the vast complex of thirty sub-camps into three main sections.

On November fifteenth, Himmler issues orders to the effect that effective immediately, Gypsies and part Gypsies are to be considered as the same as Jews and placed into concentration camps.

* * * * *

- Ghettos -

- Baltic Countries -

By forty-three, only about forty thousand Jews had survived the earlier operations by the *'Einsatzgruppen'* units. These had been concentrated in the Vilna, Kovno, Siauliai and Svencionys ghettos and various Lithuanian labour camps. During the year the Vilna and Svencionys ghettos had been destroyed and those of Kovno and Siauliai had been converted into concentration camps. Fifteen thousand Lithuanian Jews had been transported to labour camps in Latvia and Estonia. Five thousand had been deported to the extermination centers in Poland. Only about five thousand Jews remained in Latvia and these were concentrated in the Riga, Dvinsk and Liepaja ghettos.

* * * * *

- Concentration Camps -

- Janowska -

The evacuation of the Janowska Labor Camp located in the suburbs of Lvov, began in November of forty-three. Under *'Aktion 1005'* prisoners were forced to open the mass graves and burn the bodies. With a good idea of what their fate after the fact would be, on November nineteenth, the prisoners involved staged an uprising and escape attempt. A small number were successful but the vast majority was recaptured and as they had expected, promptly received *'special treatment'*.

* * * * *

- Majdanek -

On November third, as part of *'Aktion Erntfest'*, all remaining prisoners, approximately eighteen thousand, were shot and buried in large ditches near the crematorium.

* * * * *

- Extermination Camps -

Gassing operations at Sobibor ceased. Burial pits where exhumed and the bodies cremated as part of *'Aktion 1005'*.

* * * * *

- The Family -

- Karl and Wilhelm -

Karl's plan to avoid attending Himmler's October Posen speech had worked exceptionally well, with General Bichler confirming that the order, coming directly from Hitler, had reached Himmler's staff quickly and had been promptly handled on a junior level.

Father and son had been struck from the original list for attendance and the SS-Reichsfuhrer had been neither consulted nor advised as to this adjustment.

On the twenty-sixth, Karl and Wilhelm were summoned to join Hitler when he attended a demonstration flight of the new Messerschmitt 262 jet fighter. Hitler had attended a previous demonstration of an earlier model of the aircraft in May, which had been marred with mechanical failures, but had nonetheless been greatly impressed by it. While the machine had been designed as a fighter, Hitler saw it as a good platform for a medium bomber and expressed this view at the time.

During November there had been few other official occasions that had demanded their attention and the two of them had managed to spend almost half the month at the castle with the rest of the family.

* * * * *

- Eric -

Seemingly overnight Heidi's shape had ballooned and she was now finding it necessary to curtail her physical activities due to swelling in her legs and feet plus a general sense of clumsiness when moving about.

With plenty of family a hand, she was surrounded on an on-going basis by female relatives, organized by her mother, who nonetheless personally stood most of the watches over her daughter.

Eric, somewhat at loose ends over the physical changes and concerned for her, had been strongly encouraged by Heidi's mother, to fret less. After a week of being surrounded by women, he accepted the fact that she was in good hands and acquiesced, returning to his responsibilities of overseeing both mine and research center during the day and spending his nights with Heidi.

* * * * *

- Friedrichshafen -

A fully-committed Ursula had reached the stage where she was drawing out final plans for specifically where on the castle grounds the various new facilities, envisioned for the self-sufficiency of the castles' table supplies, were to be placed.

Breeding stock had been researched and sourced and were scheduled to arrive in the spring. Construction crews were busy preparing foundations for new barns and out-buildings which were to be placed behind the original horse barns and finding the necessary farm implements for her proposed endeavor now tended to fill her days. Used farm equipment had had to do, as base materials were restricted for military-only production now and no newly manufactured implements were available.

Seed for the projected gardens had also been difficult to find, but Ursula had presumed upon her father to use his influence in that regard and as a result, suitable amounts were already beginning to arrive at the castle.

The other members of the family had all settled into a comfortable routine with regard to their chosen responsibilities and with the Count and Wilhelm able to spend more time with them, the family unit had slipped into a regular day to day existence in a reasonable degree of comfort.

CHAPTER TWENTY-TWO

- November -

- Allied Air Operations -

- Europe -

RAF Bomber Command targets Berlin, Dusseldorf and Frankfurt, dropping a total of fourteen thousand, five hundred tons. Berlin alone is hit with four thousand tons. US heavy bombers drop six thousand, three hundred tons against both Norway and Germany. Targets include Ryukan and Knaben in Norway and the German targets being Wilhelmshaven and Munster.

American medium bombers drop thirteen tons over the Low Countries and France and over the same period, RAF aircraft go after communications targets in these areas.

* * * * *

- Mediterranean -

Allied air forces in this area make pinpoint attacks on communications targets in Italy, primarily in Toulon, Sofia and Turin. These are set to co-ordinate with the moving Allied ground forces. In the Middle East shipping is the main target.

* * * * *

- Battle of the Atlantic -

Seventy-eight convoys cross the Atlantic without a single sinking as Allied shipping losses drops to sixty ships for a total tonnage of three hundred and thirteen thousand tons. Seventeen U-boats are sunk.

* * * * *

- Pacific -

Japanese losses amount to two hundred and sixty-three thousand tons, most of this due to the activities of US submarines.

* * * * *

- November First -

- Solomons -

Executing *'Operation Goodtime'* US marines make a successful landing on Bougainville.

* * * * *

- Eastern Front -

The Russians take Perekop and push on to Armiansk to cut off the Crimea.

* * * * *

- Italy -

British forces take Roccamonfina.

* * * * *

- November Second -

- Eastern Front -

Russian forces take Kakhovka.

* * * * *

- November Third -

- Italy -

The British X Corps, fighting with the American Fifth Army, take Sessa Aurunca.

* * * * *

- November Fourth -

- Italy -

The British X corps takes Monte Massico and Monte Camino and the American V1 Corps capture sector Venafro and Rocavirondola.

* * * * *

- November Fifth -

- France -

Resistance fighters place bombs in the Peugeot factory at Sochaux. Equipment used in the construction of tank turrets is destroyed and when the Germans bring in replacement equipment it is promptly sabotaged.

* * * * *

- Eastern Front -

Russian forces cut the Kiev-Zhitomir rail line threatening to encircle Kiev and in the south they overrun the area between the Crimea and the lower Dniepr.

* * * * *

- Italy -

The US Fifth Army begins its offensive against the mountainous German defensive positon of the *'Reinhard line'*. The initial attacks are against the critical center where the British 56th Division takes on Monte Camino and the US 3rd Division goes against Mignano. These attempts have very little success.

In the sector where the British Eighth Army face the Germans, Vasto, Torrebruna and Palmoli are taken.

* * * * *

- November Sixth -

- Eastern Front -

The Russians liberate Kiev. All but six thousand of the occupying German troops manage to avoid being taken prisoner.

* * * * *

- November Eighth -

- Italy -

The American Fifth is having no success in reaching the *'Reinhard line'*.

* * * * *

- November Ninth -

- Solomons -

The American beachhead on Bougainville is extended and the 37th Infantry Division arrives as reinforcement.

* * * * *

- Italy -

The Eighth Army's 8th Indian Division takes Castiglione.

* * * * *

- Free French -

Generals Giraud, Georges and three others resign and de Gaulle becomes President of the French Committee of National Liberation.

* * * * *

- November Eleventh -

- New Britain -

Two naval task forces intensify the American attack against the Japanese base at Rabaul. Five carriers send one hundred and eighty-five aircraft in a single mission. The defending Japanese lose seventy of their defending Zero fighters, one of their light cruisers and two destroyers are damaged.

* * * * *

- Eastern Front -

Russian troops pushing out west of Kiev take a bridge and cross the River Teterev to capture Radomyshl.

* * * * *

- Italy -

Forces of the British Eighty Army capture Casalanguida in their push forward against the German defensive line at Sangro.

* * * * *

- November Twelfth -

- Aegean -

German troops land against the British defenders on the Dodecanese Island of Leros which is situated just off Turkey. Over the next four days they overwhelm the British and Italian troops to capture their objective.

* * * * *

- Eastern Front -

The Russians take Korostyshev and then begin to move on Zhitomir, a strategic rail center, severing the Germans last available rail line east of the Priopet marshes.

* * * * *

- Italy -

The British 56th Division is forced to retreat from some of its positions on Monte Camino as the Allied attack runs into a brick wall at the defensive German defensive *'Reinhard line'*.

* * * * *

- November Thirteenth -

- Gilbert Islands -

US Flying Fortresses begin a week long bombing campaign to soften up the Tarawa Atoll in preparation for invasion.

* * * * *

- Italy -

US Fifth Army Commanding General Clark, tells Alexander that he has to halt his ineffective attacks against the *'Reinhard line'* for the present. The British Eighth captures Atessa.

* * * * *

- November Fourteenth -

- Italy -

The Eighth Indian Division, supported by the Second New Zealand Division, takes Perano.

* * * * *

- November Fifteenth -

- Italy -

Alexander agrees with Clark's assessment of the situation. Backed by the rugged terrain and horrid weather, the Fifth has been mauled and is suffering from heavy casualties. He calls off their attack against the *'Reinhard line'*.

* * * * *

- November Sixteenth -

- Norway -

In a move to set back the German Atomic program, one hundred and sixty US bombers strike the hydro-electric power facility and heavy water factory in German occupied Vemork.

* * * * *

- November Seventeenth -

- Eastern Front -

Russian troops take Novodichi.

* * * * *

- November Eighteenth -

- Berlin -

The British launch the *'Battle of Berlin'*, sending four hundred and forty bombers against the heavily anti-aircraft fortified capital city. The launch proves to be costly in that only light damage is caused and one hundred and thirty-one are killed. This, for the loss of nine aircraft and fifty-three fight crew.

* * * * *

- Eastern Front -

The Russians capture Korosten and Ovruch north of Kiev and

Rechtisa, cutting the railroad west of Gomel.

* * * * *

- November Nineteenth -

- Italy -

General Clark had asked to have the joint Canadian and American FSSF (First Special Service Force) sent to him in Italy and they arrived in Naples on this date. He immediately sends them into the *'Reinhard line'*, at the point being held by the US 36th Infantry Division.

Clark then orders them to tackle something that several much larger formations, containing thousands of infantrymen, have been unable to achieve.

He tasks the elite and as yet unproven eighteen hundred man Force with designing and executing a plan to take Monte La Difensa, the naturally fortified mountain peak held by German positions in the Italian mountains.

These positions are being defended by the seasoned 104th Panzer Grenadier Division with the elite Herman Goering Paratroop Division in reserve. Both of these units are experienced armored divisions.

* * * * *

- Eastern Front -

The Russians realize that they have overextended themselves and back out of Zhitomir as the Germans move into the city.

* * * * *

- Poland -

Ordered to begin closing the facility, prisoners at the Janowska concentration camp start a mass uprising and escape attempt. All but a few are rounded up and executed.

* * * * *

- November Twentieth -

- Gilbert Islands -

The *'Battle of Tarawa'* begins. US marines land on Tarawa and Makin atolls and meet fanatic resistance. Their losses are extremely high.

* * * * *

- Aegean -

The British evacuate Samos and the Germans move in two days later and quickly disarm the twenty-five hundred defenders and take them prisoner.

* * * * *

- November Twenty-First -

- Gilbert Islands -

Marine reinforcements land on Betio Island, Tarawa Atoll. Initially they sustain heavy casualties as did the first landing. However, by midday there is a change in the tide and a steady flow of troops begin to converge into the beachhead. Additional US forces land on nearby Bairiki.

American troops are now firmly ashore on Butaritari Island, Makin and are pressing forward against strong Japanese resistance.

* * * * *

- New Guinea -

Near Sattelberg the Australian 9th Division is slowly but surely gaining the upper hand against the Japanese defenders.

* * * * *

- Eastern Front -

Emboldened by taking Zhitomir, German forces are now gaining momentum and begin a push toward Korosten.

* * * * *

- November Twenty-Second -

- Egypt -

The Cairo Conference, codenamed *'Sextant'*, commences in Cairo. This meeting is set to outline the Allied position against Japan and to make decisions about postwar Asia. President Franklin Roosevelt, Prime Minister Winston Churchill, and Generalissimo Chiang Kai-shek attend. Soviet leader Joseph Stalin will not attend the conference because he does not want to cause friction between the Soviet Union and Japan, with whom he had signed the Soviet-Japanese Neutrality Pact in forty-one. This pact provided for a five-year agreement of neutrality between the two nations, therefore the Russians were not at war with Japan, whereas the other three nations represented at the conference, were.

* * * * *

- Gilbert Islands -

The earlier US landings are now going well and additional troop landings are made on Abimama Atoll.

* * * * *

- November Twenty-Third -

- Gilbert Islands -

By midday the battle on Tarawa is over. The Americans have suffered one thousand killed and twice that number wounded and the Japanese garrison is all but wiped out, with only seventeen wounded Japanese taken prisoner along with one hundred and twenty-nine Korean labourers.

US forces also capture Makin Island, with two hundred dead or wounded.

* * * * *

- November Twenty-Fifth -

- New Guinea -

Australian troops overrun the final Japanese positions at Sattelberg.

* * * * *

- Rangoon -

The city is hit by American heavy bombers.

* * * * *

- November Twenty-Seventh -

- Cairo Conference -

The conference ends with some broad agreement but no firm plan of action.

* * * * *

- Berlin -

The city suffers huge civilian losses as the heavy bombing raids continue.

* * * * *

- November Twenty-Eighth -

- Iran -

At the commencement of the German-Soviet war, Churchill had offered assistance to the Soviets, and an agreement to this effect had been signed on July twelfth nineteen forty-one. Since that time, delegations had been traveling between London and Moscow to arrange the implementation of this support. When the United States joined the war, these delegations had met in Washington as well.

As a result, a Combined Chiefs of Staff committee had been created to coordinate British and American operations as well as their support to the Soviet Union.

The consequences of a global war, the absence of a unified Allied strategy and the complexity of allocating resources between Europe and Asia had not yet been sorted out however. This had quickly led to mutual suspicions arising between the Western Allies and the Russians.

There remained the question of opening a second front to alleviate the German pressure on the Russian forces and the question of mutual assistance.

Both Britain and Russia were looking towards the United States for credit and material support. There was ceaseless tension between the United States and Britain since Washington had no desire to prop up the British Empire in the event of an Allied victory. Additionally, neither the United States nor Britain were prepared to give Stalin a free hand in his dealings with Eastern Europe at war's end and lastly, there was no common policy on how to deal with Germany after Hitler had been defeated.

Communications regarding these matters between Churchill, Roosevelt, and Stalin had been ongoing by way of telegrams and emissaries, but it was evident that direct negotiations between the three leaders were urgently required.

Such a meeting had been difficult to arrange. Stalin obsessively wished to control everything from Moscow and was unwilling to risk journeys by air. Roosevelt was physically disabled and found travel grueling. Churchill was an avid traveler and, as part of an ongoing series of wartime conferences, had already met with Roosevelt in North America on five occasions and twice in Africa. He had also held two prior meetings with Stalin in Moscow.

In order to arrange this urgently needed meeting between the three men, Roosevelt had endeavored to persuade Stalin to travel to Cairo, but Stalin had turned down this offer as he did additional offers to meet in Baghdad or in Basra. The Russian leader had finally agreed to meet in Tehran, Iran.

The *'Tehran Conference'*, codenamed *'Eureka'*, commenced on this date at the Russian Embassy in Tehran, Iran. It was a strategy meeting held between Stalin, Roosevelt, and Churchill, scheduled to run from November the twenty-eighth to the first of December.

The United States and Great Britain wanted to secure the cooperation of the Soviet Union in defeating Nazi Germany. Stalin was willing to agree to this, but he had his price. In exchange, he demanded that the US and Britain would have to support the Yugoslav Partisans and after the war had been won, accept Russian domination of Eastern Europe and agree to a westward shift of the border between Poland and the Soviet Union.

The leaders then turned to the conditions under which the Western Allies would open a new front by invading northern France, something that Stalin had been pressing them to do since forty-one.

Up to this point Churchill had been advocating the expansion of joint operations of British, American, and Commonwealth forces in the Mediterranean. This, with an eye to bolstering British interests in the region. Roosevelt wasn't interested and insisted that *'Operation Overlord'*, the invasion of Europe should go forward. In the end, the leaders agreed that *'Overlord'* should be launched by May of forty-four. Stalin agreed to support the invasion by launching a concurrent major offensive on Germany's eastern front with a view to diverting German forces from northern France.

Iran and Turkey were discussed in detail. Roosevelt, Churchill, and Stalin all agreed to support Iran's government.

In addition, the Soviet Union was required to pledge support to Turkey if that country entered the war. Roosevelt, Churchill, and Stalin agreed that it would also be most desirable if Turkey entered on the Allies' side before the year was out.

Despite accepting these arrangements, Stalin dominated the conference. He used the prestige of the Russian victory at the *'Battle of Kursk'* to get his way. Roosevelt had hoped to deal firmly with Stalin's onslaught of demands, but in the end he did little but appease the Russian leader. Churchill mostly argued for his Mediterranean plan instead of the launching *'Operation Overlord'*.

The lack of a united front presented by the two western leaders served to play into Stalin's hands.

In the end, Roosevelt and Churchill accepted Stalin's demands regarding Poland's post-war boundaries, which would give the Soviets Lwów, Wilno, and Poland's eastern Kresy territory which had been occupied by Stalin under his thirty-nine alliance with Nazi Germany. Churchill proposed that Poland, in return, be compensated with a corresponding slice of Germany. The leaders agreed to this idea without bothering to first discuss the proposal with Polish government-in-exile.

At a dinner held for the leaders and their entourages at the Russian embassy, the discussions moved to the aftermath of war and Stalin suddenly proposed executing fifty to one hundred thousand German officers, so that Germany could not in the foreseeable future, plan for yet another war.

Churchill was outraged. He denounced *'the cold blooded execution of soldiers who fought for their country*, saying *that 'only war criminals should be put on trial in accordance with the Moscow Document'. (*A document which he himself had written).

The British leader had then abruptly stood up and stormed out of the room. Stalin, who had been testing the waters as to what else he could get out of the meeting, followed Churchill and told him that he was only joking, before urging him back into the room.

* * * * *

- November Twenty-Ninth -

- Italy -

British forces begin their offensives, taking Mozzogrogna and Fossacesia.

* * * * *

- New Guinea -

The Australians capture Gusika and Bonga.

* * * * *

- November Thirtieth -

- Eastern Front -

The Russian are unable to hold Korosten and lose it to the advancing Germans.

CHAPTER TWENTY-THREE

- December -

- Hitler -

As the end of nineteen forty-three approached the Fuhrer was increasingly surrounded by an atmosphere of doom and gloom.

Berlin was been destroyed by Allied bombers. His forces were facing more setbacks at Leningrad and across the Ukraine. There was every indication that Germany's forces faced yet another disastrous winter on the Eastern Front. *'SS-Sturmbannfuhrer'* Konrad Morgen's investigations into criminal activity within the SS had uncovered a large network of SS corruption at Buchenwald concentration camp, which was bringing unwanted attention to the operations of his extermination program.

Since the start of the Russian campaign, Hitler had changed his normal method of working. Previous to that, the Fuhrer had worked in staccato fits of intense activity separated by relatively long periods of indolent relaxation. By this point in the war, he was undertaking an enormous amount of daily work, without relief.

Before *'Barbarossa'*, he had been willing to allow others to do much of the mundane decision making, but now, at a time when there were far more decisions to be made on a twenty-four hour basis, he was determined to take personal responsibility for even the minor matters. As anxieties mounted he'd forced himself to adopt a strictly disciplined work ethic. This approach was unnatural for him and it inevitably affected the quality of his decisions.

Even before the war started, Hitler had begun to demonstrate signs of overwork. On occasion he had become hesitant to make decisions or would appear absent-minded. He had often lapsed into laborious monologues, or drifted off into a world of his own where he made no response or would simply utter an occasional *'Ja'* or *'Nein'*. At these times is seemed apparent that he had stopped listening or that his mind was elsewhere.

When this type of situation had taken hold of him in those early days, Hitler would head for *'Berchtesgaden'* for a rest and when he returned a few weeks later, he would be refreshed and relaxed and ready to eagerly step back into his busy schedule.

During forty-three, at the signs of overwork, those in his entourage would frequently urge him to take a vacation. He often agreed and would move his headquarters, often spending weeks at *'Berchtesgaden'*, but once there, unlike before, he would refuse to change his daily routine. Bormann now never left his side and proffered a continual stream of questions which only the Fuhrer could settle. His military staff would travel with him and those responsible for domestic affairs, who were unable to see him at *'Wolfsschanze'* would soon arrive in streams for an audience.

When those close to him began to express concerns over his workload even while at *'Berchtesgaden'* and his declining health, Hitler responded.

"It's easy to advise me to take a vacation. But it is it's impossible. I cannot leave current militarily decisions to others even for twenty-four hours."

Hitler's overwork and isolation had led to a strange state of mental incapacity, consistency and objectivity. A man who had previously been revered as an Icon, a Messiah, a Demigod, was revealed to all close to him as simply a human being and one with all the needs and shortcomings that entailed.

One thing had not changed over time however. Hitler's authority remained intact.

As the year came to a close, those around him could not help but note his ever growing tendency to cocoon himself, his preferring to keep his own company when not attending his military conferences. Gone were the eager discussions around the meal table about day to day activities or predictions about the future. There was no defeatism talk however; he steadfastly maintained his confidence in ultimate German victory, but he no longer expanded on exactly just how or when that was to come about.

Even among those who had previously been close to him, there was a growing inaccessibility. Hitler now deliberately made his decisions in isolation. In addition, his thought processing appeared slower and he exhibited a reduced inclination to develop new ideas or concepts. He was no longer able to think out of the box, seemingly locked into tunnel vision and unable to vary his committed path forward.

In December, the atmosphere at his *'Wolfsschanze'* headquarters was glum. Hitler completely ignored the holiday season. At his order, there was to be no Christmas tree, nor decorations or candles to celebrate the festival of love and peace.

* * * * *

- Inner Circle -

Hitler alone seemed to have fully understood the ramifications of the Allied demand for Germany's unconditional surrender. He had no illusions as to the seriousness of this ultimatum.

Goering, Goebbels and the other German leaders still spoke of the possibility of somehow exploiting the political differences and disagreements between the Allied countries and clung to the belief that the Fuhrer would, as he had done many times previously, manage to find a method of cutting a chasm between them by means of some political device that would turn the tide and remove the threat of their joint military threat.

They based this on Hitler's historic ability to create political miracles. After all, he had duped the Allies again and again, accomplishing just such miracles; the occupation of Austria and the non-aggression pact with Russians were prime examples. What he had done before, he could do again.

Those who attended the daily military conferences however, had little reason to share this blissful hope. They were in the thick of things and well aware of the reality of the current battle fronts. Hitler made little attempt to hide the fact that, despite the situation Germany now faced, he was firmly committed to his intentions of destroying both bolshevism and the sub-human Jewish race. Any idea that he was prepared to back off from either of these crusades in order to reach some form of peace initiative was out of the question.

During one such conference he put it succinctly.

"Don't fool yourself. There is no turning back. We can only move forward. We have burned our bridges."

* * * * *

- Georg Konrad Morgen -

Morgen was born in Frankfurt on June ninth of nineteen-nine. He graduated from the University of Frankfurt and The Hague Academy of International Law, before becoming a judge in Stettin Germany. A pacifist, he wrote a book entitled *'War Propaganda and the Prevention of War'* about a year after he met Hitler in nineteen thirty-five. The book argued against the militarization of Germany.

Morgen was a staunch believer in the principles of the law. As a judge, while he did not believe that he should question the laws themselves, he resolutely based his decisions strictly upon the evidence presented to him and refused absolutely to make any distinction based on a person's wealth or position.

When he was appointed as an assistant SS, despite having a reputation as a pacifist, he nonetheless felt compelled to enforce the laws which the Nazis had enacted and he did so without favoritism.

It was due to this inflexible determination not to show favoritism for those with ties to the Nazi Party that his frustrated superiors eventually ordered *'SS-Sturmbannfuhrer'* (Major), Morgen to serve in the *'Wiking Division'* on the Eastern Front as punishment for insubordination.

By nineteen forty-three, Morgen had been made a Judge-Advocate in the *'Hauptamt SS-Gericht '*(SS Court Head Office), while retaining his military rank and had been transferred to the *'Financial Crimes Office'* with the clear understanding that he was not to deal with any political cases.

In this position, Morgen was to give judgment over other SS members who faced charges of corruption or crimes under current Nazi law. In this capacity, he had no difficulty gaining access to the concentration camps in eastern Germany, which held primarily anti-Nazi Germans and other political prisoners, but during a mid-forty-three attempt to enter the Jewish extermination camp at Treblinka, which was located in central Poland, he and his associates were refused entry. A dedicated and determined man, this minor setback was not about to prevent him from doing his job.

Although he discovered early on that the Final Solution of the Jewish problem through physical extermination was beyond his jurisdiction, and advanced no legal objections to the large-scale, centrally-authorized anti-Jewish operations like Harvest Festival, Morgen went on to diligently prosecute any criminal activity he found. Over the next two years he conducted over eight hundred investigations into such crimes committed at concentration camps. Morgen's tenacity in prosecuting corruption and murder charges against SS members earned him the nickname 'The Bloodhound Judge'.

As an example of his tenacity, consider that among others he investigated in mid and late forty-three was the commandant of Buchenwald and Majdanek, Karl Otto Koch, as well as the Buchenwald concentration camp's doctor Waldemar Hoven, who was accused of murdering both inmates and camp guards who threatened to testify against Koch. Koch was also accused of embezzlement of in excess of one hundred thousand marks.

At every turn this investigation ran into brick walls and Morgen's own investigations were unable to find any evidence of wrongdoing. It seemed that every witness they attempted to interview died before they could get to him. Clearly warned off, the investigators refused to pursue the case and as a result, a determined Morgen decided to go undercover and become his own investigator.

Undaunted, he ensconced himself in a hotel near the camp and went to the local banks where he flashed official looking documents and led the managers to believe that he was acting on Himmler's direct orders to examine Koch's accounts. He eventually found what he was looking for and personally gathered undisputable evidence that Koch had indeed embezzled over one hundred thousand marks. In addition he dug deep into the camps records and was able to determine that possible witnesses to Koch's criminal activity had been taken to a secret cell within the camp and eliminated before they could be interviewed.

He arrived in Berlin with a bulging briefcase full of records and affidavits which he took directly to his superior, the Chief of the Criminal Police. The man was aghast at what Morgen had been able to put together and wanted no part of the situation. He promptly sent Morgen and his briefcase directly upstairs to Kaltenbrunner himself. Kaltenbrunner was just as shaken by the evidence and he too backed away from the *'hot potato'*, stating *'That's not my business, take it to your boss in Munich'*.

No quitter, Morgen did exactly that, taking the material to the head of the SS legal Department, who also had no intention of becoming involved in the matter. His comment:
"You'll have to tell all that to Himmler."

Morgen then prepared a carefully worded telegram outlining the facts and with the assistance of a friend on Himmler's personal staff, the telegram surprisingly made its way through the massive SS bureaucracy and actually onto the SS-Reichsfuhrer's desk.

Himmler, to the amazement of everyone so far involved in the matter and very probably due to his strange sense of honor, summoned Morgen and immediately gave him complete authority to proceed against Koch and everyone else associated with the repugnant case.

Morgen went on to convict those involved, successfully accomplishing what he had set out to do. There is little doubt that the fallout from of Morgen's determination to carry out his mandate led to an expansion in the leakage to others as to the facts surrounding the *'Final solution to the Jewish Question'* and it did so far more rapidly than the Nazis had planned.

* * * * *

- Cairo Conference -

The *'Cairo Declaration'* is issued and released on December first of forty-three.

It firmly states that the Allies will continue deploying military force against Japan until it accepts unconditional surrender.

The main clauses of the declaration state that the three great allies are fighting this war to restrain and punish the aggression of Japan, they covet no gain for themselves and won't involve themselves in territorial expansion wars after the conflict. Japan is to be stripped of all the islands in the Pacific which she has seized or occupied since the beginning of the Great War in nineteen fourteen and all the territories Japan has stolen from the Chinese, including Manchuria, Formosa, and the Pescadores, shall be restored to the Republic of China. Japan will also be expelled from all other territories which she has taken by violence and the parties agreed that *"in due course Korea shall become free and independent"*.

* * * * *

- Tehran Conference -

On December the first of forty-three, on conclusion of the conference, a declaration is issued by the three Allied leaders. It records the following military conclusions:

The Yugoslav Partisans should be supported by supplies and equipment and also by commando operations.

It would be desirable if Turkey should come into war on the side of the Allies before the end of the year.

The leaders took note of Stalin's statement that if Turkey found herself at war with Germany, and as a result Bulgaria declared war on Turkey or attacked her, the Soviet Union would immediately be at war with Bulgaria. The Conference further took note that this could be mentioned in the forthcoming negotiations aimed at bringing Turkey into the war.

The cross-channel invasion of France would be launched during May of nineteen forty-four, in conjunction with an operation against southern France. The latter operation would be undertaken in as great a strength as availability of landing-craft permitted. The Conference further took note of Joseph Stalin's statement that the Soviet forces would launch an offensive at about the same time with the object of preventing the German forces from transferring from the Eastern to the Western Front.

The leaders agreed that the military staffs of the *'Three Powers'* should keep in close touch with each other in regard to the impending operations in Europe. In particular it was agreed that a cover plan to mislead the enemy about these operations should be concerted between the staffs concerned.

Although all three of the leaders had arrived with differing objectives, the main outcome of the conference was the commitment to the opening of a second front against Nazi Germany by the Western Allies. The conference also addressed relations between the Allies and Turkey and Iran, operations in Yugoslavia and against Japan as well as the envisaged post-war settlement.

A separate protocol signed at the conference pledged the Allies recognition of Iran's independence.

* * * * *

- Nebelwerfer -

This weapon was initially developed for the use of the Wehrmacht's *'Chemical Troops'*. They were primarily intended to deliver poison gas and smoke shells, although a high-explosive shell was developed from the beginning of the design process.

Two different mortars were fielded before they were eventually replaced by a variety of rocket launchers ranging in size from fifteen to thirty-two centimeters. The thin walls of the rockets had the great advantage of allowing much larger quantities of gases, fluids or high-explosives to be delivered than artillery or even mortar shells of the same weight.

* * * * *

- FSSF -

The commanders of the FSSF returned to General Clark with their plan to breach the *'Reinhard line'* by taking the strong defensive German position holding the high ground at Monte La Difensa.

The importance of this mountain lay in its position relative to Hitler's *'Gustav Line'*, which was the German Winter line and the last entrenched defensive line before the Gustav. An allied push through the mountains here would enable them to move on to Cassino and the Liri valley and thence to Rome.

Strategically, the mountain provided a commanding view of the countryside and highway, giving the German artillery on the mountain control of the surrounding area. The German artillery atop La Defensa was also equipped with a new weapon, the *'Nebelwerfer'* (Smoke Mortar).

The FSSF commanders had determined that the best way to approach the entrenched enemy was by avoiding a frontal attack and instead scaling the almost vertical escarpment over the right side of the hill mass. By doing this, they hoped to catch the Germans off guard, as the previous allied attacks on the mountain had always met the enemy head on.

In conjunction with their attack there would be a coordinated move by the rest of 36th Division on the FSSF's right in attacking Monte Maggiore, the British 56th Division attacking Monte Camino and the British 46th Division holding the ground on the FSSF's left.

The assault was planned for December second. Meanwhile the men were trained in mountain climbing and fighting tactics at their temporary barracks at Santa Maria. FSSF's plan of attack was as follows:

At 16:30 hours on December first, 2nd Regiment would be trucked to within six miles of the base of the mountain and then begin the six hour march the rest of the way to La Difensa.

1st Regiment, coupled with 36th Infantry Division would be the reserve units for the 2nd Regiment. 3rd Regiment would be split in two, half to supply the 2nd Regiment following the initial assault and the other half to be reserves with the 1st Regiment and 36th Infantry Division.

All identification on Force soldiers was to be removed except for their dog tags.

Clark approved the plan.

After reaching the base of the mountain and having had a single night's rest, under cover of a heavy artillery barrage, 2nd Regiment, consisting of six hundred men, began their ascent of La Difensa at dusk on December second.

They came within range of the German positions at midnight and began to climb the final cliff, which jutted upwards at an angle of sixty-five degrees for the last one thousand feet. The men worked under appalling conditions, climbing with ropes tied to one another in the freezing rain.

Upon reaching the top the first group of men moved forward into a depression in front of the German entrenchment. The plan had been for them to hunker down and wait until everyone had reached the top and taken up positions for the attack. However the last few members up, tripped over loose gravel while moving along the mountaintop, giving away the surprise and as German flares shot into the air, the battle for the hilltop began.

The defenders were crack German troops with a good deal of experience and they quickly opened up with gun and mortar fire. Despite this devastating barrage, the men of the 2nd Regiment managed to set up machine guns and begin returning fire rapidly enough to recoup the loss of surprise and with fierce determination they rapidly overwhelmed the Germans.

Their accomplishment was astounding. The 5th Army Staff had guessed that the battle to take the stronghold would last a minimum of four to five days, but within two hours the FSSF men had not only forced the defending Germans on La Difensa off the top of the mountain, but sent them in full retreat to La Remetanea.

Anticipating a counterattack, the Force immediately dug in at Defensa. The German's did exactly that but the FSSF held their ground and with the help of massive allied artillery barrages and the flooding of both the Rapido and Garigliane rivers, the Germans were prevented from reforming, and were turned back each at every attempt.

While waiting for the orders to attack Remetanea, the 2nd Regiment was resupplied by the 1st and 3rd Regiments, who also brought them whiskey to celebrate and condoms to keep the barrels of their guns dry in the pounding rain.

Once the British forces had broken through the German lines at Monte Camino, the Force was ordered to attack their next objective, which was referred to as *'Hill 907"*. Without a breather, the FSSF immediately continued to attack, successfully assaulting Monte La Remetanea between December sixth and ninth.

The Force had proven its worth and earned the right to be classed as elite troops. They had breached the line, taken the choke point, and done so in short order.

It had cost them dearly, but they were far from finished. There were more crack German troops, holding seemingly impassable defensive positions between this mountain and Rome, and they would be called upon again and again.

* * * * *

- British Commonwealth Air Training Program -

Due to the possibility of enemy attack, the strain caused by wartime traffic at airfields and the unpredictable climate, Britain was deemed as an unsuitable location to carry out the massive air crew training that would be needed to fight the war.

It was suggested that a plan be drawn up to set up training facilities within the British Dominions where, in isolation from the main theatres of war, it would be possible to safely train British and other Allied countries aircrews.

Negotiations regarding joint training, between the four governments concerned, took place in Ottawa during the first few months of the war.

On December the seventeenth of thirty-nine, they signed an agreement aimed at accomplishing this task. It stated that these new training facilities would be based on the training methods currently in use by the RAF. Under a parallel agreement, South Africa was also to participate in the program.

The plan was to be called the British Commonwealth Air

Training Plan (BCATP). It was to be an immense military aircrew training program, jointly created by the United Kingdom, Canada, Australia and New Zealand. Under the plan, three initial training schools, thirteen elementary flying training schools, sixteen service flying training schools, ten air observer schools, ten bombing and gunnery schools, two air navigation schools and four radio operator schools were to be created.

The BCATP quickly became one of the single largest aviation training programs in history and was responsible for training nearly half the pilots, navigators, bomb aimers, air gunners, radio operators and flight engineers who served with the Royal Air Force (RAF), Royal Canadian Air Force (RCAF), Royal Australian Air Force (RAAF), and Royal New Zealand Air Force (RNZAF) during the war.

Students from many other countries attended schools under these plans. They included Argentina, Belgium, Ceylon, Czechoslovakia, Denmark, Finland, Fiji, France, Greece, the Netherlands, Norway, Poland and the United States, where the similar *'Civilian Pilot Training Program'* had been underway since the end of thirty-eight.

The British Commonwealth Air Training Plan was viewed as an incredibly ambitious program which envisioned the training of approximately fifty thousand aircrew each year, for as long as necessary. Twenty-two thousand were to come from Great Britain, thirteen thousand from Canada, eleven thousand from Australia and thirty-three hundred from New Zealand. The air crews were to receive elementary training in the various Commonwealth countries and then would be sent to Canada where advanced courses would be instructed. Training costs were to be divided between the four governments.

The agreement stipulated that aircrew graduates belonging to Dominion air forces, where they were assigned for service with the RAF, were to be placed into new squadrons and then identified as members of the RCAF, RAAF and RNZAF respectively. The British government would be wholly responsible for the pay and entitlements of graduates, once they had been placed with either RAF or Commonwealth units. Pre-war regular RCAF and RAAF squadrons were also serving under RAF operational control, while New Zealand

and Rhodesian personnel were frequently assigned to RAF squadrons which reflected their nationality by having *'NEW ZEALAND'* or *'RHODESIA'* in their names. However, in practice most personnel from other Commonwealth countries, while they were under RAF operational control, found themselves assigned to British units.

The initial negotiations for *'The Plan'* were held in Ottawa for good reason. Canada would be taking the major role in completing it. This large country had been chosen as the primary Commonwealth location for several reasons:

It offered ideal weather, and the wide open spaces that would be required for advanced flight and navigation training. On its own, the country could supply sufficient fuel and had industrial facilities already in place for the production of needed trainer aircraft, parts and supplies. Its location also guaranteed that there would be no the realistic threat from either the Luftwaffe or Japanese fighter aircraft and it offered reasonable proximity to both the European and Pacific theatres of war.

The Canadian government had agreed in December of nineteen thirty-nine to join the British Commonwealth Air Training Plan, operate its bases in Canada, and pick up a large proportion of the costs. Canada had agreed to accept most of the costs of the plan but in return insisted that air training would be Canada's primary war effort. While it agreed with the British expectation that the RAF would absorb Canadian air training graduates without restriction and distribute them across the RAF, it demanded that Canadian airmen be identified as members of the RCAF and would keep its own distinct uniforms and shoulder badges.

Its part in the plan cost Canada one point six billion out of the total plan cost of two point two billion and employed one hundred and four thousand Canadians in airbases across the land.

It was agreed that the RCAF would run the plan in Canada, but to satisfy RAF concerns, a senior RAF commander, who just happened to be a Canadian, was posted to Ottawa as Director of Training and commencing in nineteen forty, he directed BCATP training.

At its height of the British Commonwealth Air Training Plan, one hundred and thirty one thousand five hundred and thirty-three

Allied pilots and aircrew were trained in Canada. Of these, seventy-two thousand, eight hundred and thirty-five were in fact Canadian. At the plan's high point in late forty-three, an organization of over one hundred thousand administrative personnel operated one hundred and seven schools and one hundred and eighty-four other supporting units at two hundred and thirty one locations spread across Canada.

The necessary infrastructure required to meet the plans needs included construction of over eight thousand buildings, seven hundred of these being hangars, and fuel storage of more than twenty six million gallons. Three hundred miles of water mains and a similar length of sewer mains were laid, a process which entailed the excavation of two million cubic yards of material. One hundred sewage treatment and disposal plants and one hundred and twenty water pumping stations were completed; and more than two thousand miles of main power lines and five hundred and thirty miles of underground electrical cable were placed, in order to service a total connected electrical power load of over eighty thousand horsepower.

On the twenty-ninth of April of nineteen-forty, the first Canadian training course got officially underway. It contained two hundred and twenty-one recruits, and took its training at 'No. 1 Initial Training School RCAF', which was initially located at the Eglinton Hunt Club in Toronto. Out of this class, on September thirtieth of that year, thirty-nine men received their wings as aircrew. All of these graduates were retained by the BCATP in Canada, as instructors or staff pilots.

On October twenty-seventh of nineteen forty, the first BCATP personnel were sent to the Britain as observers. These thirty-seven men had received their wings at RCAF Trenton, which was located near Trenton, in Ontario. The first BCATP-trained pilots posted to Europe as a group were thirty-seven RAAF personnel who had graduated in November of forty-one, from 'No. 2 Service Flying Training School, RCAF Uplands' in Ottawa.

By the end of the war, over one hundred and sixty-seven thousand students, including over fifty thousand pilots, had trained in Canada under the program. While the majority of those who successfully completed the program went on to serve in the RAF, over half of the one hundred and thirty-one thousand, five hundred and fifty-three graduates, were Canadians.

Prior to the inception of the BCATP, the RAAF had trained only about 50 pilots per year. Under the new agreement, Australia undertook to provide twenty-eight thousand aircrew over three years, representing which would represent thirty-six percent of the total number trained by the BCATP. During the war, more than thirty-seven thousand, five hundred Australian aircrew were given initial training in Australia; a majority of these, over twenty-seven thousand, had also graduated from schools in Australia.

During nineteen-forty, Royal Australian Air Force (RAAF) schools were established across Australia to provide for initial training, elementary flying training, service flying training, air navigation, air observer, bombing and gunnery and wireless air gunnery. The first Australian flying course commenced on April twenty-ninth of nineteen forty.

For a period, most RAAF aircrews received advanced training in Canada. During mid-nineteen-forty, however, some RAAF trainees began to receive advanced training at RAF facilities located in southern Rhodesia.

On November the fourteenth of nineteen forty, the first Australian contingent to graduate from advanced training in Canada embarked for the UK.

Following the outbreak of the war in the Pacific, a majority of RAAF aircrews completed their training in Australia and served with RAAF units in the South West Pacific Theatre, and an increasing number of Australian personnel were transferred there from Europe and the Mediterranean to RAF squadrons moved there as well. A significant proportion of RAAF personnel remained in Europe and RAAF squadrons continued to be formed there.

During the war, the RNZAF contributed two thousand, seven hundred and forty-three fully trained pilots to serve with the RAF in Europe, the Middle East, and Far East. An additional one thousand, five hundred and twenty-one pilots who completed their training in New Zealand were retained in country; either as instructors, staff pilots, or manning operational squadrons formed during the latter half of the war.

By nineteen forty, before the British Commonwealth Air Training Plan had been fully developed, New Zealand also trained one hundred and eighty-three observers and three hundred and ninety-five air gunners for the RAF. From forty-three onwards, the training of wireless operator/air gunners, and navigators was carried out in New Zealand for Pacific operations. In addition, some two thousand, nine hundred and ten pilots were trained to elementary standards and then sent on to Canada to continue their training. More than twenty-seven hundred radio operator/air-gunners, eighteen hundred navigators, and five hundred bombardiers passed through the Initial Training Wing (ITA) before proceeding to Canada.

Of the one hundred and thirty-one thousand trainees who graduated in Canada under the Commonwealth Air Training Plan, New Zealanders formed five point three percent.

Under a parallel agreement to the BCATP, South Africa trained thirty-three thousand aircrew for the South African Air Force and other Allied air forces. They were second only to Canada in output.

At the time Southern Rhodesia was a British Crown Colony and was not involved in the negotiation or signing of the BCATP. The Southern Rhodesia Air Force was absorbed by the RAF in nineteen forty. Rhodesia provided significant initial training facilities and contributed personnel to British units.

By mid-nineteen forty, Canadian flying instructors employed in the BCATP were finding it impossible to keep up with the training demands. To increase the numbers of flying instructors, the RCAF began a campaign aimed at recruiting American pilots.

In response to the campaign, Americans began crossing the border and appearing at the nearest recruiting centers: 'in such numbers that they caused some embarrassment to Canadian authorities'.

President Roosevelt, when confronted with this mass exodus, ordered that Americans going to Canada to join the RCAF or RAF, were to be granted exemption by the US draft board. After Pearl Harbor, one thousand, seven hundred and fifty-nine American members of the RCAF transferred to the armed forces of the United States, another two thousand made the transfer later on in the war and about five thousand chose to complete their service with the RCAF.

On the third anniversary of the British Commonwealth Air Training Plan, US president Franklin D. Roosevelt publicly recognized this massive effort that Canada had undertaken. He avouched that his northern friend and neighbor, Canada had become *'the Aerodrome of Democracy',* a play on his earlier description of the United States as *'the Arsenal of Democracy.'*

* * * * *

- Deportations -

On December second the first transport of Jews from Vienna arrived at Auschwitz.

On December sixteenth, the Chief Surgeon at Auschwitz reported the completion of one hundred and six castrations.

* * * * *

- The Family -

- Karl and Wilhelm -

Early in the month, the Count and his son had been summoned to a meeting with Albert Speer, Minister of Armaments and Munitions. When they'd arrived they'd found Speer in his office with Luftwaffe *'Generalleutnant'*, Adolf Joseph Ferdinand Galland.

Karl was on good terms with Speer, although, as was generally the case when it came to those of Hitler's inner circle, he had made no overt attempts at achieving anything more than a professional relationship with him. He had no idea why he and Wilhelm had been summoned but in view of the continues intrigues of the top Nazi leaders, he had advised his son to keep his thoughts to himself and only respond briefly and to direct questions should they arise during the meeting.

Speer greeted them warmly and introduced Galland, who neither of them had met previously although they were both well aware of the German air ace's accomplishments and the high esteem in which he was held by all Germans.

Ensconced at a circular table, the four men were served coffee while exchanging the usual chitchat as to the current situation. Karl was polite in response but took great care not to offer opinions that might be taken the wrong way. Wilhelm smiled, nodded and kept his mouth shut as his father had advised. In view of his junior rank among those at the table, this response was a given and was in fact expected.

Once they had finished their coffee, Speer cleared his throat and moved directly into the reason for the meeting.

"Feldmarschall von Stauffer, I have asked you here today to seek your assistance in dealing with a slight conundrum that has recently arisen."

Here, Speer paused to give Karl an opening to respond. The Count smiled and nodded.

"Anything I can do assist you in any way, Herr Minister."

Speer smiled, but the expression on Galland's face had not changed since the coffee cups had disappeared. Karl knew that Galland had a reputation for speaking his mind and was somewhat surprised that the *'Generalleutnant'* had said very little so far. Galland appeared to be watching him and his son very carefully, looking for a readable facial reaction from either of them which might indicate how Speer's words were being received.

The Count noted that Speer was choosing his words judiciously as he continued, and all Karl's senses told him that he should take great care to weigh his answers to whatever requests for assistance might be forthcoming.

"I understand you watched the Me 262 demonstration with the Fuhrer last month..."

Karl nodded but said nothing.

"...the Fuhrer was impressed with the aircraft, did you share his enthusiasm?"

Karl weighed his answer and made it brief.

"Yes, it is a fine aircraft, well ahead of anything the Allies have."

Galland, a man of action, who no doubt had little patience for this type of verbal foreplay, gave a deep sigh and spoke.

"Herr Feldmarschall, do you support the Fuhrer's order that the craft be built as a medium bomber rather than the fighter it was specifically designed to be?"

A little taken aback by the General's frankness and lack of tact, Speer quickly interjected.

"Galland is a fighter man as you know, Count. He favors using the craft as it was initially designed. Reichsmarschall Goering however is in agreement with the Fuhrer on this."

Galland waved his hand in dismissal.

"When does the Herr Reichsmarschall not agree with our esteemed leader? This is the same man who refuses to believe that Allied fighters can now penetrate deeply into Germany. One would think that the two of them are unaware of the fact that our cities are being bombed into oblivion. We cannot consider the offensive at this point in the air war, we must build a sufficient number of these superior fighters now in order to have any hope of shooting down the Allied bloody bombers which are destroying our factories and flattening our cities. We must have fighters now, or we will be destroyed from the air. Give me these jet fighters and I will accomplish that and then we can worry about producing bombers once that has been done."

Speer was obviously shaken by the outburst but he put has best face on and smiled.

"In view of the destruction raining down on us from the skies, I'm sure you can understand the *'Generalleutnant's'* frustration over the situation. I asked you here in order to seek out your advice as to the varying views as to the use of these new planes. In your position you have a good overview of the general research and development of new super weapons and you have been at the forefront of advancing new designs for production since the war began. Confidentially and for our ears only, I would ask you to share with us exactly where you stand on this question."

Karl took the time to light a cigarette before he responded to the direct question. It was patently obvious to him what answer these two men wanted from him and anyone living in the real world had to know what the sensible answer was, however he wasn't about to jeopardize his position by bluntly saying so.

"Gentlemen, I am a facilitator, I do not involve myself in political or military decision making. I am not qualified to do so and I am happy to leave that to those like yourselves to determine. I might suggest that under the circumstance a reasonable path to take in the manufacture would be to develop both types. The numbers of each type built would of course have to be determined by you, Minister.'

He turned to address Wilhelm.

"Can what I am suggesting be accomplished without too much redesign of the 262?"

Wilhelm locked his gaze with his father before responding.

"Yes of course. The necessary changes would be relatively simple to accomplish."

The count nodded and turned to face the other two men.

"There you have it then. Ask for the design changes for bombers to be created and in the meantime, build fighters that can easily be converted to bombers as and when needed. General Galland will have his superior fighter planes and the Fuhrer will have his medium bombers, when and if he needs them. If you come to that conclusion, I cannot see any reason or any set of circumstances that would lead me to question, or discuss it with the Fuhrer. My job is to see to it that Germany is kept on the cutting edge of research and development. You are duty bound to decide what will be manufactured"

The meeting ended shortly thereafter and both Karl and Wilhelm were glad to leave the office as both were beginning to perspire heavily.

Once they were safely in Karl's staff car he heaved a sigh of relief.

"Damn these palace intrigues...Oh well it's done now and all things considered, I think it went as well as could be expected."

Wilhelm nodded.

"Well I think you managed to give them an out that will allow them to build fighters without Hitler noticing what they are doing. Imagine him and Goering wanting bombers. My God! Are they both blind as to what is going on?"

Over the rest of the month Karl and Wilhelm spent their time holding their pattern in the balancing act of keeping up with the appearance of being good Nazis and ensuring that they remained in both Hitler and Himmler's good books. They were finding it a difficult act to maintain, both men becoming frustrated with the exercise, although fully understanding that for the sake of the family's future, they had no option but to keep to this path until wars end and Karl believed that would take at least one more year, if not more.

They continued to spend as much time as possible out of bomb-torn Berlin and in the relatively safe surrounds of castle von Stauffer.

* * * * *

- Eric -

Nearing term, Heidi was beginning to be both tired and exasperated. She was easily brought to tears and very much looking forward to having the whole business over with.

Eric empathized with her frustration and was eagerly waiting the birth of their first child. He found himself going out of his way to make her last days easier and the two of them often spent the early evening in their new home alone, preparing for their upcoming parenthood.

Eric now took pains to cater to her every desire and repeatedly told her that her suggestion that she was ugly and undesirable to him was ridiculous, that he had never seen her more beautiful and that his desire for her had never been stronger, something he was prepared to prove to her any time she wished, provided that it was all right with her doctor. This never failed to perk Heidi up and more often than not, led to some form of safe sexual contact between them and afterward, satisfying hours of lying cradled in each other's arms.

* * * * *

- Friedrichshafen -

Ursula had done all she could regarding her latest project. She oversaw construction of the new farm buildings on a daily basis but pretty well everything to do with the future implementation of the plan for them to be food self-sufficient at the castle, would have to wait for spring to arrive.

The Count had taken notice of her frustration at waiting and had provided some relief by asking her to organize the shipment of some of their personal family and *'Operation Fatherland'* treasure across the lake and into Switzerland where he had secured sufficient vaults to hold it safely until war's end.

CHAPTER TWENTY-FOUR

- December -

- Allied Air Operations -

- European Theatre -

Bomber Command and the US Eighth Air force drop a total of twelve thousand tons of bombs. The RAF targets Berlin, Leipzig and Frankfurt with seven thousand tons and the US bombers strike at Kiel, Emden and Bremen.

Both Air Forces bomb targets in the Pas de Calais area late in the month as they work to destroy the launching pads that have been constructed there for the V1 flying-bombs.

The new variant of the Mustang fighter boasting a Merlin engine is used operationally for the first time in a Fighter sweep over Belgium on the first of the month and, on a subsequent bombing mission over Kiel on the thirteenth, this new Mustang takes up its first bomber escort duties.

* * * * *

- Mediterranean Theatre -

Allied air forces face terrible weather over the month, however several sorties are made over Augsburg, Innsbruck and Turin.

* * * * *

- December First -

- Italy -

Allied forces are in the final stages of preparations for a resumption of their offensive.

* * * * *

- December Second -

- Italy -

Overnight there is a very successful German air raid on Bari. Eighteen transports making up a total of seventy thousand tons are sunk and thirty-eight thousand tons of supplies are lost. One of the bombs dropped hits an Allied ammunition ship carrying mustard gas. The resulting release of gas kills eighty-three Allied soldiers in one fell swoop and a total of one thousand troops are killed before the raid ends.

The British take Lanciano and Castelfrentano.

* * * * *

- New Guinea -

The Australians take Huanko.

* * * * *

- December Third -

- Eastern Front -

The Russians capture Dovsk.

* * * * *

- Italy -

The British take San Vito.
The FSSF pushes the Germans off the peak of Monte la Difensa.

* * * * *

- December Fourth -

- Pacific -

US submarine *'Sailfish'* sinks the Japanese escort carrier *'Chuyo'* in Japanese home waters.

* * * * *

- Bolivia -

This South American country declares war on all Axis powers.

* * * * *

- December Sixth -

- Italy -

After ferocious fighting the British take Monte Camino.

* * * * *

- December Eighth -

- New Guinea -

Australian forces take Wareo.

* * * * *

- Italy -

The Allied forces in this campaign begin to suffer more serious constriction in their makeup and supply as the upcoming European invasion codenamed *'Operation Overlord'* begins to take serious precedent over the Italian theatre of operations. French and Italian troops begin to move into the line as experienced units are ferried back to Britain to prepare for *'Overlord'*. The US fifth Army's attacks continue but make little progress. Canadian troops operating with the British Eighth Army begin attacks over the Moro River.

* * * * *

- December Ninth -

- Eastern Front -

The Russians take Mederovo and move on toward Znamenka.

* * * * *

- December Tenth -

- Eastern Front -

Znamenka is captured by the Russians.

* * * * *

- Italy -

The Canadians breach the bottleneck at the Moro River and shove the German troops back far enough to allow the following units of the British Eighth Army to cross the river in strength.

* * * * *

- Solomons -

The first US planes arrive at the newly constructed Cape Torokina airfield as the marines continue to push the Japanese forces back and gradually extend the American held territory.

* * * * *

- December Twelfth -

- Berlin -

Feldmarschall Erwin Rommel is appointed head of *'Fortress Europe'* as chief planner for the defense against an expected Allied invasion of Europe.

* * * * *

- December Thirteenth -

- Greece -

German forces carry out the *'Massacre of Kalavryta'* in southern Greece.

* * * * *

- December Fourteenth -

- Eastern Front -

Russian forces take Cherkassy.

* * * * *

- December Fifteenth-

- New Guinea -

The Australians take Lakona.

* * * * *

- December Sixteenth -

- Eastern Front -

The Russians take Kalinin.

* * * * *

- December Seventeenth -

- Italy -

Monte Sammucro falls to the Allies.

* * * * *

- December Eighteenth -

- Italy -

The US fifth Army takes Monte Lungo.

* * * * *

- December Nineteenth -

- New Britain -

American troops take the Japanese airstrip.

* * * * *

- December Twenty-Second -

- Italy -

The Eighth Army's 2nd Canadian Brigade fights its way into Ortona, which is being defended by a unit of the crack German 1st Paratroop Division. Fierce street-fighting ensues.

* * * * *

- December Twenty-Third -

- Italy -

The 1st Canadian Division from Eighth Army joins the fight and takes control over the majority of Ortona and further inland, other Eighth forces take Arielli.

* * * * *

- December Twenty-Fourth -

- London/Washington -

As the massive preparations for the upcoming invasion of Europe consume Allied planning and troop movements, a series of announcements starting this date and ending on the twenty-ninth, are made with regard to changes in Allied commands.

US General Dwight D, Eisenhower is appointed the Supreme Allied Commander in Europe. British Air Marshall Tedder is to be his deputy. British Admiral, Sir Bertram Ramsey and Air Marshall Leigh

Malory will lead the naval and air forces respectively. General Montgomery will lead the British ground forces.

British General, Sir Henry Maitland Wilson becomes Supreme Allied Commander for the Mediterranean with General Devers as his deputy. British General Alexander will command in Italy. US Army Air Force General Ira Eaker takes over the command of all Allied Mediterranean Air Forces. British General Oliver Leese will take over the command of the Eighth Army. American Army Air Force General Carl Andrew Spatz is to command all the US Strategic Bomber Forces against Germany and US Gerald Doolittle will now lead the Eighth Air Force. British General, Sir Arthur Bernard Paget takes up the positon of Supreme Commander in the Middle East.

* * * * *

- December Twenty-Fifth -

- Eastern Front -

The Russian cut the Vitebsk-Polotsk rail line.

* * * * *

- December Twenty-Sixth -

- New Britain -

US Marines land on Cape Gloucester.

* * * * *

- Artic -

The British battleship HMS *'Duke of York'* engages the German pocket battleship *'Scharnhorst'*. The British ship gains the advantage and eventually after a prolonged bombardment and torpedo attacks between the ships and their escorts, *'Scharnhorst'* is reduced to a burning wreck and sinks. Only thirty-six men of her two thousand man crew survive. She was the last Nazi capital warship in a position to threaten the Artic convoys and the British give a grateful sigh of relief at her demise.

* * * * *

- Eastern Front -

The Russians take Radomyshl.

* * * * *

- Italy -

Monte Sammucro and the surrounding hills are cleared of German defensive units.

* * * * *

- December Twenty-Seventh -

- Bay of Biscay -

The German blockade runner *'Alsterufer'* is sunk by Allied aircraft.

* * * * *

- December Twenty-Eighth -

- Bay of Biscay -

The eleven destroyers and accompanying torpedo boats, which have been sent out to run escort for the *Alsterufer'* are intercepted by the British cruisers HMS *'Enterprise'* and *'Glasgow'*, who promptly sink three German ships before the Germans abandon the fight and run.

* * * * *

- Italy -

After days of ferocious house-to-house fighting, the Canadians complete the capture of Ortona.

* * * * *

- December Twenty-Ninth -

- Eastern Front -

Russian forces retake Korosten and Chernakov northwest of Kiev and Skvira to the southwest.

* * * * *

- December Thirtieth -

- New Britain -

US Marines take the Japanese airfield at Cape Gloucester.

* * * * *

- Eastern Front -

The Russians capture Kazatin.

* * * * *

- December Thirty- First -

- Eastern Front -

Russian forces take Zhitomir.

* * * * *

- Italy -

By year's end, the reduced Allied forces in both the US Fifth and British Eighth Armies find themselves exhausted and now on the back burner to the upcoming *'Overlord'* European invasion and making little progress against the German defenses.

Other books by Patrick Laughy

Paperbacks

Alumni

The Little Black Book

The 4th Reich Book 1

The 4th Reich Book 2

The 4th Reich Book 3

The 4th Reich Book 4

E-books

Alumni

The Little Black Book

Atlantis Ship of the Gods

The 4th Reich series Books 1-5

www.ingramcontent.com/pod-product-compliance
Lightning Source LLC
Chambersburg PA
CBHW070804180626
46818CB00001B/90